Virginia Woolf's Ethics of the Short Story

Christine Reynier

palgrave
macmillan

First published 2009 by
PALGRAVE MACMILLAN

Palgrave Macmillan in the UK is an imprint of Macmillan Publishers Limited, registered in England, company number 785998, of Houndmills, Basingstoke, Hampshire RG21 6XS.

Palgrave Macmillan in the US is a division of St Martin's Press LLC, 175 Fifth Avenue, New York, NY 10010.

Palgrave Macmillan is the global academic imprint of the above companies and has companies and representatives throughout the world.

Palgrave® and Macmillan® are registered trademarks in the United States, the United Kingdom, Europe and other countries.

ISBN-13: 978–0–230–22718–7 hardback
ISBN-10: 0–230–22718–X hardback

This book is printed on paper suitable for recycling and made from fully managed and sustained forest sources. Logging, pulping and manufacturing processes are expected to conform to the environmental regulations of the country of origin.

A catalogue record for this book is available from the British Library.

A catalog record for this book is available from the Library of Congress.

10 9 8 7 6 5 4 3 2 1
18 17 16 15 14 13 12 11 10 09

Printed and bound in Great Britain by
CPI Antony Rowe, Chippenham and Eastbourne

To Olivier

Contents

List of abbreviations   ix

Introduction 🗡   1
   The uncertain boundaries of Virginia Woolf's short stories   1
   The reader and Woolf's short stories   4
   Woolf's short stories: a territory difficult to map out   10
   Towards an overall vision and synthetic appraisal of
     Woolf's short stories   13

1 Virginia Woolf's Definition of the Short Story   18
   Woolf's essays about the short story   18
   Appraising Woolf's definition of the short story   22
   The short story redefined as an ethical space   28

**2 Woolf's Short Stories as a Paradoxical and
   Dynamic Space**   36
   Transmuting the story-telling process   36
   From the fragment to the whole: the associative method   37
   A whole made of fragments: the method of interruption   44
   Woolf's short story as literary fragment   55
   Woolf's short story as a paradoxical and dynamic space   56

**3 Conversation, Emotion and Ethics or
   the Short Story as Conversation**   60
   "Form is emotion": conversation as the form of
     the encounter between the self and the other   63
   The role of the party: the short story as an ethical and
     aesthetic space   75
   "A Dialogue upon Mount Pentelicus" or
     conversation redefined   79

4 Woolf's Ethics of Reading and Writing   90
   Conversation as the encounter between creator and reader   90
   Staging the story-telling process and the story-teller   90
   Staging the origin of the creative process   98

Staging the reader and the reading process   99
× The short story as a moment of being   102
"A Haunted House": the short story as a "house of Love"   105

5 **Woolf's Short Story as a Site of Resistance**   **111**
The short story as a site of resistance against silence   114
The short story as a site of resistance against authority 125
Conclusion   146

Notes   149

Bibliography   168

Index   177

Abbreviations

CSE: *The Complete Shorter Fiction*
AHH: *A Haunted House and Other Stories*
MDP: *Mrs Dalloway's Party*
DIARY: *The Diary of Virginia Woolf*
LETTERS: *The Letters of Virginia Woolf*
ESSAYS: *The Essays of Virginia Woolf*
C.E. II: *Collected Essays II*

Introduction

The uncertain boundaries of Virginia Woolf's short stories

Although she is better known as a novelist, Virginia Woolf wrote from the beginning to the end of her career many short stories, the number and variety of which seem to preclude any overall reading that would lead to the definition of the Woolfian short story as a specific literary genre. She herself liked to think that short story writing was a recreational process. When the writing of a novel had been particularly demanding and exhausting, she liked to turn to a shorter form that did not require such a long-term investment and rest her mind in that way. In a letter to her friend Ethel Smyth, she significantly writes: "These little pieces in Monday or (and) Tuesday were written by way of diversion; they were the treats I allowed myself when I had done my exercise in the conventional style".[1]

She sometimes wrote short stories on an impulse—as she did with "The Mark on the Wall" which was written in one day "all in a flash"[2]—published them or put them aside, and only finished them when a literary agent asked her to. According to Leonard Woolf, "Virginia Woolf used at intervals to write short stories. It was her custom, whenever an idea for one occurred to her, to sketch it out in a very rough form and then to put it away in a drawer. Later, if an editor asked her for a short story, and she felt in the mood to write one (which was not frequent), she would take a sketch out of her drawer and rewrite it, sometimes a great many times".[3]

1

This is confirmed by Virginia Woolf's diary in which she notes, for example, on 22 November 1938, that she is "rehashing 'Lappin and Lapinova', a story written I think at Asheham 20 years ago or more: when I was writing *Night and Day* perhaps";[4] and "Lappin and Lapinova" was published in April 1939. Similarly "The Duchess and the Jeweller" was first drafted in 1932, revised in 1937 and published in 1938.[5]

Woolf's diary, in an entry of 17 August 1937, further reveals that if she could be enthralled by writing short stories, she could also feel excited at the prospect of making some money out of them:

> This morning I had a moment of the old rapture—think of it!— over copying *The Duchess and the Jeweller* for Chambrun, N.Y. ... there was the old excitement, even in that little extravagant flash—more than in criticism I think. Happily—if that's the word—I get these electric shocks—Cables asking me to write. Chambrun offer £500 for a 9.000 word story. (*Diary* V: 107; 17 August 1937)

In the wake of feminist critics, Elena Gualtieri argues that "[t]hroughout her career, from her beginnings as a reviewer to her most famous feminist essays, writing for money always represented for Woolf the mark of professionalisation, a legitimation of women's 'scribbling' into an acceptable and socially recognised occupation".[6] Nevertheless, by referring repeatedly to her short story writing as a recreational and lucrative process and above all, by neglecting to publish all of her short stories, Woolf may have somewhat downplayed the importance of these texts, reducing the short story to a minor genre or, more accurately, accepting the place ascribed to it by the literary canon.

This casually dismissive attitude, noted by many critics, may account for the relative neglect of her short stories. Even if some of her short stories are frequently reprinted in anthologies, "Woolf is not covered in most histories of the short story form".[7]

However, Woolf's attitude to short story writing is more ambiguous than it may first appear since her diary and letters are also proof to her anxiety on the eve of the publication of her short stories not only because the printing may not be very good[8] or the book may not sell very well[9] but mainly because of the harsh criticism she may have to face. Such was the case with "Kew Gardens", on 12 May 1919: "I read a bound copy of Kew Gardens through.... It seems to me slight & short; I dont see how the reading of it impressed Leonard so much ... one depends so much upon praise. I feel rather sure that I shall get none for this story; & I shall mind a little" (*Diary* I: 271). When *An Unwritten Novel* was about to be published, on 15 April 1920, she noted: "*An Unwritten Novel* will certainly be abused" (*Diary* II: 29). And again when *Monday or Tuesday* was about to come out, she wrote on 6 March 1921:

> I now wonder a little what the reviewers will make of it—this time next month. Let me try to prophesy. Well, *The Times* will be kindly, a little cautious, Mrs Woolf, they will say, must beware of virtuosity. She must beware of obscurity. Her great natural gifts etc.... She is at her best in the simple lyric, or in *Kew Gardens*. *An Unwritten Novel* is hardly a success. And as for *A Society*, though spirited, it is too one-sided. Still Mrs Woolf can always be read with pleasure. Then in the *Westminster, Pall Mall* and other serious evening papers I shall be treated very shortly with sarcasm. The general line will be that I am becoming too much in love with my own voice.... The truth is, I expect, that I shan't get very much attention anywhere. (*Diary* II: 98)

After publication, she was prey to "the twitching and teasing of private criticism" (*Diary* II: 108; 10 April 1921) as well as of public criticism, Lytton Strachey's, Roger Fry's or T. S. Eliot's comments affecting her as much as any reviewer's. She carefully records in her diary her friends' reactions to "Kew Gardens": "I've had Roger's praise of Kew Gardens" (*Diary* I: 273; 16 May 1919); "I had a surfeit of praise for Kew Gardens ... highly admired by Clive & Roger ... Forster approves too" (*Diary* I: 276; 22 May 1919). Later, on a par with the reviewers', her friends' comments on *Monday or Tuesday* are reported: "a mildly unfavourable review of Monday or Tuesday reported by Leonard from the Dial, the more depressing as I had vaguely hoped for approval in that august quarter" (*Diary* II: 166; 17 February 1922) is followed by "L. [Leonard] ... dropped into my ear the astonishing news that Lytton thinks the String Quartet 'marvellous'.... And then there was Roger who thinks I'm on the track of real discoveries, & certainly not a fake" (*Diary* II: 109; 12 April 1921); "And Eliot astounded me by praising Monday & Tuesday! This really delighted me. He picked out the String Quartet, especially the end of it. 'Very good', he said, and meant it, I think. The Unwritten Novel he thought not successful: Haunted House 'extremely interesting'" (*Diary* II: 125; 7 June 1921). Understandably sensitive to praise, especially from friends who were also writers, she can also feel the pinch of jealousy when Hamilton Fyfe in the *Daily Mail* predicts that Leonard's story "Pearls and Swine" "will rank with the great stories of the world" while hers are read in the *Daily News* as a "bereft world of inconsequent sensation" (*Diary* II: n. 116; 3 May 1921). However, she is comforted when *Monday or Tuesday* starts selling and happy not to have been "dismissed as negligible", whatever the reviewers' opinion (*Diary* II: 109; 12 April 1921).

And when in 1985, Susan Dick published *Virginia Woolf. The Complete Shorter Fiction,* she brought for the first time to public notice, through the numerous notes appended to her volume, the extensive and careful process of revision the short stories were submitted to. Woolf henceforth appeared to have been as scrupulously careful in her writing and revisions of her short stories as of her novels.

Woolf's anxiety and meticulous revisions are clearly at odds with the light-hearted approach of the short stories initially noticed in the diary and letters and show that she took short story writing more seriously than she chose to say.

The reader and Woolf's short stories

In July 1917, Woolf's contemporary readers discovered Woolf's first short story, "The Mark on the Wall", along with Leonard Woolf's "Three Jews" in *Two Stories,* the first publication of the Hogarth Press. Later, in May 1919, they could read *Kew Gardens* and in 1921 *Monday or Tuesday,*[10] the only volume of short stories published by Woolf herself and her own press, the Hogarth Press; they could also discover a few short stories in English or American periodicals such as *The Athenaeum, Criterion, Forum, Harper's Magazine* or *Harper's Bazaar.* It is only after Woolf's death that her readers were allowed to discover that she had written far more than 18 short stories. In 1944 Leonard Woolf undertook to publish *A Haunted House and Other Stories,* which includes *"A Haunted House", "Monday or Tuesday", "An Unwritten Novel", "The String Quartet", "Kew Gardens", "The Mark on the Wall",* "The New

Dress", "The Shooting Party", "Lappin and Lapinova", "Solid Objects", "The Lady in the Looking-Glass", "The Duchess and the Jeweller", "Moments of Being", "The Man who Loved his Kind", "The Searchlight", "The Legacy", "Together and Apart", and "A Summing Up".[11] It has long been the authoritative edition until Stella McNichol published *Mrs Dalloway's Party*[12] in 1973, and most of all, Susan Dick brought out in 1985 *Virginia Woolf. The Complete Shorter Fiction*, a volume including 46 works, seventeen being published for the first time. This ground-breaking edition, revised and expanded in 1989, revealed the enormous body of short stories written by Woolf. It brought to the public's attention the early stories ("Phyllis and Rosamond", "The Mysterious Case of Miss V.", "The Journal of Mistress Joan Martyn", "A Dialogue upon Mount Pentelicus", "Memoirs of a Novelist"), written between 1906 and 1909 and hitherto unpublished,[13] as well as the latest ones ("Gipsy, the Mongrel", "The Symbol, "The Watering Place") and a number of others ("The Evening Party", "Sympathy", "Nurse Lugton's Curtain", "The Widow and the Parrot",[14] "Happiness", "A Simple Melody", "The Fascination of the Pool", "Scenes from the life of a British Naval Officer", "Miss Pryme", "Ode Written Partly in Prose on Seeing the Name of Cutbush Above a Butcher's Shop in Pentonville", "Portraits", "Uncle Vanya"). Forty-four years after Woolf's death, her readers could discover those texts together with a number of incomplete pieces, which Dick did not hesitate to include in abundant appendices. Since then the various collections which have been published have not brought any major changes except for David Bradshaw's 2003 volume, *Carlyle's House and Other Sketches*,[15] which is a collection of seven hitherto unpublished texts.

Rather than coming back to the complex history of the composition and publication of Woolf's short stories which has been thoroughly charted by Susan Dick in the substantial notes appended to her scrupulously rigorous volume, I would like to have a close look at the editorial choices which the different editors made. Indeed, each edition of Woolf's shorts stories necessarily has a different impact on the reader through the selection criteria that have been adopted. While all the editors, from Leonard Woolf onwards, have stated their desire to respect Woolf's intention,[16] they have all chosen to include in their collections texts that had been unpublished in Woolf's lifetime and therefore not finally revised. Such a choice proceeds from a legitimate desire to provide an interesting insight into the author's way of working while running the obvious risk that the notion of "work in progress" may gradually be lost in the reading of texts that the hasty "common reader" will not immediately identify as unrevised.

Stella McNichol's decision to put together in *Mrs Dalloway's Party* seven short stories ("Mrs Dalloway in Bond Street", first published in *The Dial* in 1923, "The Man who Loved his Kind", "Together and Apart", "The New Dress" and "A Summing Up", first published in *A Haunted House*, and two unpublished texts, "the Introduction" and "Ancestors") is amply accounted for in her introduction where she explains that all the stories are connected with Mrs Dalloway's Party; the original title of *Mrs Dalloway* was *At Home* or *The Party*; the position of the stories in the Berg Manuscripts suggests a close connection with the novel and finally, some of Woolf's compositional notes for *Mrs Dalloway* present:

> a short book consisting of six or seven
> chapters, each complete separately.
> Yet there must be some sort of fusion!
> And all must converge upon the party at the end. (*M.D.P.* 15)

The arrangement of the short stories, according to McNichol, follows this initial plan for *Mrs Dalloway*.[17] However coherent it may be, this choice necessarily orientates the reading, suggesting these seven short stories constitute a sequence or cycle and are connected with *Mrs Dalloway* while the others may not be—which is already a critical stance.

In a more ambitious move, Susan Dick tried to solve the problem of the persistent dissemination of Woolf's short stories by publishing a volume including all of Woolf's short fiction. She decided to include all the short stories that Woolf wrote from the beginning of her career, in 1906, to the end of it, in 1941:

> In deciding to mix the unrevised stories and sketches with those which Woolf had published, rather than group them in a separate section, I have viewed these works as documents that will best enrich and inform the context in which the more polished stories and sketches are read when they are placed in close conjunction with them. (Dick 5)

She opted for a chronological order, systematically privileging the latest version revised by Woolf herself. Yet her attempt at a *Complete Shorter Fiction* has been in some measure defeated by Bradshaw's latest find, which may not be the last.[18]

These various collections necessarily orientate the reading and give a different image of Woolf's short stories, whether the reader be aware of it or not. Susan Dick chooses to follow a chronological order so that the reader can "follow the amazing evolution of [Woolf's] genius as a writer" (Dick 1) and divides her book into four chapters, starting with "Early Stories"; going on with the 1917–21 period, in which "The Mark on The Wall" points to "an important new stage" (Dick 2); then the 1922–5 period, mostly constituted of the Dalloway's stories; and concluding with the 1926–41 period. She thus introduces, in an eminently subjective move, landmarks such as "The Mark on The Wall",[19] divisions that mark out the first two periods as the most prolific (25 short stories written within the space of eight years whereas only 17 were written in the last 16 years), and counterbalances the quantitative appraisal by a qualitative one through the introduction of the notion of "evolution", connoting progress, instead of favouring a more neutral approach to a writers' varied experiments.

Furthermore, by choosing to include in her volume stories previously published in collections of essays—"A Woman's College from Outside", "In the Orchard", and "Three Pictures"—Dick points at the thin line separating Woolf's fiction from her essays and she justifies her choice by offering a definition of Woolf's "shorter fiction": "those short pieces...are, to my mind, clearly fictions, that is, works in which the characters, scenes, and actions are more imaginary than they are factual, and in which the narrator's voice is not necessarily identical with the author's" (Dick 2).

Dick's chronological arrangement and careful annotations that crisscross the reading of the different holograph drafts and typescripts with the reading of Woolf's diary or letters, also suggest that if short stories can pave the way to novels, they can also, more often than not, grow out of them. Stella McNichol's volume had already pointed out that if *Mrs Dalloway* had been preceded by "Mrs Dalloway in Bond Street", it had also been followed by short stories related to it. By collecting short stories that surround the writing of *Mrs Dalloway*, McNichol suggested that there is an original form of circulation and exchange between Woolf's short stories and the novel. And if we look carefully at Dick's edition and footnote apparatus, we can see that this phenomenon, which may be rare in the history of writing,[20] was not unusual in Woolf's career. *Night and Day, Jacob's Room, To the Lighthouse, The Waves* or *Between the Acts* are all surrounded by short stories, leading to them[21] and sprouting from them.[22] This would deserve a study of its own,[23] presenting as it does short stories as "pre-texts" and "post-texts" and subsequently raising the problem of the autonomy of the novel and of its complete or incomplete nature. In her letter to Ethel Smyth dated 16 October 1930, just before presenting *Monday or Tuesday* as a diversion, Woolf explains how, when she was ill, she thought of writing short stories like "Kew Gardens" and then, when she recovered, afraid that she might have been flirting with insanity in such pieces, she came back to a more conventional style of writing in *Night and Day*.[24] In that case, the novel rather than the short story came as a rest and a diversion.

If we now turn to *Carlyle's House and Other Sketches*, we can see that David Bardshaw offers seven texts from Woolf's 1909 notebook that "would have been included in Leaska's volume,[25] presumably, had its existence been known about" (Bradshaw 2003: xvii). Leaska's volume being *Virginia Woolf. A Passionate Apprentice: The Early Journals 1897–1909*, these texts therefore belong to Woolf's early journals. However Bradshaw refers to them as sketches because they are "rough" (Bradshaw 2003: xviii) early texts and because "Woolf's 1909 notebook…functioned primarily as a verbal sketch-book" (Bradshaw 2003: xvii), the analogy between writing and painting being introduced by Woolf herself in her 1903 journal from which he quotes. The word "sketch" being also the word Jean Guiguet uses to define Woolf's short stories,[26] the reader is led to read these seven journal entries as so many short stories. Each editor thus chooses, more or less explicitly, to highlight the affinities that the short story may have with another literary genre, whether it be the essay, the novel or the journal.

This observation is to be linked with the varying terminology the editors resort to. While Leonard Woolf opts for the term "stories" in *A Haunted House and Other Stories*, Susan Dick prefers the word "shorter fiction" where the word "fiction" certainly enlarges the definition of the short story to something other than the "story" but the adjective "shorter", containing as it does an implicit comparison with Woolf's longer fiction, that is, the novels, definitely orientates and even limits the reading to a comparison with the novels (and an unresolved contradiction, or at least hiatus, then appears between this choice and her introduction where the essays, not the novel, are said to be close to the shorter fiction). David Bradshaw, through the term "sketch", points to a different direction reducing on the one hand the texts to mere sketches, incomplete forms, while enhancing their visual aspect and underlining the analogy with painting. The term "sketch", as we have just seen, was first used by Guiguet who refers to Woolf's short stories as "sketches" or "impressionist pochades" and "tales" and studies them briefly along this division.[27] According to him, the sketches—"Blue and Green", "A Haunted House", "Monday or Tuesday", "Kew Gardens" and "The String Quartet"—all belong to an early period of experimentation eventually leading to *The Waves* while the tales, beginning with some form of mystery or uncertainty and ending with the dispelling of the enigma, all tell stories. Guiguet clearly uses the analogy with painting to signal the absence of narrative in some texts. Susan Dick more or less takes up this distinction when she divides Woolf's shorter fiction into three categories: "short stories in the traditional sense, narratives with firm story lines and sharply drawn characters", "fictional reveries which in their shifts of perspective and lyrical prose recall the autobiographical essays of some nineteenth-century writers, de Quincey in particular", and finally " 'scenes' or 'sketches', [that] probably owe a debt to Chekhov" (Dick 1). In introducing these distinctions she indirectly justifies the use of the umbrella-term "shorter fiction".

What is striking is that through each of these different terms, each editor or critic foregrounds certain aspects or qualities of Woolf's short stories, thus betraying a very different and subjective conception of the short story. Both the terminology and the selection criteria which they adopt point to the fact that they tend to see Woolf's shorts stories as being separated only by a very thin line from another genre (the essay for Dick, the novel for McNichol, the journal for Bradshaw), a tendency that can be found in critics as well: Gualtieri, in her analysis of Woolf's essays, stresses "the fluidity of generic boundaries between Woolf's early journals, her essays, and her short stories" (Gualtieri 18) and focuses on "the most sustained and most visible of these generic cross-overs", that between short stories and essay-writing (Gualtieri 30); and while restricting her approach to the short story and the essay, Leila Brosnan phrases this as "Woolf's innovative generic smudging".[28]

To read Woolf's short stories in terms of generic blurring would lead to analyse the way in which reflections on how to write modernist fiction, generally pertaining to the essay, are woven into the fabric of short stories while elements of fictionality (story, characters, etc.) are introduced into the essays. Hence similarities between, for example, "Mr. Bennett and Mrs. Brown" and "An Unwritten Novel". This would lead one to conclude, with Brosnan, that "self-conscious experimentation with the short story destabilises its fictionality" (Brosnan 139) and vice-versa. The same type of analysis could be carried out with the short stories which are connected with the novel *Mrs Dalloway* or the 1909 journal. The editorial choices I have examined and their underlying assumptions about the short story thus pave the way for a reading in terms of generic destabilisation, the short story and the essay, the short story and the novel, the short story and the journal being in turn destabilised as genres. And one could imagine other editorial criteria and classifications that would add to the list of genres blurred by the short story.

The question is whether one should be content with such conclusions. Can generic blurring and destabilisation be accepted as satisfactory answers and as providing the necessary critical tools to read Woolf's short stories efficiently? This is a point which, to my mind, has not been sufficiently addressed by Woolfian criticism and which I would like to broach, probe and question.

Woolf's short stories: a territory difficult to map out

The various selections of texts that the editors have come up with suggest Woolf's short stories are a territory with uncertain boundaries and the terminological variations in the editors' titles or introductions indirectly point out the difficulty of mapping out this territory. Moreover, instead of opting for a thematic arrangement, as in *Mrs Dalloway's Party*, most collections show, through their titles, that one short story has been selected to announce a series, as in *A Haunted House and Other Stories* or *Carlyle's House and Other Sketches*. They thus call attention to the heterogeneity of the collected texts and the absence of an overall project on the author's part. All this may account for the relative critical neglect of Woolf's short stories since the very idea of embracing such disparate material may be rather daunting. Indeed, only two book-length studies have so far been devoted to Woolf's short stories: Dean R. Baldwin's *Virginia Woolf: A Study of the Short Fiction*[29] and Nena Skrbic's *Wild Outbursts of Freedom. Reading Virginia Woolf's Short Fiction,* respectively published in 1989 and 2004. Baldwin first presents a critical analysis of Woolf's short stories before reproducing, in the next two chapters, two of Woolf's essays ("Mr. Bennett and Mrs. Brown" and "Modern Fiction") and six critical essays on specific short stories. The initial critical analysis consists in examining briefly, if perceptively, each short story in turn, following Guiguet's division of Woolf's short story writing into three periods (1917–21; 1927–9; 1938–40), updated by the author after Dick's publication of *The Complete Shorter Fiction* to 1917–21; 1923–9 and 1938–41. According to Baldwin, during the first period, "Woolf was searching for fictional techniques to express new vision"; the second period "includes all the stories gathered in Stella McNichol's collection of Mrs Dalloway stories.... These stories subject the form to less pressure than the earlier ones"; the last period contains Woolfs' "conventional short fiction" (Baldwin 4). Although Baldwin is interested in Woolf's experimentation in short story form and technique, his approach is openly chronological and biographical; the variety of texts is put forward and no attempt at a synthesis is made; the latter is even defeated since he writes: "As yet, no definitive study of Woolf's short fiction has appeared to focus and unify the critical process. Given the variety of Woolf's stories, such a study may be unlikely" (Baldwin xiii).

Nena Skrbic, in her 2004 *Wild Outbursts of Freedom. Reading Virginia Woolf's Short Fiction,* provides an insightful analysis of Woolf's short stories as exercises in artistic freedom that flout tradition and preconceptions through generic nonconformity while foregrounding the poetic, the visual, and the cinematic. Skrbic deals with their deconstructive strategy as being in keeping with a post-war vision of the world, analyses the early short stories in feminist terms and reveals the existence of unpublished juvenilia before exploring Woolf's fascination with the uncanny as well as her reformulation of the ghost in her ghost stories, and finally focusing on the short story cycle, Mrs Dalloway's Party. Rather than giving a systematic reading of the short stories, Skrbic wishes "to foreground how Woolf's wider objectives as a writer are conveyed more concentratedly (though not exclusively) in her short fiction than in her novels" (xviii) and renders a vibrating homage to these short texts.

Apart from those two books,[30] quite a number of articles have been written on individual short stories, a field which seems to be developing at the moment as witness the number of proposals received for the special 2008 issue of the *Journal of the Short Story in English* devoted to Woolf which I edited.[31] This may signal a change compared to what Daugherty noticed in 2004:

> Though not ignored entirely, the stories averaged about three entries a year in the *MLA Bibliography* between 1990 and 2003 (ranging from a low of one to a high of eight); one to two articles (out of approximately forty-five) in the annual Woolf conference *Selected Papers*; and one essay, one manuscript transcription, and one essay on the short fictions editorially labeled "Portraits" in the nine volumes of *Woolf Studies Annual* to date. (Daugherty 102)

And she adds that *The Cambridge Companion to Virginia Woolf* has no chapter on the short stories.[32] Daugherty's essay is included in *Trespassing Boundaries. Virginia Woolf's Short Fiction*, edited by Kathryn N. Benzel and Ruth Hoberman and published in 2004, a volume which stands out as a most valuable addition to Woolf criticism and as "the first collection of essays to be published that is devoted solely to Woolf's shorter fiction" (xv). After a foreword by Susan Dick who traces the history of the writing of the short stories, the essays examine Woolf's texts as "ambitious and self-conscious attempts to challenge generic boundaries, undercutting traditional differences between short fiction and the novel, between experimental and popular fiction, between fiction and non-fiction, and, most of all, between text and reader" (2) and put forward the instability of the genre.

We could say that in a way, Skrbc's book and these essays make explicit what had been implicit in Dick's choice to bring together, in The *Complete Shorter Fiction*, texts published by Woolf as short stories and acknowledged as such ("The Mark on the Wall" or "Kew Gardens", for example) and texts such as "Ode Written Partly in Prose on Seeing the Name of Cutbush Above a Butcher's Shop in Pentonville", "Portraits" or "Uncle Vanya" that do not fit the conventional pattern of the short story, not even the new modernist one embodied by Katherine Mansfield's. In so doing, Dick suggested how free Woolf was with the genre and how easily she could play with it.

Benzel and Hoberman also challenge what had been, until recently, the underlying *a priori* of most criticism on Woolf's short stories, that is that the latter are experimental texts, mere laboratories leading to the writing of novels. As Baldwin characteristically writes, noting "Virginia Woolf's restless experimentation in short story form and technique" (Baldwin 6): "Her place in literary history will ultimately depend almost entirely on the novels, with the stories providing interesting sidelights" (Baldwin xii). Such an approach implicitly reduces the short story to a minor literary genre without any value of its own, a point of view Benzel and Hoberman counteract vigorously: "The essays in our collection seek to read Woolf's stories within the context of their chosen genre rather than as second best, as poor reflections of or preparation for her novels" (6).

Towards an overall vision and synthetic appraisal of Woolf's short stories

What is needed is clearly both a reevaluation and an overall vision and synthetic appraisal of Woolf's short stories. If Baldwin and Skribc made the first attempts, Dick's edition of the short stories is probably the most valuable contribution in that respect, albeit in a very indirect way. Her extremely careful editorial work and the abundance of information she provides is particularly enlightening as to Woolf's own perception of the short story. Indeed, she tells us that a number of short stories were initially designed as chapters of novels: "A Woman's College from Outside" was first meant to be chapter X of *Jacob's Room*;[33] "Mrs Dalloway in Bond Street" was first designed as the first chapter of a book called "At Home: or The Party" and, curiously enough, this first chapter appears in the holograph of *Jacob's Room*, part III;[34] as for "Nurse Lugton's Curtain", "[a] holograph draft of this story is located in volume II of the holograph of *Mrs Dalloway*, pp. 104–6, and was probably written in the fall of 1924. The untitled story interrupts the scene in which Septimus watches Rezia sewing a hat for Mrs Filmer's daughter. On p. 107 VW returns to this scene" (Dick 306). Dick's findings suggest how fluctuating the boundaries between short stories and novels (or between the novels themselves, in the case of *Jacob's Room* and "At Home") could be for Woolf. Dick also mentions that several holograph versions of the short stories were written by Woolf directly on the verso side of some other work of hers or are intertwined in some way with novels or essays and Dick uses such information to date the composition of some undated stories. About "The Symbol" and "The Watering Place", she writes

> Undated holograph drafts of these stories are located at the back of a writing book that VW entitled "Essays". The front of the book contains drafts of essays published in 1931 and 1932, and a portion of the holograph of *Flush*. At the back are drafts of five unpublished pieces, only two of which, the first, entitled "Sketches" ["The Symbol"] and the second, entitled "The Ladies Lavatory" ["The Watering Place"], appear to be complete. The other three are "Winter's Night", "English Youth" and "Another Sixpence". These five sketches may be the last works of fiction that VW wrote. (Dick 318–19)

and she adds that, as far as "The Symbol" is concerned, "[t]he text given here is that of the typescript with holograph revisions, dated 1 March 1941, and typed on the verso side of pages from the later typescript of *Between the Acts* and 'Anon'" (Dick 319) while, for "The Watering Place", "[t]he text given here is that of the undated typescript which was typed on the verso side of pages from the later typescript of *Between the Acts*" (Dick 321). In this specific case, we can surmise that Woolf was saving on paper in times of war but this cannot be the case for, for example, "The Shooting Party", about which Dick explains: "Both the holograph draft and the first of two typescripts with holograph revisions are dated 19 January 1932. One page of a draft of 'A Letter to a Young Poet' (published in July 1932) precedes the final page of the holograph of the story" (Dick 315).

Dick's work of genetic criticism gives us many valuable hints. Indeed, Woolf's way of writing on the back of pages where other texts had already been consigned points out how much she favoured circulation (not only thematic but also physical circulation) between her various pieces of writing. However genre-conscious she may have been, her manuscripts show that for her, there were no tight boundaries between her various pieces of writings. Although essays, novels or short stories are all distinct, they all belong to the same work, an immense text, a "whole made of fragments". To recognise this is to acknowledge that, far from being marginalia, her short stories definitely belong to her work. And here Woolf may take a different standpoint from women writers of her generation who, as Hanson shows, opted for the short story because it was a "marginalised" genre that fitted their marginalised social status.[35] Woolf, on the contrary, physically weaves her short stories into her novels and essays, thus refusing all distinction between so-called major and minor genres, and situating them in a new space where circulation prevails, an open space. This space she occasionally opens further when she suggests, as she does in her diary,[36] that writing and painting, the two sister(s') arts, may come together when she draws a sketch of the widow and her parrot on the first page of the typescript of the short story "The Widow and the Parrot"[37] or when she writes "Portraits" and "Uncle Vanya" as "part of a collaborative work called 'Faces and Voices' with Vanessa" (Dick 313). The many drafts and revised versions of the short stories that Dick reveals are also proof to Woolf's taste for incompletion and inconclusion.[38] For her, the very notion of a finished text was meaningless since a text was always in progress, was liable to be revised, added to or pruned, and endlessly transformed. The many reworkings of "The Searchlight", from the earliest draft in 1929 to those of June 1930, December 1930, January 1939, and 1941, offer one of the best examples of this endless process.[39]

Woolf's short story, as presented in *The Complete Shorter Fiction*, thus comes out as belonging to a space characterised by circulation, incompletion and inconclusion. Such a definition of the short story, deriving from Dick's editorial work, needs to be confronted with what Woolf herself tells us about the short story.

Indeed, in the light of the observations made previously about the editors' coherent yet necessarily subjective and restrictive choices, and instead of taking for granted, as Baldwin amongst others does,[40] one editor's conception of Woolf's short story, I would rather turn to Woolf herself in order to find out what she herself calls a short story. Is it a "story", a "sketch", a "short fiction" or something else? If an answer could be found to these questions, the reader would see his way more clearly among these texts and would be able to assess Woolf's short story writing more easily.

The only volume of short stories Woolf published in her lifetime provides an embryo of answer. Indeed, the author chose to publish her own texts under the title of one of them, *Monday or Tuesday*, without adding, as was later the case, *and Other Stories*. This choice may appear as non-committal or, on the contrary, as a way of calling the reader's attention to the impossibility of using the term "short story". Woolf's dissatisfaction with this conventional term and the meaning assigned to it would then be voiced here.

If we thumb through Woolf's diary, we see, as we have done at the beginning of this introduction, that while she refers to the writing of her short stories, to their publication and reception, she does not say much about the genre itself. In her letters, she calls for a new form without being too explicit about it. Similarly, the index of her essays edited by Andrew McNeillie has entries about essays, letters, novels, poetry and prose, but none about the short stories. Which, understandably enough, leads Baldwin to assert:

> Unfortunately, she left few direct statements about her theory of the short story; there are no manifestos like "Modern Fiction" or "Mr. Bennett and Mrs. Brown" regarding the short story. Comments about her experiments in short fiction, therefore, must be related to her pronouncements about the novel and to what can be inferred from the stories themselves. (Baldwin xii)

Yet the reading of some of these essays may prove fruitful, even if the word "short story" does not appear in their titles. Indeed, while referring to Maupassant, Flaubert, Chekhov or Mansfield, Woolf tries to define this new genre which has not yet found a name of its own, the old term "short story" emphasising, as she points out in "Modern fiction,"[41] the story-telling—something which may no longer be adequate when dealing with modernist texts. She also attempts to define the reading contract upon which this new genre is based. As she writes about Chekhov's stories:

> But it is impossible to say "this is comic", or "this is tragic", nor are we certain, since short stories, we have been taught, should be brief and conclusive, whether this, which is vague and inconclusive, should be called a short story at all. (*Essays* IV: 163)

A close reading of a selection of significant essays, in Chapter 1 will aim at delineating Woolf's own conception of the short story. What she thinks about the traditional definition and conventional boundaries of the genre will be examined along with the way in which, as a critic of the genre, she redefines it. We shall see that far from retaining formal generic criteria and defining the short story in terms of generic transgression or even generic bending, Woolf defines it as combining contradictory but dialogic impulses and maps out its territory as a paradoxical and fundamentally ethical space. Woolf's own conception of the short story will tell us a great deal about the place she ascribes to it within her whole work, whether fictional or non fictional. Thus equipped with a provisional definition, we shall go back to her short stories and, rather than offering a detailed commentary on each text, we shall provide a guideline to their reading while attempting to reappraise them. Such will be the aim of this book. For individual studies of Woolf's short stories, for a reading of these texts in context and a comparison with contemporary short story writers, alluded to here in passing, the reader should turn to the fairly numerous articles already published. In the present study, a synthetic reading of Woolf's short stories will be aimed at. We shall first show, in the second chapter, that Woolf conceives her own short stories mainly as a space of tension which, at a structural level, both plays fragmentation against wholeness and combines them, which certainly requires a specific type of reading. This paradoxical and dynamic space will be analysed as a space of encounter, staging as it does the encounter between the self and the other, whether these are defined as characters (Chapter 3) or as writer and reader (Chapter 4). Conversation, redefined by Woolf, will appear to be the form of this encounter as well as the locus of emotion, that is, an eminently aesthetic and ethical space. Conversation will prove to be the very form Woolf chooses for her short story, "a form without formalism", which finally, as we shall argue into our last chapter, turns the short story into a site of resistance against all form of political and literary monologism and totality. The short story as conversation will thus be read as a deeply committed form where the aesthetic, the ethical and the political are brought together.

1
Virginia Woolf's Definition of the Short Story

Woolf's essays about the short story

Virginia Woolf's essays are written, like most essays of her time, in a style both polemical and metaphorical, extremely different from the cut-and-dried scientific style most literary critics and theoreticians adopt today.[1] Yet such a style should not blind us to Woolf's aim and competence. In some of these essays, such as "Is Fiction an Art?", she laments the lack of all theory of fiction:

> For possibly, if fiction is, as we suggest, in difficulties, it may be because nobody grasps her firmly and defines her severely. She has had no rules drawn up for her. And though rules may be wrong, and must be broken, they have this advantage—they confer dignity and order upon their subject; they admit her to a place in civilised society. (*Essays* IV: 460)

And in "On Re-Reading Novels", she opposes fiction to drama which has found its own theory:

> The drama, however, is hundreds of years in advance of the novel....But so far we have swallowed our fiction with our eyes shut. We have not named and therefore presumably recognized the simplest of devices by which every novel has come into being.[2]

I would like to show that in her essays, Woolf goes on elaborating her own "theory" of fiction and particularly, a "theory" of the short story.

No definition of the genre is stated explicitly in any particular essay and if we browse through the index of McNeillie's edition of Woolf's essays, we find that none of them is devoted to this topic even if several mention specific short stories. What I mean to show, in the wake of Nena Skrbic stimulating insights into Woolf's comments on the genre in her essays, reviews and correspondence,[3] is that Woolf's definition of the short story is present but disseminated in her essays and is there for the reader to reconstruct. Like Woolf's common reader, he must "create for himself, out of whatever odds and ends he can come by, some kind of whole—..., a theory of the art of writing" (*Essays* IV: 19), or more exactly, a "theory" of the short story. While occasionally referring to various other essays, I will base my present study on three essays mainly: "An Essay in Criticism",[4] published in 1927, "The Russian Point of View",[5] published in 1925 and "On Re-Reading Novels", published in 1922.[6] In the first essay, Woolf deals with Ernest Hemingway's short stories *Men without Women* (1927); in the second, Chekhov's short stories mainly are analysed and the last one focuses on Gustave Flaubert's "Un Cœur simple". Many of the remarks she makes concern fiction as a whole and novels in particular as the title of the third essay, "On Re-Reading Novels", points out, but the various statements she makes on the short stories of the writers mentioned above, if put together and examined closely, constitute a coherent and stimulating definition of the short story. From essay to essay, Woolf keeps asking the same type of question: why do I like Chekhov better than Hemingway? Why do I like Flaubert's story? These lead her to define her conception of the short story albeit in a diffuse way, through answers disseminated in the essays. If we are patient enough and if we listen to her call for a less indolent, more receptive reader who should turn into a critic, we can trace the outline of Woolf's "theory" of the short story. Although Woolf uses this word herself in "The Common Reader" (1925), we should keep in mind that she resists all form of system threatening to enclose and stifle thought. What we find in the essays mentioned above are Woolf's own reflections about other short story writers. Whether she praises or criticises them, what comes out in-between the lines is the pattern of the short story as Woolf herself conceives it, in a way the ideal pattern for her own short stories. This pattern is what she had in mind in the 1920s and if we can assume that it is what Woolf aims at in her own texts, we can also surmise that Woolf's ideal may have changed from the beginning to the end of her career. We shall therefore consider that these essays provide not so much a strict definition of the short story genre as broad, flexible guidelines that will help us to read the wide range of Woolf's short stories in a comprehensive way while respecting their diversity. They provide a working framework that can be accepted as such or adapted and extended as we go along.

In "An Essay in Criticism", Woolf makes a distinction between two types of short stories: those in the French and those in the Russian manner, yet she refuses all normative judgment: "Of the two methods, who shall say which is the better?" (*Essays* IV: 454). Mérimée and Maupassant's short stories are "self-sufficient and compact" (454) and come to clear rounded conclusions: "when the last sentence of the last page flares up, as it so often does, we see by its light the whole circumference and significance of the story revealed" (454); whereas the Russian type is inconclusive, "cloudy and vague, loosely trailing rather than tightly furled" (454). Woolf then proceeds to read Hemingway's short stories, *Men without Women,* as stories written with great skill in the French manner but failing to satisfy her. This is not only due to the writer's "display of self-conscious virility" (454), but also to a formal flaw in the short stories themselves. Indeed, Hemingway resorts to excessive and superfluous dialogue; and superfluity leads to lack of proportion. Although his short stories are "quick, terse and strong" (454), they are not, unlike Mérimée's or Maupassant's, perfect in shape:

> And probably it is this superfluity of dialogue which leads to that other fault which is always lying in wait for the writer of short stories: the lack of proportion. A paragraph in excess will make these little craft lopsided and will bring about that blurred effect which, when one is out for clarity and point, so baffles the reader. (*Essays* IV: 455)

Lack of proportion and too much dexterity turn his short stories into "dry and sterile" pieces (454) which fail to provide the reader with any real lasting emotion (unlike bullfighting which in *The Sun Also Rises* is supposed to provide emotion to the spectator and which Woolf adopts as a metaphor throughout her essay).

What Hemingway fails to achieve, Flaubert and Chekhov succeed in achieving. In "On Re-Reading Novels", Woolf takes a close look at

Flaubert's "Un Cœur simple", the story of "an old maid and a stuffed parrot" (*Essays* III: 344),[7] and demonstrates that the story hinges on the following phrase, appearing when "The mistress and the maid are turning over the dead child's clothes. 'Et des papillons s'envolèrent de l'armoire' " (340),[8] a phrase which accounts for the characters' behaviour, especially the servant's devotion to her mistress: "Félicité lui en fut reconnaissante comme d'un bienfait, et désormais la chérit avec un dévouement bestial et une vénération religieuse" (340).[9] The intensity of the phrase "Et des papillons s'envolèrent de l'armoire" contains all the repressed emotion of the characters and explains away all that precedes and follows in the story. This phrase also creates in the reader a deep emotion and "a flash of understanding" (340) which reveals the meaning of the story, the necessity of the various previous observations finally radiating from that intense phrase, all this amounting to a necessary re-reading of the short story. From then on, everything falls into place: the reader is granted a moment of understanding and a moment of being, in other words aesthetic emotion, coinciding with the characters' own emotions. And Woolf concludes that "both in writing and in reading it is the emotion that must come first" (341).

Woolf uses this reading of Flaubert's short story to show that Percy Lubbock, in *The Craft of Fiction*, is wrong when he argues that only by stripping our reading from all emotional reaction can we get at the form of the book, what he calls "the book itself" (*Essays* III: 339), its shape and outline, what we would call its structure. She bluntly rejects Lubbock's understanding of form in visual terms and his subsequent formalism before redefining form as the arrangement of emotions: "we feel with singular satisfaction, and since all our feelings are in keeping, they form a whole which remains in our minds as the book itself" (*Essays* III: 340). In the revised version of the same essay, "On Re-reading Novels", she phrases this even more explicitly: "when we speak of form we mean that certain emotions have been placed in the right relations to each other" (*C.E.* II: 129). And for Woolf, "the book itself' is not form which you see, but emotion which you feel" (*Essays* III: 340). Rejecting pure formalism, Woolf foregrounds emotion in the short story (as in the novel). Refusing to dissociate form from emotion, she comes close to Clive Bell's concept of "significant form"[10] in painting—provided we accept that "once the apostles of 'form' begin to talk about 'significant form', they cease to be pure formalists"[11]—or, more obviously, to Roger Fry's statement in *Vision and Design*: "I conceived the form and the emotion which it [the work of art] conveyed as being inextricably bound together in the aesthetic whole".[12]

Emotion is also at the heart of Chekhov's short stories, even more prominently than in Flaubert's. This is what Woolf discusses in "The Russian Point of View". According to her, Chekhov is characterised by his "simplicity". Chekhov's simplicity, in Woolf's terms, first refers to the bareness of his style, a quality she also grants Hemingway. Simplicity further refers to the ordinariness of the situations his short stories are based on (for example, "A man falls in love with a married woman, and they part and meet, and in the end are left talking about their position..." [*Essays* IV: 184]), the same ordinariness as in "Un Coeur simple". And more unexpectedly, simplicity becomes synonymous with "humanity" (182), a call "to understand our fellow-sufferers" (183), a form of sympathy "not with the mind—for it is easy with the mind—but with the heart" (183).[13] In other words, Chekhov's short stories, through their characters' portrayals, represent a shift from intellectual to emotional understanding and require a similar shift in the reader. Indeed, the soul which Chekhov is interested in "has slight connection with the intellect" (186). Chekhov, and Woolf in her reading of Chekhov, operates a displacement, in the definition of the soul, from the intellect to affects. In other words, the soul becomes the locus of affects. And by making the soul his prominent concern, Chekhov foregrounds emotion. Emotion in the characters creates emotion in the reader, what Woolf calls "the pleasure of reading", an intense feeling.

Appraising Woolf's definition of the short story

Through her appraisal of Flaubert, Hemingway and Chekhov's short stories, Woolf indirectly defines the short story genre and delineates a sort of model for the short story as an impersonal art of proportion and emotion.[14] Once established, Woolf's pronouncements on the short story should be closely examined not only in the light of the essays devoted to this literary genre but also of other non-fictional writings of the author's as well as of other later theories. This should enable us both to illuminate and synthesise Woolf's disseminated statements about the short story and provide adequate, if still flexible, critical tools with which to read her own short stories.

First, the short story should be an art of proportion, which is not exactly the same as an art of brevity. It is true that in "On Re-Reading Novels", Woolf chooses to illustrate her point by the analysis of a short story for the following reason: "and, not to strain our space, let us choose a short story, *Un Cœur Simple* (sic)" (*Essays* III: 339). Gustave Flaubert's short story is chosen as an example only because it saves space; in other words, Woolf does not seem to make any difference here between novels and short stories except in terms of length. Brevity seems to be retained as the first defining trait of the short story, just as it was by Woolf's ancestor Edgar Allan Poe, who claimed that a short story should be read "at one sitting".[15] However clear and simple, this trait is not specific enough and tends above all to reduce the short story to a genre that can only be appraised in comparison with the novel and its length. Yet, further on in the same essay, she writes: "Flaubert introduces a number of people for no purpose, as we think; but later we hear that they are now all dead, and we realise then for how long Félicité herself has lived. To realise that is to enforce the effect", thus implying that nothing is gratuitous in a short story. In "An Essay in Criticism", Woolf comes back to the notion of brevity and far from defining the short story as a novel in miniature she grants brevity a value of its own which makes it synonymous with formal purity and perfection,[16] much as writers like Alberto Moravia or Julio Cortazar have more recently defined the short story as a "pure genre"[17] and a "perfect form".[18] Indeed, the art of brevity is enlarged to an art of proportion, devoid of excess and superfluity, simple and perfect in shape, the very qualities Woolf admires in Greek literature.

Second, the short story should be an impersonal art, an art where the writer should not, through too much involvement, betray his sex, no more than he should in a novel. Indeed, in "An Essay in Criticism", Woolf takes Hemingway, as well as D. H. Lawrence and Joyce, to task for "their display of self-conscious virility" (*Essays* IV: 454). Echoing a former entry of her *Diary* where she laments "the damned egotistical self; which ruins Joyce and Richardson to my mind" (*Diary* II: 14; 26 January 1920), she writes that "any emphasis laid upon sex is dangerous. Tell a man that this is a woman's book, or a woman that this is a man's, and you have brought into play sympathies and antipathies which have nothing to do with art. The greatest writers lay no stress upon sex one way or the other"

(*Essays* IV: 453–4). Indeed, they are, like Shakespeare, androgynous, "man-womanly" or "woman-manly".[19] Woolf's ideal for the short story and fiction in general is Greek literature, "the impersonal literature" (*Essays* IV: 39), where hardly anything is known about the life of Aeschylus or Euripides: "we have either no sense or a very weak one of the personality of the Greek dramatists" ("Personalities", *C.E.* II: 274). This yearning for the erasure of the author's self is reminiscent of T. S. Eliot's call for depersonalisation, for "a continual extinction of personality",[20] in his 1919 essay "Tradition and the Individual Talent". However, personality may not have exactly the same meaning for Woolf and Eliot.[21] If, for Woolf, impersonality is synonymous with ungendered anonymity, a form of bareness and purity,[22] it is also equated with universality. In her essay "Personalities", Woolf examines Shakespeare's case and notices that, although "very little is known of him biographically...one has the certainty of knowing him" (*C.E.* II: 275). She concludes that Shakespeare and his like are "great artists who manage to infuse the whole of themselves into their works, yet contrive to universalize their identity so that, though we feel Shakespeare everywhere about, we cannot catch him at the moment in any particular spot....All has been instilled into their books" (*C.E.* II: 275–6). Woolf's universality does not presuppose a unified subject; for her, a universal art form cannot be ascribed to a single voice but to a double one, both male and female, and even to a pluralist voice. In other words, instead of being emptied out and disappearing as in Eliot's case, the authorial voice becomes an anonymous and universal or collective voice, "the common voice singing out of doors",[23] the voice of a multiple self and multiple selves, a polyphonic voice, what Gillian Beer calls "the nameless multiple author" in reference to Woolf's "Anon" that she compares with Walter Benjamin's "storyteller".[24]

Third, the short story should be an art of emotion rather than of thought, both in the writing and the reading. "Learn to make yourself akin to people.... But let this sympathy be not with the mind— for it is easy with the mind—but with the heart, with love towards them". Woolf selects this quotation from "A Village Priest", a short story by Elena Militsina[25] and uses it in "The Russian Point of View" (*Essays* IV: 183) just as she had in her early 1919 essay "Modern Fiction" (*Essays* IV: 163) where she discusses Chekhov's short story

"Gusev", and in "The Russian View" (*Essays* II: 342). Through repetition, emotion is foregrounded, both the short story writer's emotional understanding of characters and, as we saw earlier, the reader's emotional response.

At this point, the model of the short story Woolf provides is not so much a formal one (since both conclusive and inconclusive short stories in the French or Russian manner can be accepted; and she herself will write short stories belonging to these two categories) as a model where emotion is foregrounded, which places her within the history of sensibility that goes back to the Romantics and even to earlier eighteenth-century thinkers.

Emotional intensity directly derives from the perfect shape or "proportion" of the short story and turns it into a meaningful whole. By selecting this criterion, Woolf points to the short story as being a moment of emotional intensity, of represented as well as of experienced emotion, that is, a "moment of being"; the moment of being is then both the one evoked by the narrative and the narrative itself (a perfect form transmitting a perfect moment), which in turn creates an intense emotion in the reader. One could therefore say of the short story writer that, like the poet's, "his power [is] to make us at once actors and spectators" ("How Should One Read a Book?", *C.E.* II: 8). The intensity of the text produces an intense emotion in the reader very much like the violent shock produced by a personal emotion: "Our being for the moment is centred and constricted, as in any violent shock of personal emotion" (*C.E.* II: 7); and this comes before any sort of understanding: "Afterwards, it is true, the sensation begins to spread in wider rings through our minds; remoter senses are reached; these begin to sound and to comment and we are aware of echoes and reflections" (*C.E.* II: 7); and Woolf concludes: "we learn through feeling" (*C.E.* II: 9). In this evocation of the different phases of the creative process, from conception to reception, Woolf gives a central place to feeling, in the wake of the Romantics[26] and also of G. E. Moore who associated feeling or emotion with the cognitive element in aesthetic appreciation: "It is plain that in those instances of aesthetic appreciation … there is a bare cognition of what is beautiful in the object, but also some kind of feeling or emotion".[27] Emotional intensity is also linked, through the words "a flash of understanding" and "sudden intensity" used in "On Re-reading Novels" (*Essays* III: 340), with speed and rhythm, and Woolf comes back to this even more explicitly in "How Should One Read a Book?":

> Thus the desire grows upon us to have done with half-statements and approximations; to cease from searching out the minute shades of human character, to enjoy the greater abstractness, the purer truth of fiction. Thus we create the mood, intense and gen-eralised, unaware of detail, but stressed by some regular, recurrent beat, whose natural expression is poetry…. The intensity of poetry covers an immense range of emotion. (*C.E.* II: 6–7)

Here intensity is linked both with abstraction ("enjoy the greater abstractness…the mood, intense and generalised") and with rhythm ("stressed by some regular, recurrent beat"). Through semantic or structural repetitions, variations and echoes,[28] rhythm, born from the conjunction of brevity and intensity, structures the text and brings about the climactic emotional shock. Rhythm for Woolf, just as it is for E. M. Forster, is the basis of all true feeling in writing. As for abstraction, it is defined here in pictorial terms as the non-figurative, the non-representational and as synonymous with impersonality:

> So drastic is the process of selection that in its final state we can often find no trace of the actual scene upon which the chapter was based…. Life is subjected to a thousand disciplines and exer-cises. It is curbed; it is killed…. There emerges from the mist some-thing stark, something formidable and enduring, the bone and substance upon which our rush of indiscriminating emotion was founded.[29]

The process of selection and elimination allows the transcription of the intensity of affects while turning the text into "a sort of imper-sonal miracle" (*Essays* IV: 404). And it is thanks to this emotional intensity that the paradoxical nature of Woolf's aesthetics, with its combination of two apparently incompatible notions—abstraction and emotion, resulting from two contradictory impulses, elimin-ation and saturation[30]—can be perceived.

Finally, this definition of emotional intensity opens onto ques-tions of literary genres and shows that the short story is much closer to poetry than to the novel, with which it was initially compared in the same essay, "On Re-Reading Novels". And Woolf confirms this in "Notes on an Elizabethan Play": "The extremes of passion are not for the novelist" (*Essays* IV: 66); they are characteristic of drama and poetry and she adds, about Elizabethan drama: "the emotion [is] concentrated, generalised, heightened in the play. What moments of intensity, what phrases of astonishing beauty the play shot at us" (*Essays* IV: 66). Owing to this intensity, "the play is poetry" (*Essays* IV: 66). Intensity, in the end, is a characteristic of poetry, the supreme form of writing.

Woolf points to the generic hybridity of the short story which she conceives as being closer to poetry and drama than to the novel, very much like the "play-poem" her later work *The Waves* is meant to be. Aesthetic purity is thus closely linked by Woolf to generic hybridity. In other words, for her hybridity and cross-fertilisation become the necessary conditions of beauty and purity. Woolf thus goes against the grain and deprives hybridity of all derogatory connotations (just as she does in "Walter Sickert" where "the hybrids, the raiders" [*Essays* IV: 243] are praised or in *Flush,* where Flush is shown to be much happier among the Italian mongrels than the English pure-breds) in a move which is not without ideological implications.[31]

The definition Woolf gives of the short story through the joint concepts of proportion and intensity can be compared with the definition some critics or writers have given more recently. For some, like John Wain and much like the first theoretician of the short story, E. A. Poe, "the literary form that the short story most resembles is poetry".[32] Others, like Jean-Marie Schaeffer, draw a list of generic characteristics that do not allow a distinction between the short story and the novel. Only the five characteristics selected by Eileen Baldeshwiler (chronological disruptions, the use of images, the emphasis laid on inner life, open endings and meaning, a greater emotional intensity)[33] seem to match Woolf's definition, yet they do not take into account the relationship Woolf establishes between the new type of short story, the Russian one, and the old realist type, the French one. In the end, John Gerlach and Pierre Tibi's definitions seem more adequate. Gerlach writes: "The short story blends the brevity and intensity of the lyric poem with the narrative traits (plot, character and theme) of the novel"[34] and Tibi adds: "the short story seems to be the space of a confrontation between poetry and narrativity".[35] Yet for Woolf, it is not always narrativity which is so much at stake as its erasure; and where Tibi chooses to talk about "confrontation" between genres within the short story, Woolf prefers to think in terms of cross-fertilisation. And eventually, none of these definitions mentions the other genre with which short stories converse, that is, drama. In the end Woolf's theory of the short story differs from them all while combining them in a theory of her own where formal considerations of generic hybridity and proportion are intertwined with the notion of emotion, thus illustrating her demonstration in "On Re-Reading Novels" that form and emotion—what we could rephrase as form and content or form and meaning—are one and the same thing.

The short story redefined as an ethical space

Woolf gives further clues as to her own ideal short story through her recurrent references to Chekhov. In "The Russian Point of View", she discusses his short stories in terms of "humanity" and "honesty", terms which belong to a humanist tradition and are saturated with moral implications but which she redefines in her own way. What Woolf likes in Chekhov's short stories is their "humanity" and understanding of "fellow-sufferers", in other words, their openness and attentiveness to the other, their ethical faculty if, with Levinas and in Gibson's words, we define ethics as the moment when "the ego is deposed, gives up its drive to sovereignty and enters into ethics, into social relationship, dialogue, disinterestedness".[36] In the same way, she takes us a step further than "On Re-Reading Novels" in the definition of the ideal short story—although not in a very explicit manner. She first proceeds by elimination: if Chekhov is successful as a short story writer, it is neither because he is interested in social satire—even if he is "aware of the evils and injustices of the social state" (*Essays* IV: 185); nor because he is a psychological writer: "The mind interests him enormously.... But again the end is not there" (185). "Is it that he is primarily interested", Woolf wonders, "not in the soul's relation with other souls, but with the soul's relation to goodness? These stories are always showing some affectation, pose, insincerity. Some woman has got into a false relation; some man has been perverted by the inhumanity of his circumstances. The soul is ill; the soul is cured; the soul is not cured. Those are the emphatic points in his stories" (185). Chekhov's interest in "the soul's relation to goodness" is what Woolf calls the fundamental "honesty" of Chekhov's method.

Thematic honesty—the denouncing of "affectation, pose, insincerity" (*Essays* IV: 185)—goes together with formal honesty, that is, inconclusiveness and all types of resistance to formal manipulations. Indeed, Woolf shows how Chekhov's honesty exposes in return the falsity of conclusiveness; in this light, "the general tidying up" of the ending, "the marriage, the death, the statement of values so sonorously trumpeted forth'" (in Victorian and Edwardian fiction especially) appear as a mere "affectation of goodness", "nauseating in the extreme" (183). Conclusiveness, answering all questions, appears as a form of manipulation (whereas Chekhov indirectly warns the writer: "let us never manipulate the evidence so as to produce something fitting, decorous, agreeable to our vanity", 185). Unlike manipulation, inconclusiveness leads not to artifice but to a new form of "truth to life", Woolf explains in "Modern Fiction": "It is the sense that there is no answer, that if honestly examined life presents question after question which must be left to sound on and on after the story is over" (*Essays* IV: 163). Woolf thus indirectly advocates in the short story both an openness to the other as human being (or, more exactly, as human-like being) and an openness to the other as unfamiliar, innovative literary devices, bringing together, as it were, Hegel's definition of the other with more recent ones, as Derek Attridge does in *The Singularity of Literature*:

> In many discussions from Hegel to the present, "the other" (or "the Other")…indicates an already existing entity which the self encounters; most obviously, another human being. "The other" in Levinas's writing, for example—frequently called "Autrui" rather than "l'Autre" in order to bring out its human dimension— is linked closely to the biblical "neighbor", even though ultimately the otherness in question is that of God…. Whatever its precise complexion, the other in these accounts is primarily an impingement from outside that challenges assumptions, habits, and values, and that demands a response.[37]

And Attridge goes on explaining that "the encounter with a human other is not different in its essentials from the experience of the other as one attempts creatively to formulate fresh arguments or to produce an original work of art or philosophy" (Attridge 2004: 33) and he adds that the "process of responding to the other person through openness to change is not dissimilar, then, to the one that occurs when a writer refashions norms of thought to realize a new possibility in a poem or an argument" (Attridge 2004: 34).[38] Woolf can therefore be said to conflate Hegel and Levinas's definitions of the other as having a human dimension and Attridge's definition of the other as the breaking down of the familiar in a work of art; in his own words: "the act of breaking down the familiar is also the act of welcoming the other" (Attridge 2004: 26). Woolf's notions of humanity and honesty can therefore be seen as ways of discarding morality in favour of ethics, and an ethics that is, as in Attridge's case, indistinguishable from aesthetics.

Moreover, with Chekhov's inconclusiveness and unanswered questions, "the soul gains an astonishing sense of freedom" (*Essays* IV: 185). What Woolf means by "freedom" has to do both with morals and with the reading process. Morals first. In the same essay, Woolf goes on trying to define the soul, "the chief character in Russian fiction" (*Essays* IV: 185), and finds a clearer definition in Dostoevsky. The soul is a "medley of beauty and vileness" (*Essays* IV: 186); in the soul, the mind, according to the Russians, "[t]he old divisions melt into each other. Men are at the same time villains and saints; their acts are at once beautiful and despicable. We love and we hate at the same time. There is none of that precise division between good and bad to which we are used" (*Essays* IV: 187). It comes out that what Woolf likes in Chekhov and Dostoevsky is their lack of Manichaeism.[39] In their world, good is not opposed to bad, a criminal can be liked, moral categories are questioned. Their vision, unlike the Victorians', is not moral and moralising. Far from being Cartesian, their vision which questions the moral, Cartesian prejudice, appears to us closer to Spinoza's a-moral ethical vision: "il n'est aucune chose que nous sachions avec certitude être bonne ou mauvaise...";[40] or as Deleuze puts it: "l'Ethique...remplace la Morale, qui rapporte toujours l'existence à des valeurs transcendantes. La morale, c'est le jugement de Dieu, le *système du Jugement*. Mais l'Ethique renverse le système du jugement".[41] It is a vision which does not privilege the either/or logic, typical of closure, but "the compromised binary"[42] which, according to Harpham, is the paradigm of the ethical, linked as it is with openness and the welcoming of the other, whatever the latter' s form.

Such an ethical vision can only be inscribed within a textual space which permits questions and the questioning of conventional literary assumptions, that is, a space of freedom. It is a space without closure where thematic honesty is inscribed within the bounds of an honest form: "It is the sense that there is no answer, that if honestly examined life presents question after question", Woolf writes in "Modern Fiction" (*Essays* IV: 163). Like the Russian short stories, this space "flood[s] us with a view of the infinite possibilities of the art and remind[s] us that there is no limit to the horizon, and that nothing—no 'method', no experiment, even of the wildest—is forbidden, but only falsity and pretense. 'The proper stuff of fiction' does not exist; everything is the proper stuff of fiction, every feeling, every thought" (*Essays* IV: 164). With such a pronouncement, the writer's wide-ranging freedom is proclaimed and Woolf rejects all notion of hierarchy between methods and topics: there are no more noble forms, genres or subject-matters; everything is welcome, from "simplicity", bareness of style and ordinary situations, to generic impurity, which allows for the re-definition of the short story as, for instance, a play-poem.

If welcoming the other, whatever its shape, pertains to the writing, it also pertains to the reading of short stories. As Woolf explains, the openness to the other that Chekhov achieves in his short stories requires an emotional and inventive response from the reader or, as she shows in her discussion of Lubbock, form cannot be dissociated from emotion, whether it be the character's or the reader's emotion. Woolf's notion of form as emotion, or "form without formalism" (Attridge 2004: 119), enables her to re-think the old dualism of the aesthetic tradition between form and content. Form as emotion is best exemplified in the art of proportion that the short story is, where the experience of writing and reading is made more intense by the concision of the text. As Woolf writes in a letter about Robert Louis Stevenson, form cannot be dissociated from meaning: "I don't believe you can possibly separate expression from thought in an imaginative work".[43] For Woolf, as for Attridge, "Formal inventiveness is not merely a matter of finding new ways of constructing sentences or managing verbal rhythms" (Attridge 2004: 108); form is emotion or, in Attridge's words and definition of form, "sounds and shapes are nexuses of meaning and feeling" and "the new form that emerges…is…a new content—an open set of fresh possibilities of meaning, feeling, perceiving, responding, behaving" (Attridge 2004: 108).

In such a form, literary conventions are refashioned: the omniscient narrator gives way to a plural voice, exemplifying the interaction of the self with the other; silent and spoken words intermingle, creating a dialogue between inner and outer voices; the fictional, the metafictional, the historical or the autobiographical are woven together in total disregard of generic laws; allusion, quotation, and creation are intertwined in an interplay between the old and the new. Although the list is far from exhaustive, these are some of the ways in which short stories welcome the other, in its multiple shapes.

Such a new literary space is more demanding for the reader who needs to change his reading habits: "we raise the question of our fitness as readers.... We have to cast about in order to discover where the emphasis in these strange stories rightly comes" (*Essays* IV: 184). One sentence echoes what Woolf writes in "Modern Fiction" about Chekhov's "Gusev": "The emphasis is laid upon such unexpected places that at first it seems as if there were no emphasis at all" (*Essays* IV: 162). The reader's first impression of Chekhov's short stories is one of "bewilderment" (*Essays* IV: 183): "What is the point of it, and why does he make a story out of this? We ask as we read story after story" (*Essays* IV: 184). On unfamiliar ground with Chekhov's inconclusive stories, the reader must question his critical assumptions, shaped by Victorian fiction. Similarly, the emphasis on the heart rather than the mind, on the ordinary rather than the extraordinary, and the use of a bare style instead of an ornate one calls the reader's attention to what had been hitherto despised or set aside as uninteresting. The writer then "frees us to take delight, as we do when ill or travelling, in things themselves. We can see the strangeness of them only when habit has ceased to immerse us in them" ("Phases of Fiction", *C.E.* II: 82). Just as illness, by breaking our habits of perception through fever or a recumbent position, discloses "undiscovered countries" and brings to light the "wastes and deserts of the soul" ("On Being Ill" [*Essays* IV: 317]), this type of writing results in bewilderment and defamiliarisation.[44] Chekhov's method destabilises the reader, a most welcome moment of "bewilderment" for Woolf as it is for Spinoza: "[i]l y a Etonnement [*Admiratio*] quand à l'imagination d'une chose l'Ame demeure attachée, parce que cette imagination singulière n'a aucune connexion avec les autres" (Spinoza 198).[45] Bewilderment[46] or *Admiratio* is the moment when the mind loses its bearing and is ready to accept new landmarks, a new way of thinking, here a new frame of criticism. As Vinciguerra writes about Spinoza's concept: "L'étonnement, non seulement marque ponctuellement une rupture dans le cours de la pensée, mais il peut aussi être le critère autour duquel se cristallise une nouvelle habitude de pensée".[47] The emphasis Woolf lays on bewilderment in the reading of successful short stories reads as a call for the suspension of fixed reading habits— which goes together with the questioning of fixed moral categories— and for the necessity of responding fully to the alterity of the text. As Woolf explains in "Phases of Fiction": "Hence, we are at once conscious of using faculties hitherto dormant, ingenuity and skill, a mental nimbleness and dexterity such as serve to solve a puzzle ingeniously; our pleasure becomes split up, refined, its substance infinitely divided instead of being served to us in one lump" (*C.E.* II: 81). Destabilisation is thus turned into a most welcome writing and reading principle and bewilderment becomes the sign of successful writing. Through suspension of reading habits, Woolf asks for a form of passivity while requiring full response, that is, a most active participation of the reader. Woolf's short story reader must therefore be active and passive, what she calls, in "The Moment: Summer's Night", a "passive participant" (C.E. II: 293), what Attridge phrases in the following way: "[creative reading] requires a peculiar kind of passivity that does not preclude a high degree of alertness—what Wordsworth meant by 'wise passiveness' perhaps" (Attridge 2004: 80), or, more probably, we could add, what Keats meant by "negative capability", a receptive and outgoing capacity, both assimilative and dynamic, "capable of being".[48]

Woolf's reflection on inconclusiveness may come as a forerunner of Umberto Eco's definition of the open text but her appreciation of the reader's passive participation it necessitates is more qualified than the difference Roland Barthes will make between passive and active reading in the readerly and the writerly texts,[49] even if she couples the reader's activity with his pleasure and writes that a short story that follows these rules makes "exciting reading" and provides the reader with "giddy rapture" (*Essays* IV: 186), a truly and early Barthesian erotics of reading. She even goes further by introducing a reader who has to reinvent his reading assumptions and his frame of criticism, that is, a reader who enjoys a newly discovered freedom: "as we read these little stories about nothing at all, the horizon widens" (*Essays* IV: 185). Such a reader is no other than the "responsible reader" Derek Attridge defines as a reader able "to read inventively, to respond to the inventiveness of the work in an inventive way, and thus affirm and prolong its inventiveness", and such reading, according to him, is the locus of the ethical.[50]

If we know how to read her essays carefully, Woolf provides us with far-reaching conclusions: although the terse, compact, conclusive French-style short story has its merits, the inconclusive Russian-type one finally has her favour. Not simply because its form is new, but mainly because it adumbrates a new reading process while operating a shift from the intellect to affects and from morality to ethics. In those pages we have looked closely at the various terms (impersonal, proportion, emotion, humanity, simplicity, honesty) that Woolf uses to refer to the genre of the short story and at the meaning she ascribes to them. In a move typical of her ability not only to play on the polysemy of words but also to add new personal meanings, Woolf rejuvenates "old words" for, as she writes in "Craftsmanship", "they hate anything that stamps them with one meaning or confines them to one attitude, for it is their nature to change" (*C.E.* II: 251). She redefines these terms in such a way that they can all be brought under the banner of the ethical, as redefined by Attridge. Concomitantly, rather than discarding it as a term which has become inadequate, Woolf rejuvenates the term "short story" by redefining it as an impersonal art of proportion and emotion, with an "honest", inconclusive and a-moral method. Seen in terms of openness to the other and as requiring a similar openness from the reader, the short story appears as a space where the reader's responsibility is acknowledged and where the other, as the breaking down of the familiar, is welcome. Such a space is a space of freedom both for the writer and the reader, a space where form, emotion, and "honesty" are finally indistinguishable, that is, both an aesthetic and ethical space.

Such a definition, in all its nuances and complexities, places the short story at the very centre of Woolf's aesthetic quest, presenting it neither as simple entertainment nor as standing in any sort of hierarchical relation with another genre, but as participating fully in the creative process. As such, in its redefined meaning, the term "short story" will be retained, rather than any other. By thus delineating the contours of the short story, Woolf meets other twentieth-century theoreticians or writers. She lays the emphasis on the short story as an art of proportion, much as Cortazar, in the 1980s, will define the short story as an art of perfection. By envisaging the short story as an impersonal art, Woolf anticipates on the Structuralists' erasure of the author, especially in Barthes' 1968 article, "The Death of the Author"; she also echoes T. S. Eliot's theory of impersonality developed in "Tradition and the Individual Talent", an essay in which he shows that the surrender of the writer's self will allow "significant emotion" (Eliot 1999: 49), the impersonal "art emotion" (Eliot 1999: 47) to come to the fore; yet, as we have seen, she never meets them completely. Woolf also insists on the importance of emotion, both in the writing and the reading process, thus inscribing herself within the English tradition of sensibility as well as pointing, through the link she makes between emotion and ethics, towards the works of Gilles Deleuze or, in another field, Antonio Damasio, who have recently rediscovered Spinoza's ethics, or of Andrew Gibson, who is arguing in favour of "an ethics of affect" (Gibson 162), and of Derek Attridge. Woolf also grants pride of place to the reader of short stories. The emphasis that she lays on bewilderment in the reading of successful short stories reads as a call for the stripping away of fixed reading habits, which goes together with the questioning of fixed moral categories: destabilisation is thus turned into a most welcome writing and reading principle. A short story that would follow these rules would make, in Woolf's own words, "exciting reading" and provide the reader with "giddy rapture" (*Essays* IV: 186), a truly and early Barthesian erotics of reading. What now remains to be seen is whether and how Woolf's own short stories match her definition.

2
Woolf's Short Stories as a Paradoxical and Dynamic Space

By defining in her essays the short story as an impersonal art of proportion and emotion, Woolf puts together terms that seem to jar with each other. Proportion suggests symmetry, balance, some form of rational organisation at odds with emotion, which is generally connected with excess, passion and intensity, the very opposites of rationality. Similarly, impersonality suggests an absence of personal involvement, an "extinction of personality" in T. S. Eliot's words,[1] and therefore a lack of emotion or at least, an attempt at depersonalisation and at erasing emotion or keeping emotion under control.

By bringing these apparently contradictory notions together, Woolf implicitly defines the short story in terms of tension, that is, of simultaneous opposition and connection, in other words as a paradoxical or oxymoronic form combining contraries. The dialectics of proportion, impersonality and emotion are what we are going to address now, confronting Woolf's "theory" with her practice and analysing the story-telling process in an attempt at delineating Woolf's short story more accurately.

Transmuting the story-telling process

The variety of Woolf's short stories is a challenge and seems to preclude any overall reading. However, there are some recurrent features worth thinking about and analysing to highlight the writer's story-telling process. Using such a term as story-telling obviously suggests Woolf tells stories in her short stories, which seems to go against her essays and novels where she repeatedly denounces story-telling as well as the plot that is at the heart of it. In her early essay, "Modern Fiction", she vigourously derides the misplaced labour of the writer who "seems constrained, not by his own free will but by some powerful and unscrupulous tyrant who has him in thrall, to provide a plot, to provide comedy, tragedy, love interest, and an air of probability embalming the whole so impeccable [sic] that if all his figures were to come to life they would find themselves dressed down to the last button of their coats in the fashion of the hour" (*Essays* IV: 160). And she yearns for a type of literature where "there would be no plot, no comedy, no tragedy, no love interest or catastrophe in the accepted style, and perhaps not a single button sewn on as the Bond Street tailors would have it" (160). And down to her last novel, she will denounce plot: "Don't bother about the plot: the plot's nothing".[2] However, when we come to her short stories, we cannot help noticing that she keeps telling stories: the story of the duchess and the jeweller, the story of Mabel and her new dress, the story of Minnie Marsh or Milly Masters, the story of Gipsy the mongrel, etc. The question is whether those stories match the conventional definition of what a story and its plot are. The terms "story" and "plot" are defined by E. M. Forster in *Aspects of the Novel* in the following way: "We have defined a story as a narrative of events arranged in their time-sequence. A plot is also a narrative of events, the emphasis falling on causality. 'The king died and then the queen died' is a story. 'The king died, and then the queen died of grief' is a plot".[3] I would like to show that in her short stories, even more clearly than in her novels, Woolf does not so much discard the notions of story and story-telling as re-appropriates them by transmuting them in many different ways. And because she re-appropriates and redefines the "story" and "story-telling", I will argue, as I already did in Chapter 1, although for different reasons, that the term "short story" should be retained to refer to her own short texts.

From the fragment to the whole: the associative method

The paradigmatic moment

When we browse through Woolf's short stories, we can see that she writes about a few days in John's life ("Solid Objects"), one day on the slopes of Mount Pentelicus ("A Dialogue upon Mount Pentelicus"), a few hours spent by various guests at Mrs Dalloway's party ("The New

Dress", "Ancestors", "The Introduction", etc.) or by different characters in Kew Gardens ("Kew Gardens"), a "moment (the 20th June,
1906)" in "Phyllis and Rosamond". Woolf selects a slice of life, a
moment or a series of moments in her characters' lives and organises
her short story around it. The chosen moment can both span a
restricted length of time while expanding it. A linear development
can then be adopted and the doings of a character are exposed in a
chronological order. In "Phyllis and Rosamond" we follow the two
young ladies' "progress throughout the day" (*CSE* 18),[4] from break-
fast through lunch and tea to an evening gathering, the conventional pattern of the story matching the conventional life of the
characters. However, while the conventional time-pattern of the
short story contains and restrains it in the same way as social conventions constrain the two girls, the limits of the short story are
expanded. The day in Phyllis and Rosamond's lives singled out by
the narrative becomes emblematic of their daily life, just as the June
day in *Mrs Dalloway* becomes emblematic of Clarissa's days.
The same paradigmatic quality is attributed to the days selected in
John's life in "Solid Objects". "John had been that day to Barnes
Common, and there under a furze bush had found a very remarkable
piece of iron" (106): what John does on that very day is similar to
what he did the day before or will do the next day, that is, walk
around collecting objects. The same is true of the brief encounter
between the duchess and the jeweller: the duchess who is a compul-
sive gambler ("Been gambling again had she?", 252), regularly comes
to the shop to sell her jewels and Oliver always buys them, pretending to help her while accepting to be cheated by her for the sake of
her daughter with whom he is in love ("each felt this and knew this
every time they touched hands thus in the little back room", 251).

In such short stories, the life of a character is contracted and
reduced to a specific moment which is in turn expanded through its
paradigmatic qualities. Two contradictory impulses go into the making of the moment and contribute to give the reader the feeling that
a story is being told and that he knows the characters well. A fragment in a character's life is thus turned into a whole.

Intensity

In many other short stories, Woolf chooses not so much to endow
the moment with paradigmatic qualities as to highlight its uniqueness

and intensity. Many short stories are centred on a moment of intense emotion: the suffering of Lily Everit in "The Introduction" or of Mabel Waring in "The New Dress", the ecstasy of human intercourse in "Together and Apart", the discovery of love in "Moments of Being: Salter's Pins Have No Points", happiness in the story of the same name, hatred and unhappiness in "The Man who Loved his kind", etc. The moment—a few hours or a few minutes—is enlarged; "actual time" is forgotten and "mind time"[5] considerably expands the narrow limits of the moment so that life is measured not by time but by "value" or intensity, as E. M. Forster suggests:

> there seems something else in life besides time, something which may conveniently be called *"value"*, something which is measured not by minutes or hours, but by *intensity*, so that when we look at our past it does not stretch back evenly but piles up into a few notable *pinnacles*, and when we look at the future it seems sometimes a wall, sometimes a cloud, sometimes a sun, but never a chronological chart. (Forster 1974: 19; emphasis mine)

Value or intensity, in E. M. Forster's words, prevails in Woolf's short stories and the emotion experienced by the characters takes on hyperbolic dimensions: humiliation, for Mabel, becomes "the whole horror" (171); Lily Everit in front of Bob Brinsley feels like a fly that is being killed and "the yoke that had fallen from the skies onto her neck crushed her" (188). Conversely, Fanny Wilmot surprises Miss Craye "in a moment of ecstasy" (220) and Miss Anning and Roderick Serle, while talking with each other, feel "the old ecstasy of life" (193). Ordinary feelings take on the dramatic intensity of raw emotions as in Greek plays, where "emotions stand still and suffer themselves to be looked at" (*Essays* IV: 48), or Elizabethan plays where "the dramatist…shows us not Annabella in love, but love itself" (*Essays* IV: 66). Through such intensity, the short story is given the dramatic quality of a scene as well as some theatricality, especially when pitches of intensity are reached. Such is the case of Gilbert Clandon's phone call to Sissy Miller, in "The Legacy", and his rage at discovering the truth about his wife's death:

> He could not bear it. He must know the truth. He strode to the telephone.

"Miss Miller!" There was silence. Then he heard someone moving in the room.

"Sissy Miller speaking"—her voice at last answered him.

"Who", he thundered, "is B. M.?"

He could hear the cheap clock ticking on her mantelpiece; then a long drawn sigh. Then at last she said:

"He was my brother". (287)

In some short stories, intensity is conveyed through pictorial means, as in "Three Pictures", a triptych-like short story, where *hypotyposis* brings home the young couple's happiness in the rather conventional first picture that "might have been called 'The Sailor's Homecoming'" (228) before giving way to an expressionistic picture, in the style of Edvard Munch's *The Cry* (1893), where "inexpressible horror" (229) is voiced by a loud sexless cry rending "the dead silence", a prosopopoeia accounting for the horror of the scene; finally, in the third picture, *hypotyposis* conveys a visual sense of peace: in the graveyard, the grave-digger's family is having a picnic while the sailor's grave is being dug. Happiness and unhappiness, life and death are brought together while the pictorial qualities of this third moment offer indirect comments on the deceptiveness of appearances and the reversibility of signs: what can be a peaceful moment for the gravedigger's family is a tragic one for the sailor's wife. This short story, like most of Woolf's, seems to illustrate Woolf's saying in *Between the Acts*: "Love. Hate. Peace. Three emotions made the ply of human life" (Woolf 2000: 57), provided we understand the word "hate" as encompassing hate and what is hateful, horror, suffering and unhappiness; peace being the peace of happiness, love and life as well as the peace of death, whether natural or tragic.

Woolf's short story is certainly an art of emotion, as the author suggests in the essays initially examined. And through the intensity of emotion, a moment, a fragment in a character's life is turned into a self-contained and autonomous whole, or as Woolf herself writes about Mérimée and Maupassant's stories, a "self-sufficient and compact" whole (*Essays* IV: 454).

The associative method

However, this self-contained moment bursts out of its limits, reaching out as it does into other moments, other scenes or pictures.

Indeed, although she steeps her characters in the present moment, Woolf implements the same "tunnelling process" (*Diary* II: 272; 15 October 1923) as in her novels, "dig[ging] out beautiful caves behind [her] characters" (*Diary* II: 263; 30 August 1923), and through these forays into their past, she manages to tell their stories or life-stories, "scene making [being her] natural way of marking the past".[6] In "Kew Gardens", for instance, through the mechanism of memory, the past resurfaces and its very presence enriches the present moment. Strolling in Kew Gardens among butterflies zig-zagging from flower-bed to flower-bed, Simon remembers the dragon-fly which kept circling round Lily and himself; a love-scene of his youth delicately traced through the metonymy of the square silver shoe-buckle that encapsulates "the whole of [Lily]" (91), and of the dragon-fly whose dance metaphorises Simon's desire for Lily. Strolling is a situation conducive to thinking and Simon appears as the *flâneur par excellence*. The setting, the gardens where he had come 15 years before, the butterflies and their irregular movements channel his thoughts towards a similar moment in the past, a moment of sexual desire. As for Simon's wife, Eleanor, she is also strolling and sensitive to the men and women lying in the grass but as a *flâneuse*, the memory prompted in her by the situation is more heretical: "the kiss of an old grey-haired woman with a wart on her nose, the mother of all my kisses all my life" (91), certainly not the kiss of a mother. Both Simon and Eleanor, like Baudelaire's *flâneur* according to Benjamin, read the past in the city gardens while existing fully in the present.[7]

The situation is similar in "Mrs Dalloway in Bond Street" where Mrs Dalloway is walking in Westminster and the June morning, "fresh" and "unused" (152), brings back memories of her happy childhood just as "a leaf of mint" or " a cup with a blue ring" (152) would. Walking together with the quality of the morning, the sensation of freshness and novelty allow the past to become present again, as the madeleine does for Marcel. The next moment Big Ben strikes ten and its "leaden circles" (152) make Mrs Dalloway stand erect as her harsh education has taught her to. Discipline and its attendant suffering lead her to think of Mrs Foxcroft's own suffering at the death of her son, or rather at the loss of her property ("Mrs Foxcroft at the embassy last night decked with jewels, eating her heart out, because that nice boy was dead, and now the old Manor House (Durtnall's van passed) must go to a cousin", 152).

Here a more recent past invades the present, the two being closely knit together as the parenthesis where Mrs Dalloway registers the passing of a van suggests, and finally opens onto a heart-rending future. Later the statue of Queen Victoria will remind her again of her childhood and her nanny ("Victoria's white mound, Victoria's billowing motherliness ... always ridiculous, yet how sublime, thought Mrs Dalloway, remembering ... being told by Nanny to stop dead still and bow to the Queen", 153). Alternately, a sensation, a sound or a sight, make the past come back to the surface and invade the present so that the limits of the present moment are pushed back and it comes to contain both the present, the past, and occasionally the future as in T. S. Eliot's poem:

> Time present and time past
> Are both perhaps present in time future
> And time future contained in time past.[8]

In these two short stories, external events—sights, sensations—prompt memory, an involuntary and random process analogous to the erratic movements of the walkers that leads to the interweaving of past and present. Similarly, in "The Searchlight", the light of the searchlight that "falls here and there" (272) will metaphorise the randomness of involuntary memory[9] and the intertwining of past and present will be conveyed through Mrs Ivemey who imitates the gestures of her great-grandfather and great-grandmother and wears "something blue over her shoulders" (270), like her ancestor.

The power of the past to enrich the present and the interactive nature of the relation uniting the past and the present is proved *a contrario* in a caricature, "Ancestors". Mrs Vallance spends her evening at Mrs Dalloway's party remembering her happy childhood in Scotland and criticising the triviality of the party ("all *this* seemed to her so trivial", 180), the stuffiness of the room where she is standing and the foolishness of the young men surrounding her. Unable to enjoy the present moment, she takes refuge in the past, an idealised past: "that garden (which now appeared to her the place where she had spent her whole childhood, and it was always starlit, and always summer, and they were always sitting out under the cedar tree smoking ..." (183). The way in which she looks at the party, the room and the guests becomes significant of her own life built on a stultifying nostalgia for the past ("dreaming of the past, which is, Mrs Vallance thought, somehow so much more real that the present", 182)—that is, a dead petrified present or an absence of life ("life had passed over her like a wheel", 182). The caricatural portrait of this character who cannot reconcile past and present, points to the necessary intertwining of past and present and their mutual power of enrichment.

The present moment can also extend its limits by reaching out into other moments, without necessarily privileging the temporal dimension. Such is the case of "A Simple Melody", one of the short stories revolving around Mrs Dalloway's party.[10] Caught in the middle of a conversation with Miss Merewether, Mr Carslake is looking at "a picture of a heath" (201); some element in it—its soothing beauty—sets him thinking and dreaming about bringing some of the party's guests (Mabel Waring, who appears in "The New Dress"; Stuart Elton, who appears in "Happiness", etc.) to such a heath and walking with them. After a while, he looks back at the picture and another element—its sadness—makes his thoughts drift in another direction; again and again, the circling movement is repeated. Like the mark on the wall in the 1917 short story, the picture serves as the starting-point of the thinking process and regularly sets it going again. It is a focal point to which the character's gaze and thoughts converge and from which they diverge repeatedly. The picture, like the mark, is both the catalyst of thought and the connecting link between various "trains of thought" (88). It is also comparable to the letter which, in "Sympathy", prompts the narrator's conjectures, with its name and date suggesting that the person mentioned has just died: "Hammond, Humphry, on the 29th of April, at the Manor, High Wickham, Bucks" (108). The narrator slowly drifts from the supposedly deceased Humphry to his wife, Celia, to reflections on death and back to Humphry before her mistake is finally revealed and Humphry Hammond appears to be not Celia's husband but her father-in-law.

Whether the character is caught in the middle of a conversation, reading a letter or dreaming about a mark, the beginning is an abrupt *in medias res* one and so is the ending of those short stories: Mr Carslake and Miss Merewether resume their conversation; the whole letter is finally read and the error dispelled; the nail finally proves to be a snail. In between the beginning and the end, the same method can be observed: a similar drifting and circling process where an object, an image, a word or a state of mind is associated with another and so on, in a chain-like fluid movement: the flux and flow of random thought and association, whether it be a first or third person narrative, what has been aptly called the stream of consciousness technique. It is the method Rosamond Merridew, a historian specialising in "the system of land tenure in mediaeval England" (33), has adopted: "If you read my work called 'The Manor Rolls' you will be pleased or disgusted according to your temperament by certain digressions which you will find there" (34). If this method is close to that developed by some historians in Woolf's time, it also enlightens us about Woolf's own writing method. However, the word "digression" underlines the diverging movement and not the concomitant converging one.

Rather than adopting her words in "The Journal of Mistress Joan Martyn" and calling her method a digressive one, I will say Woolf privileges an associative method. Her short stories are primarily based on connection and, as such, constitute moments of harmony and unity. Woolf's short stories cannot therefore be defined as stories or plots. Woolf certainly does not favour the linearity and causality underlined by E. M. Forster in his definition of these two notions but redefines in her short stories the story-telling process in terms of association, connection, expansion, of moments shooting out into other moments. This process could be compared to Deleuze's rhizomatic thinking which promotes becoming and is structured by moments of synthesis, "the rhizome operat[ing] by variation, expansion, conquest, captures, offshoots".[11]

A whole made of fragments: the method of interruption

But to be content with this would be to betray Woolf's writing practice as a short story writer since the feeling of wholeness the reader derives from his reading is counterbalanced by a different one. Connection goes together with disconnection in her texts and the feeling of fluidity is counteracted by a feeling of fragmentation. Indeed, Woolf's short stories always expose some form of fragmentation. Far from adopting only a seamless progression, they also favour what we could call a method of interruption. Whether they stage a character's stream of consciousness or a conversation between characters, they show how the flow of thoughts or of words unfolds and is simultaneously interrupted.

At a micro-structural level, stylistic and thematic fragmentation is quite frequent; disruptions, interruptions or disconnection pervade conversation and can become a satirical device. In "The Evening Party", disruption is at the core of the moment described, the evening party. Two characters, one of them a writer, try to have a conversation with a professor about Shelley's use of punctuation. Although the conversation does take place, it is constantly interrupted by references to the external world—draughts, lost glasses, the discomfort of evening dress, modern print, rheumatism, etc.—which keeps impinging on the professor's efforts at concentrating on Shelley:

> To tell the truth open windows after sunset—standing with my back—agreeable though conversation—You asked of Shelley's commas. A matter of some importance. There, a little to the right of you. The Oxford edition. My glasses! The penalty of evening dress! I dare not read—Moreover commas—The modern print is execrable (97).

Are the broken style, the nominal sentences interrupted by dashes or exclamation marks, a sign of old age? Or a satire of the professor's inability to talk of literature? Or does the passage point out the difficulty of saying what one means and reveals the inadequacy of language: "Speech is an old torn net, through which the fish escape as one casts it over them" (99)? Probably all of this at the same time.

Woolf will make a similar attempt at transcribing the way in which external elements blur a conversation, acting as parasitic noise, in a late short story, "The Watering Place" (1941). There, the narrator transcribes a conversation overheard in a ladies' lavatory in a sea-side town. While "exerting their rights upon improving nature" (291), two young ladies talk and their talk is constantly interrupted by the water gushing next door; their words are erased by this noise which is compared to the tide:

> their talk was interrupted as by the surge of an indrawing tide; and then the tide withdrew and one was heard saying:
> 'I never did care about her—the simpering little thing... Bert never did care about big women... Ave you seen him since he's been

back?...His eyes...they're so blue...Like pools...Gert's too...Both
ave the same eyes...You look down into them...They've both got
the same teeth...Are He's got such beautiful white teeth...Gert has
em too...But his are a bit crooked...when he smiles...'
The water gushed....The tide foamed and withdrew. It uncovered
next: "But he had ought to be more careful. If he's caught doing it,
he'll be courtmartialled..." (291)

Through interruption, a nondescript conversation becomes totally
disconnected and ludicrous; its very futility is turned into comic
word-play.

In "Kew Gardens", disconnection is brought to a climactic and
satirical peak when two elderly women are captured

energetically piecing together their very complicated dialogue:
"Nell, Bert, Lot, Cess, Phil, Pa, he says, I says, she says, I says, I says,
I says—"
"My Bert, Sis, Bill, Grandad, the old man, sugar,
Sugar, flour, kippers, greens
Sugar, sugar, sugar." (93)

The accumulation of names and substantives, the juxtaposition of
the verbs "he says", "I says", the repetition of "sugar", the absence of
link-words take off the substance of the conversation and reduce it to
a meaningless chaos that only "the flowers standing cool, firm and
upright in the earth" (93) can listen to without smiling.

As a satirical device, interruption points out the meaninglessness
of conversation or its absence of logic. Conversation is reduced to a
shuttlecock game in which empty words, reduced to mere sounds,
are exchanged; its power of conveying meaning disappears while
its social function of connecting people is retained, suggesting that
social connection is based not on conversation proper but on affect-
ive links: being together turns out to be more important than
exchanging meaningful words and messages. The interrupted conversation, with its jerky rhythm, its broken sentences, its gaps and
parasitic noises, becomes a Woolfian topos where the external
world and the world of language are set against each other and
intertwined.

At a macro-structural level, structural fragmentation is a frequent device. A recurrent pattern can be observed: the narrator or the characters' thoughts are presented, rather than re-presented, and a foray into the past or into an imaginary world is superseded by another; a scene is interrupted by another. For instance, in "An Unwritten Novel", the anonymous narrator gazes at a woman sitting opposite her in a train compartment and imagines her life. In the embedded story, she offers a disconnected series of slices of life (Minnie Marsh at luncheon, Minnie Marsh praying or darning a glove, Minnie Marsh's moments of boredom or hatred of her sister-in-law, etc.), further disconnected by the wild rhythm of the style and the fragmentation of sentences constantly interrupted by dashes, exclamation marks, question marks or aposiopeses ("Vows broken? Not Minnie's!... She was faithful. How she nursed her mother! All her savings on the tombstones—wreaths under glass—daffodils in jars. But I'm off the track. A crime…. They would say she kept her sorrow, suppressed her secret—her sex, they'd say—the scientific people", 115). Fragmentation is similarly exposed in "The Journal of Mystress Joan Martyn". Within the story told by the historian Rosamond Merridew, is embedded Joan Martyn's diary. Each entry focuses on a scene of Joan's daily life: the arrival of the pedlar, the midsummer pilgrimage, getting ready for marriage and ruling a house, etc. Each entry is autonomous and disconnected from the following one. The diary illustrates, amongst other things, the possible disconnected nature of story-telling, composed as it is of a series of scenes disconnected from each other yet connected through the origin of the telling, the diarist. Similar efforts at containing the exposed fragmentation can be traced in "An Unwritten Novel" through the use of leitmotivs (the "spot on the window-pane" Minnie tries to rub away, the itching spot between her shoulders which is now a "stigma", now "some stain, some indelible contamination" [113], now "the itch and the patch and the twitch", now "the stain of sin", "the crime, the thing to expiate" [115]) which provide the connecting link between disconnected scenes.

Two other examples, "Kew Gardens" and "The Mark on the Wall", will enable us to prove our point. In "Kew Gardens", the snail's progress in the flower-bed is punctuated by the movements of men and women walking past; this situation allows brief snapshots of various characters: Eleanor and Simon, the young man and the old mad one, the two elderly women, and the young couple. In other words, the short story is made of a series of fragments, each focusing on specific characters who respectively remember the past, summon the spirits of the dead, talk at random, and experience love for the first time. The snail is the slow-moving, relatively stable reference point as well as the connecting link between the various characters and scenes. The scenes are independent, whole and yet always interrupted and the characters come out of the blue only to disappear straight away: "The figures of these men and women ... those ghosts ... soon diminished in size among the trees and looked half-transparent" (91). These ghostly figures are captured briefly before they vanish like a mirage, in an optical effect due to the heat which also stands as a metaphor of the sudden birth and death of fictional characters in the creator's mind: "Thus one couple after another with much the same irregular and aimless movement passed the flower-bed and were enveloped in layer after layer of green-blue vapour, in which at first their bodies had substance and a dash of colour, but later both substance and colour dissolved in the green-blue atmosphere. How hot it was!" (95).

"Kew Gardens" combines association and interruption, something which comes out even more clearly in "The Mark on the Wall", an earlier short story. The mark on the wall prompts the narrator's thoughts; the narrator speculates about the nature of the mark (is it a nail, a leaf, a smooth tumulus, a gigantic nail or a plank in the sea?) and her thoughts start drifting (is the mark a nail meant for a miniature chosen by the people who lived in the house before the narrator did?) until they are interrupted for no apparent reason. The mark immediately sets the narrator thinking again. The narrator regularly returns to the mark and drifts away from it in a reiterated converging and diverging process. Each time, the mark initiates a new "train of thought" (88), new speculations, associations of ideas and reflections. In other words, the external world prompts thought, stimulates the inner world; one thing leads to another in a free-associative way, different from the "automatic fancy" (83) the narrator first experiences when sitting by the fireside, a familiar situation automatically bringing to mind the same clichés: "my eye lodged for a moment upon the burning coals, and that old fancy of the crimson flag flapping from the castle tower came into my mind, and I thought of the cavalcade of red knights riding up the side of the black rock" (83). Each time, the "train of thought" is brutally and unexpectedly interrupted, for no reason at all, chance merely playing its part: "he was in the process of saying that in his opinion art should have ideas behind it when we were torn asunder, as one is torn from the old lady about to pour out tea and the young man about to hit the tennis ball in the back garden of the suburban villa as one rushes past in the train" (83). Or "something is getting in the way" (89), outer reality—the mark, someone standing in front of the narrator and reminding her of the war—after a while, impinges on the world of speculation:

> Where was I? What has it all been about? A tree? A river? The Downs?...Someone is standing in front of me and saying—
> "I'm going out to buy a newspaper."
> "Yes?"
> "Though it's no good buying newspapers...Nothing ever happens. Curse this war; God damn this war!...All the same, I don't see why we should have a snail on our wall." (89)

In the end external reality, which appears to be both cut from internal reality and intertwined with it, fulfills a double function since it can both prompt and interrupt thought. As for the thinking process, it is best metaphorised by life, such as it is depicted in the short story: "if one wants to compare life to anything, one must liken it to being blown through the Tube at fifty miles an hour.... Yes, that seems to express the rapidity of life, the perpetual waste and repair; all so casual, all so haphazard..." (84). The metaphor conveys the speed and the randomness of thought as well as its accidental nature (how it focuses on one thing rather than another), its "waste and repair" (how it accumulates thoughts as human beings accumulate possessions only to lose them immediately). The double nature of the thinking process, based on accumulation and loss, association and interruption, is thus conveyed.

Virginia Woolf's short stories are based, like the movement of thought, on two contradictory and complementary strategies, an associative one and a disruptive one. They display a constant pull and counter-pull between continuity and discontinuity, between totality and fragmentation. Woolf indirectly acknowledges such a phenomenon in Chekhov's short stories when she writes in "The Russian Background": "The fragments of which it [Chekhov's short story] is composed may have the air of having come together by chance" (*Essays* III: 84). The tension between unity and fragmentation entails a tension between what Poe calls "totality" or "single effect" (Poe 446) and a multiplicity of effects, that is the possibility for the reader to hold the whole story in his mind while feeling it keeps eluding him. Story-telling is thus redefined as combining an associative method with a method of interruption, an original and paradoxical process; and the short story appears to be both a fragment turned into a whole and a whole made of fragments, "a mosaic of jagged fragments",[12] to use H. G. Well's formula about *A Portrait of the artist as a Young Man,* "fragments of eggshell—fragments of a map", to use Woolf's own words (*CSE* 117). As Patricia Laurence writes about Woolf's novels: "The seeming opposition between notions of "totality" and "fragmentation" is collapsed in Woolf's narrative techniques", something that "many critics of Woolf miss or ignore as anomaly or ambivalence rather than conscious design".[13] Woolf's short stories, like her novels, can indeed be described as a world of tension, a moving, living world whose motto could be, as in *Between the Acts,* "Unity—Dispersity".

Framing/unframing the short story

Such tension is further exposed by the presence or absence of frames. Frames in Virginia Woolf's short stories may first appear as efforts at containing fragmentation within a whole while their absence may be a way of reasserting its power. However, things may turn out to be more complex than they seem.

Framed stories

In several short stories, Woolf chooses to encapsulate her story within clearly delineated boundaries or frames. These frames may take the form of what we could call "strong frames", that is an outer narrative can contain an inner, embedded one. In "An Unwritten Novel", the narrator, sitting in a train compartment, observes a woman sitting opposite her and indulges in character-reading: "Leaning back in my corner, shielding my eyes from her eyes, seeing only the slopes and hollows, greys and purples, of the winter's landscape, I read her message, deciphered her secret, reading it beneath her gaze" (114). When the train stops, the woman gets off, the narrator realizes she has been imagining rather than deciphering the woman's life-story: "Well, my world's done for! What do I stand on? What do I know? That's not Minnie. There never was Moggridge" (121); and the story comes to an end. A similar situation is evoked in "The Shooting Party" where the narrator looks at a woman getting into the carriage with a brace of pheasants and starts imagining her life until the train stops and she gets off: "she was quite an ordinary rather elderly woman, travelling to London on some quite ordinary piece of business" (260). Again reality does not match the narrator's fiction. In "The Lady in the Looking-Glass", an observer sitting on a sofa and looking at a lady's looking-glass, imagines its owner until the latter appears and proves to be different from what she had imagined, actually extremely disappointing. In "The Searchlight", the situation is different but the device is the same. Sitting on the balcony of an old mansion-house on a moonless night, waiting for the play to begin, "Mr and Mrs Ivimey's party were drinking coffee" while "rods of light wheeled across the sky. It was peace then; the airforce was practising; searching for enemy aircraft in the sky" (269). The searchlight reminds Mrs Ivimey of her great-grandfather and she starts telling his story until "[t]he searchlight had passed on" (272) and her reminiscences come to an end: "it was time they went on to the play" (272). In each case, a neat beginning and a neat ending encapsulate a story with a development, a neat progression or a quest for some object: the nature of a character, belonging to the present or the past. Each of these stories culminates in a surprise-effect, that is, the discovery of the real identity of the character, which reads more as an anticlimax than a climax. With the discovery, the reverie comes to an end; the moment is over.

As Jonathan Culler remarks, "the frame is determining, setting off the object or event as art and yet the frame itself may be nothing tangible, pure articulation".[14] Indeed, in some of Woolf's short stories, frames can be reduced to a minimal form, an enclosing sentence or phrase marking the boundaries of a moment as in "Monday or Tuesday" where the story opens and ends with the flight of the heron: "Lazy and indifferent, ... the heron passes over the church beneath the sky ... . Lazy and indifferent the heron returns" (137); or in "Moments of Being" where the title phrase "Slater's Pins Have No Points" appears at the beginning (215) and at the end of the short story (220). Or again in "In the Orchard", each of the three pictures of Miranda opens with "Miranda slept in the orchard" and closes with "Oh, I shall be late for tea!" (150–1).

Such framing devices, whether strong or weak, contribute in one way or another to isolate a moment—a moment of fiction, a moment of the past, a moment of sleeping and dreaming, a moment of intimacy. Framing thus apparently turns the short story into a self-contained whole, a "crystal globe" (*CSE* 99), a perfect shape.

Unframed stories

However, not all of Woolf's short stories are framed; many of them offer a beginning *in medias res* and an open ending. Most of the time, when we begin reading these texts, the narration is already in full swing. The character is there without having been properly introduced or sometimes, even named : "Ah, but let us wait a little!—The moon is up; the sky is open, ... The wind blows soft round the corner of the street, lifting my cloak..." ("The Evening Party", 96). We are confronted with a place which has not been described or named ("Well, here we are; and if you cast your eye over the room...", "The String Quartet", 138). From the very beginning of her short stories, Woolf defeats the rules of conventional narration. Like her novels, her short stories begin *in medias res*, the characters being caught in the middle of an action ("Since it had grown hot and crowded indoors, ... Mr Bertram Pritchard led Mrs Latham into the garden", "A Summing Up", 208), a conversation ("'Slater's pins have no points—don't you always find that?' said Miss Craye", "Moments of Being", 215) or silent reflections ("Mabel had her first serious suspicion that something was wrong as she took her cloak off", "The New Dress", 170). Just as "Mrs Dalloway said she would buy the gloves herself", the opening sentence of "Mrs Dalloway in Bond street" (152), sends the reader back to a "pre-text", a virtual text preceding the actual one where the use of the definite article "the" would be accounted for, the *incipit* of unframed short stories always points to a "pre-text", simultaneously negating itself as a beginning and redefining the opening as an intrusion into an already existing fictional world. It thus posits the narrative to come as a fragment of a larger whole rather than an autonomous, self-contained whole.

The open ending of the unframed short stories points the same way. In some cases, the open ending introduces a sense of promise, the promise, in exchange of a £20,000 cheque for rotten pearls, of a week-end with his beloved Diana for Oliver Bacon, in "The Duchess and the Jeweller": "And again he was a little boy in the alley where they sold dogs on Sunday.

'For,' he murmured; laying the palms of his hands together, 'it is to be a long week-end'" (253). For Angela, in "A Woman's College from Outside", it is the discovery of love and the promise, symbolised by the open window and the coming of morning, of other such wonderful moments:

> she lay in this good world, this new world, this world at the end of the tunnel, until a desire to see it or forestall it drove her, tossing her blankets, to guide herself to the window, and there, looking out upon the garden, where the mist lay, all the windows open, one fiery-bluish, something murmuring in the distance, the world of course, and the morning coming. (147–8)

In these stories, both the character and reader are given a sense of expectation.

In some other short stories, inconclusive ones, the character may come to some form of conclusion while the reader is faced with inconclusion. In "Mrs Dalloway in Bond Street", Clarissa Dalloway who, while in the shop, had been wondering about the other lady buying gloves, suddenly recognises her. The moment of recognition comes at the same time as the loud noise of a car backfiring in the street: "[t]here was a violent explosion in the street outside. The shopwomen cowered behind the counters. But Clarissa, sitting very upright, smiled at the other lady. 'Miss Anstruther!' she exclaimed" (159). If the character is granted a form of revelation at the end, the reader is left wondering about this lady: who is she? And what sort of conversation is Clarissa going to have with her? The reader's imagination is solicited instead of being satisfied. And sometimes, both the reader and the character are solicited at the end. Such is the case of "A Haunted House" where the discovery of the treasure is formulated in a question ("Is this your buried treasure?") which highlights the fact that the nature of the treasure is still unknown or at least, uncertain. Or in "The Symbol", just as the lady is unable to finish the last sentences of her letter ("'...They died trying to climb the mountain... They died in an attempt to discover...'", 290), "[t]here seemed to be no fitting conclusion" (290) for the reader either. Such stories are inconclusive in the manner of Chekhov.

On the other hand, unframed short stories can be conclusive although this is hardly ever synonymous with total closure. "Lappin and Lapinova", a metaphoric rendering of the life and death of Ernest and Rosalind's marriage, comes to a clear-cut conclusion: "So that was the end of that marriage" (268). However the deictic "that" suggests the other married couples will know the same fate as Ernest and Rosalind; their marriage is therefore given a paradigmatic value which in turn prevents the closure of the short story. In the short stories revolving around Mrs Dalloway's party, closure is similarly asserted and undermined. Lily Everit is defeated by Bob Brinsley at the end of "The Introduction", Mr Serle and Miss Anning part at the end of "Together and Apart" just as, in "A Man who Loved his Kind", Miss O'Keefe and Prickett Ellis "parted for ever" (200). Closure, neat as it is, contains intimations that such moments of humiliation, happiness or hatred and egotism are not exactly over since they are both emblematic of the characters staged and have a universal value. Even in seemingly more traditional narrative short stories like "The Widow and the Parrot" where we witness the death of the two eponymous characters, closure is defeated through an acknowledgement of the haunting power of the past: "[v]isitors to Rodmell may still see the ruins of the house, which was burnt down fifty years ago, and it is commonly said that if you visit it in the moonlight you may hear a parrot tapping with his beak upon the brick floor, while others have seen an old woman sitting there in a white apron" (169).

These observations about the general absence of closure in Woolf's unframed short stories lead us to reconsider Woolf's framed short stories. If frames turn such short stories as "An Unwritten Novel", "The Shooting Party" or "The Searchlight" into self-contained wholes and bring about a sense of closure, they also, paradoxically enough, bring about a sense of continuity and promise. At the end of "The Searchlight", although Mrs Ivimey's reminiscences have come to an end, the past keeps haunting or even inhabiting the present, and the great-grandmother she has evoked lives on in her even if she is not totally aware of it. Indeed, like her ancestor, "she had something blue on her head" and her slip of the tongue is quite revealing: "'Oh the girl…She was my—'she hesitated, as if she were about to say 'myself'.

But she remembered; and corrected herself. 'She was my great-grandmother,' she said" (272). In other words, the embedded story contaminates the framing narrative, thus establishing a form of continuity and undermining all possibility of closure.

In "An Unwritten Novel", the confrontation with reality is both a source of disappointment ("Life's bare as bone", 121) and of inspiration to the narrator ("And yet the last look of them…floods me anew. Mysterious figures!", 121). Similarly, at the end of "The Shooting Party", the character both steps out of the carriage and of the story and yet murmurs " 'Chk. Chk' as she passed" (260), the very sounds that set the narrator's imagination going at first. In both those short stories, the frame is burst open, pulled apart and the story-telling promises to start again. What at first seemed to bring closure and frustration to the reader only creates further promise, an assertion of the inexhaustible power of story-telling: "it's you, unknown figures, you I adore; if I open my arms, it's you I embrace, you I draw to me-adorable world!" (121). In framed as in unframed stories, the promise of an ending eventually disappears with the ending of the short story. And fulfilment finally lies in the absence of fulfilment or more exactly, in its endless deferment. Thus, in Woolf's framed short stories, framing goes together with frame-breaking and the tension between an attempt at closure and an open ending turns a form that at first appeared to be whole into a fragment, similar to the form of the unframed short story, which is also, paradoxically enough, a whole.

Woolf's short story as literary fragment

Wholeness and fragmentation are therefore compatible in the form of the short story renewed by Woolf, and this compatibility turns Woolf's short story into a genre analogous to the literary genre of the fragment, as analysed by Philippe Lacoue-Labarthe and Jean-Luc Nancy in *L'Absolu littéraire*.[15] In this study of German Romanticism, they focus on the *Fragments critiques* published by Friedrich Schlegel in 1797 as well as the *Fragments* published in the first volume of the *Athenaeum* in 1798, and show that the fragment is the Romantic literary genre *par excellence*. The term "fragment" is never used by the German romantics as a synonym of "broken piece". According to Lacoue-Labarthe and Nancy, the fragment points both to its being an autonomous form and part of a whole: "it refers, if we may say so, both to the borders of the fracture as an autonomous form and to its shapeless or misshapen form".[16] Such is the case of the famous fragment 206 of the *Athenaeum*: "Like a little work of art, the fragment must be totally independent from the surrounding world and closed upon itself like a hedgehog".[17] This fragment is more ambiguous than it is generally said to be since it not only foregrounds total closure and posits fragmentation as a form of totality but it also posits the fragment as "a small work of art", necessarily related to a larger one. And they add: "To write a literary fragment is to write in fragments".[18] Multiplicity, plurality is at the heart of the fragment as a literary genre and each fragment is to be read both as a whole and as part of a whole. Each is a self-contained autonomous whole and the whole is a plurality, a "co-presence"—rather than an addition—of parts, something Lacoue-Labarthe and Nancy link with the essential incon- clusiveness and prospective nature of the fragment: "The frag- ment...first of all means incompletion".[19] Such a conception of the fragment could be adapted to Woolf's short stories. Defining her short stories as literary fragments would enable us to account for the plurality and essential inconclusiveness of this literary genre as well as, and mainly, for the double nature of each short story, their simul- taneous fragmentation and wholeness—"that sense of the falling petal and the complete rose" (*CSE* 178).

Woolf's short story as a paradoxical and dynamic space

The story-telling process in Woolf's short stories is indeed based on contradictory impulses; the reader registers a constant pull-counter- pull movement between completion and lack of completion, fram- ing and an absence of framing, fragmentation and unity. Woolf's short story consequently appears as a limited and limitless space, as a form that is now a fragment of a whole, now a fragmented whole, that is, a literary fragment in the sense defined by Schlegel. The term "fragment" carries with it the very notion of brevity and proportion that Woolf ascribes to short stories in her essays while the ambiva- lence of the term acknowledges the tension at work in Woolf's short stories and matches Woolf's definition of the short story in her essays as a paradoxical, and therefore dynamic space.

Indeed, we have seen how Woolf breaks down the familiar mode of short story-telling, playing an associative method against a disruptive one. She grants a large place to emotion and redefines proportion in terms of balance or tension, tension constituting the very dynamics of the short story. This first confrontation of Woolf's definition of the genre with her practice of short story writing shows that from Woolf's initial definition of the short story as an impersonal art of proportion and emotion, what should mainly be retained is, beyond the literal phrasing, her insistence on the paradoxical nature of the short story as combining opposites.

In the end, rather than the use of such devices as the beginning *in media res*, the absence of closure or the representation of the moment, that can all be found in other twentieth-century short stories by Katherine Mansfield or Elisabeth Bowen, for example, it is the way in which Woolf combines them that creates the originality and specificity of her short stories.

The "mosaic-effect"

Along with the short story, its reading is redefined. Woolf's short stories are best described, as we have just seen, in terms of disruption as well as in terms of flux. The tension at work in Woolf's short stories, the pull and counter-pull between continuity and discontinuity, could very well be compared with the movement of thought itself. Not thought conceived as a flow or continuous process, as the phrase "stream of consciousness technique" which has long been appended to Woolf's writing suggests, but thought defined both as continuity and discontinuity, as Walter Benjamin does in *The Origin of the German Tragic Drama*: "Tirelessly thought begins continually from new things, laboriously returning to the same object. [It is a] continual pausing for breath".[20]

Such continuous yet constantly interrupted movement of thought demands an unfamiliar form of understanding and reading that should be sympathetic to it. As Woolf writes in her essay "How Should One Read a Book?", "how great a part the art of not reading plays in the art of reading" (*Essays* III: 393) or, as Roland Barthes phrases it, one must read "looking up".[21] This is also what Benjamin advocates in the case of a mode of writing characterised by interruptions: "Its aim is not to sweep the reader along and inspire him with enthusiasm. ... This form can be counted successful only when it forces the reader to stop" (Benjamin 1977: 29). Interruption may well be, in Benjamin's as in Woolf's case, the trace of "the obstinate resistance" of a text which "at first trips us and blinds us" (*Essays* III: 158) and which Woolf describes in her essay "Reading". "We must stop, go back, try out this way and that, and proceed at a foot's pace", she writes (158): the type of reading Woolf advocates is a difficult and demanding process comparable to "mounting only a solemn and obstinate donkey instead of going up to town by an electric train" (158). It is a slow process that lets the reader enter the text through its loopholes. Such reading is no more linear than the short story narrative itself; it consists of "repeated shocks" (152) that come at irregular intervals, like "[t]he little irregular beam of light" that shows the children their way during the moth-hunting scene evoked in the same essay. Reading has thus to do with seeing rather than meaning, with overcoming blindness and seeing at intervals an "unknown world" (150), a world of magic such as the one the children discover at night with great "excitement" (151) in the story embedded in the essay and which functions as an allegory of reading while enacting, through its apparent unrelatedness to the reflections on the subject, the "obstinate resistance" of the text to reading. Woolf's short stories certainly require the type of reading the author evokes in her essay, that is, reading through a series of irregular shocks that call for a "shock-receiving capacity" ("A Sketch of the Past", 83) akin to the writer's.

Reading then creates what Benjamin calls the mosaic-effect: "the task of reading such a writing is comparable to being confronted with the individual pieces of ceramic tile from which a mosaic is formed".[22] However the reading process acknowledges the existence of these fragments as well as the existence of the whole mosaic, or if we refer again to Lacoue-Labarthe and Nancy's terminology, it acknowledges the existence of fragments together with the existence of the fragment. Indeed, in moments of understanding and great emotional intensity, what Benjamin calls moments of "recognition" and Woolf "moments of being" (both resorting to the same metaphor to refer to their fleeting nature, "a flash of lightning" for the first[23], "a flash of understanding" for the second[24]), "the majesty of the mosaic" appears (Benjamin 1977: 28). In such moments, the reader puts the pieces together but, to follow Benjamin's model, without acknowledging any supremacy of the whole over the fragments.[25] The moment coincides for the reader with the welcoming of the possible meaning(s) emerging from the text; and the moment being renewable, new meaning is available at each reading and for each reader. Both for Woolf and for Benjamin, and in Woolf's own words, a text is always rich "with more than one can grasp at any single reading" (*Essays* III: 149), and this is particularly true of the short story.

For Woolf, fiction, and short stories especially, are not static objects to be looked at but evolutional works of art. This is what Woolf synthesises in "The Russian Background" when she writes: "inconclusive stories are legitimate; ... somehow or other they provide a resting point for the mind—a solid object casting its shade of reflection and speculation" (*Essays* III: 84). And, as McNeillie remarks in a footnote to his edition of this essay, solid object is "[a]lmost the title of Virginia Woolf's story 'Solid Objects', begun in 1918 and published in *The Athenaeum*, 22 October 1920", at the time the essay, published in 1919, was written. Indeed, the phrase "solid object" reverberates on this somewhat cryptic short story and reveals a possible metafictional meaning. In their respective literal and etymological meanings, the words "reflection and speculation" suggest a mirror-effect that can be read as the expression of the short story's self-reflexivity or as an allusion to the images the solid object sends back. The short story is thus presented as a core surrounded by reflections, a solid object whose meaning is duplicated or multiplied. In any case, the short story appears as a resting point from where the reader's mind can start speculating, drifting, interpreting, thus expanding the solid object into a plastic and dynamic one.

3
Conversation, Emotion and Ethics or the Short Story as Conversation

Neither the space of fragmentation nor the space of wholeness, the short story has come out, in the preceding chapter, as containing both fragmentation and wholeness, like the literary fragment it has been compared with. It appears to be a space of tension where, in a more general way, opposites come together without merging into one another. It is a third space, a space of encounter between two different elements—structurally speaking, between fragmentation and wholeness, and more generally, between the self and the other, if we define these terms as Derek Attridge does in *The Singularity of Literature*. The other, Derek Attridge remarks, "is a somewhat over-worked phrase in current academic discourse" (Attridge 2004: 28) and although not as general as "otherness" or "alterity", it is certainly imprecise. Attridge then proceeds to make a list of the different meanings of the term[1]:

> In many discussions from Hegel to the present, "the other" (or "the Other") … indicates an already existing entity which the self encounters; most obviously, another human being. "The other" in Levinas's writing, … is linked closely to the biblical "neighbor", even though ultimately the otherness in question is that of God. In colonial and post-colonial studies "the other" tends to stand for the colonized culture or people as viewed by the dominant power. Whatever its precise complexion, the other in these accounts is primarily an impingement from outside that challenges

assumptions, habits, and values, and that demands a response. (Attridge 2004: 32)

Before adding his own definition: the other, according to him, "is always a *singular* encounter, and an encounter with singularity". It refers to "[t]he otherness that is brought into being by an act of inventive writing—an argument, a particular sequence of words, an imagined series of events embodied in a work" (Attridge 2004: 29). The other is the new with an irreducible singularity.

Basing my argument on Attridge's definitions, I will show that the encounter which takes place in Woolf's short stories is alternately between the self and the other as characters or narrative entities (Chapter 3) or as writer and reader (Chapter 4) or as the old and the new, that is, an encounter between the text itself and another text or between the short story and another literary genre or art form, and eventually, between them all at the same time, which creates the irreducible singularity of Woolf's work of art (Chapter 5). In the three forthcoming chapters these various types of encounter will be explored as well as the form they take which, I shall argue, is the form of conversation.

As Attridge points out, the other "is premised on a relation. To be 'other' is necessarily to be 'other than' or 'other to'" (Attridge 2004: 29). This is indeed what Woolf gives us to see in her short stories where the other is other than the self and/or related to the self and where the encounter between the self and the other—two or more characters or a narrator and one or more characters—takes the form of conversation, but conversation redefined. The Latin word *conversatio* refers to "the act of living with" and conversation originally meant "having dealings with others" before being restricted to a form of spoken exchange or dialogue between at least two persons. If Woolf stages the latter type of conversation and its commonplace meaning, she more often than not privileges an unspoken form of exchange or silent conversation which gives back its full meaning of "together" to the prefix "cum" and reactivates the initial meaning of the word conversation. Spoken dialogue refers us to the Platonic tradition, especially to *The Symposium* which, according to Clive Bell, stages "the more exquisite pleasure of serious discussion",[2] and belongs to the public sphere, the sphere of orality and even, theatricality, whereas silent conversation takes us within the private sphere, the world of a powerful but subtle and difficult to circumscribe form of communication, what Nathalie Sarraute calls "subconversation".[3] It is well-known that silence is one of the hallmarks of modernist literature: as early as 1915, Hewet, Woolf's novelist-to-be in *The Voyage Out*, claims that he "want[s] to write a novel about Silence...the things people don' say"[4] and Stephen Dedalus, Joyce's hero, followed suit in *A Portrait of the Artist as a Young Man*: "I will try to express myself in some mode of life or art as freely as I can and as wholly as I can, using for my defence the only arms I allow myself to use—silence, exile, and cunning".[5] However it would be more accurate to say that what Woolf relentlessly explores in her short stories is not so much silence as the unspoken, rich and complex relationship between the self and the other. Silent conversation as a form of sympathy or antipathy between characters is foregrounded: it stands on its own or comes as a complement to the spoken dialogue, backing it or undermining it. Very often unspoken and spoken conversation converse with each other, thus highlighting the author's doubly dialogic choice.

The very complementarity of orality and silence is pointed out in an early short story, "The Journal of Mistress Joan Martyn", written in 1906. Joan Martyn, a lady living in the fifteenth century, voices her fascination for the stories the peddler who has stopped at her place for the night tells "in a high melodious voice" (55) and adds that "the best of stories are those that are told over the fireside;...no written book can stand beside them" (62). Joan Martyn asserts the value of oral tales within the pages of her journal, an intimate space the reader is allowed to enter and which is, through its quaintness and the strange stories it tells, as fascinating for her as the peddler's tales are for Joan. The necessary complementarity of oral and written tales, of the spoken and the silent words (and worlds) is thus indirectly established in a manner comparable to what Ford Madox Ford will do in a later novel, *The Good Soldier*, where Dowell the narrator claims to be telling his story sitting "at one side of the fireplace of a country cottage, with a sympathetic soul opposite [him]...talking, in a low voice"[6] while he testifies that he has written his story: "I am writing this now, I should say, a full eighteen months after the words that end my last chapter" (Ford 1995: 149).

Similarly Woolf explores the interaction of spoken and silent conversation which takes place during the encounter between the self and the other. And whether spoken or silent, conversation appears to be the locus of the exploration of emotion. When the self comes into contact with the other or when the self discovers his own self as other, some form of emotion is born. Throughout the short stories, conversation becomes the locus of a whole range of emotions or more exactly, it becomes indistinguishable from the emotion it originates.

"Form is emotion": conversation as the form of the encounter between the self and the other

Love

A whole sample of emotions, from love to hatred, can indeed be found in the short stories. Conversation can be extremely banal and insignificant as the conversation between the young man and the young woman strolling past the flower-bed in "Kew Gardens" is:

> " 'Lucky it isn't Friday," he observed.
> "Why? D' you believe in luck ?"
> "They make you pay sixpence on Friday."
> "What's sixpence anyway? Isn't it worth sixpence?"
> "What's 'it'—what do you mean by 'it'?"
> "O anything—I mean—you know what I mean". (94)

However, while they are talking about the price one pays to enter Kew Gardens on a Friday, a silent conversation is going on between the two characters which is in keeping with their gestures and their sense of touch: "The couple stood still ..., and together pressed the end of her parasol deep down into the soft earth. The action and the fact that his hand rested on the top of hers expressed their feelings in a strange way" (94). Their nascent love is silently voiced as well as the promise of a shining future, of blooming love and full-bodied happiness, since they are now, as the flower and butterfly metaphors suggest, "in that season which precedes the prime of youth, the season before the smooth pink folds of the flower have burst their gummy case, when the wings of the butterfly, though fully grown, are motionless in the sun" (94); and the mountain metaphor comes as a contrapuntal warning of possible danger and difficulty in their blissful life: "but who knows...what precipices aren't concealed in [words], or what slopes of ice don't shine in the sun on the other side?" (94). This silent conversation is made possible both by touch and, as the butterfly metaphor points out, by the insignificant spoken words themselves: "words with short wings for their heavy body of meaning" (94), words where the signified exceeds the signifier by far, thus threatening the balance of the butterfly-words. It is this gap between the signifier and the signified that Woolf is interested in here. And only metaphors, indirect language, can explore this gap and convey the rich emotion of love which direct words would make commonplace or sentimentalise.

In "A Woman's College from Outside" (1926), Angela, a student at Newnham, is standing at the window at night and "[t]he mist was cleft as if her voice parted it" (147). The cleft mist signals an opening onto another world, the coming out of the tunnel ("after the dark churning of myriad ages here was light at the end of the tunnel; life", 147), while the window opening onto the night shows Angela is on the threshold of a new experience. Like the kerb on which Clarissa stands at the beginning of *Mrs Dalloway*, it becomes the chronotope of a moment of crisis, here, the discovery of love. During the conversation Angela has with Alice, a fellow-student, the latter "kissed her, at least touched her head with her hand" (147). Superseding words, touch leads to the discovery of a new world, the bright world of a new emotion metaphorised by the "wind-lashed sea in her heart"; the violence of this emotion can only go with ceaseless movement ("Angela...roamed up and down the room...throwing her arms out", 147), which the breathless rhythm of the sentence emphasises. The intensity of the emotion suddenly revealed to Angela ("this excitement, this astonishment") combines movement with light ("she held [the golden fruit] glowing to her breast", 147), perfection with fragility ("a thing not to be touched, thought of, or spoken about", 147) and the whole is encapsulated in "the golden fruit" that has dropped like an offering from "the miraculous tree", the symbol of this newly discovered love and of the coming together of two human beings. Violence, suddenness, movement, fragility, intensity, warm light, and perfection are the main characteristics of this moment when the character discovers love or is, as it were, struck with love; it is a moment of revelation ("Such was her discovery", 147), a moment of beauty and pure bliss, a miracle, in other words, a moment of coming together.

The same violence and intensity of feeling is Clarissa's when Peter Walsh comes back unexpectedly from India: "And Clarissa had lent forward, taken his hand, drawn him to her, kissed him,—actually had felt his face on hers before she could down the brandishing of silver flashing plumes like pampas grass in a tropic gale in her breast" (*Mrs Dalloway*, 50–1). The images used by Woolf in "A Woman's College from Outside" are also reminiscent of Katherine Mansfield's "Bliss" where Bertha and Miss Fulton contemplate the flowering pear-tree which unites them in bliss for a while; love is here presented as burning light and as an offering dropping, as it were, from the tree too:

> How long did they stand there? Both, as it were, caught in that circle of unearthly light, understanding each other perfectly, creatures of another world, and wondering what they were to do in this one with all this blissful treasure that burned in their bosoms and dropped, in silver flowers, from their hair and hands?[7]

Written six years after "A Woman's College from Outside" and published in 1928, "Moments of Being: 'Slater's Pins Have no Points'" expatiates on the same theme resorting to similar devices. "'Slater's pins have no points'—don't you always find that?'", the few words uttered by Miss Craye, the piano teacher, to Fanny Wilmot, her pupil, are enough to set the latter thinking about Julia Craye's life, a life of independence, entirely dedicated to music and the quest of beauty, but also of frustration. In the midst of her reverie and while looking for the pin on the floor, Fanny sees Julia "pick[ing] up the carnation which had fallen on the floor.... She crushed it, Fanny felt, voluptuously in her smooth, veined hands" (217) and interprets Julia's gesture as a sign of her sensuality and ability to create beauty as well as a sign of her frustration:

> The pressure of her fingers seemed to increase all that was most brilliant in the flower; to set it off; to make it more frilled, fresh, immaculate. What was odd in her, and perhaps in her brother too, was that this crush and grasp of the fingers was combined with a perpetual frustration. So it was even now with the carnation. She

had her hands on it; she pressed it; but she did not possess it, enjoy it, not altogether. (217)

When Fanny finally finds the pin on the floor, the discovery coincides with another, namely that she has been wrong throughout and that Julia is not a frustrated woman but a woman capable of love. The few spoken words about Slater's pins have led to an intense silent exchange between the two characters, a moment of communion and bliss during which Fanny sees through Julia and understands "the effluence of her spirit" (220), the truth about her, a moment of great intensity as the intense purple colour framing Julia points out: "behind her was the sharp square of the window, uncurtained, purple in the evening, intensely purple" (220).

If in "A Woman's College from Outside" the "moment of ecstasy" (220) is presented as a gift from the one to the other, here it is presented as a moment of welcoming of the other: "She saw Julia open her arms" (220)—an equally generous disposition. Moreover, in both short stories, the setting is similar, the characters being framed by a window at night. The window, "uncurtained" in "Moments of Being", opens onto the night suggesting an opening in the life of the character while giving the moment of exchange between the characters the dimension of a vision, something which is emphasised in "Moments of Being" where the moment coincides with Fanny *seeing* the pin on the floor. The vision in "Moments of Being" is a vision of light and transparency ("All seemed transparent for a moment to the gaze of Fanny Wilmot, as if looking through Miss Craye, she saw the very fountain of her being spurt up in pure, silver drops", 220), of "bareness and intensity" (220) and the metaphors used to evoke the character in this privileged moment are water metaphors ("the very fountain of her being spurt up in pure, silver drops", 220) and fire metaphors ("She ... saw her blaze; saw her kindle", 220) reminiscent of "the glow" in the earlier short story. Just as in "A Woman's College from Outside" love combines, for example, perfection with fragility, the "moment of ecstasy" is here described as a moment when usually incompatible elements, such as water and fire, come together, something finally encapsulated in the depiction of Julia at the end: "Out of the night she burnt like a dead white star" (220). This sentence conveys the coming together of life and death as well as the ephemeral quality of the moment which disappears as it unfolds in a climatic anti-climax.

The moment of being can thus be said to be a moment of encounter when spoken conversation interacts with silent conversation (banal spoken words prompting, sometimes with the help of the senses, a silent conversation), when the self meets the other, ever so briefly, and when opposites are brought together, thus creating a particularly intense emotion.

Beside this extreme form of emotion which love is, Woolf explores, through the interplay of conversation and subconversation, moments when various shades of feelings are experienced by characters, feelings of more or less blatant sympathy, moments of happiness, sharing and togetherness. Such is the case of "Happiness". In this short story, Stuart Elton and Mrs Sutton exchange a few words at Mrs Dalloway's party[8]:

> "I went to Kew this afternoon", he said ...
> "To Kew alone?" Mrs Sutton repeated. "By yourself?" ...
> "Quite alone", Mrs Sutton repeated.... "Yes", he said. ...
> "Kew was lovely—full of flowers—magnolias azaleas", he could never remember names he told her. (179–80)

These words, scattered through the short story, are echoed by the silent exchange these two characters have about the nature of happiness. Mrs Sutton, an actress who does not find employment anymore, feels the pinch of middle-age and although a mother and wife, is dissatisfied with life while Stuart Elton, who is ill and a bachelor, is pleased with his. Through Stuart Elton's internal focalisation, happiness is defined first tentatively through a series of metaphors as a sense of being one and many, whole and multiple, a rose and its many petals: "that sense of the falling petal and the complete rose" (178), "this state of being curled in rosy flakes round a bright light" (178). The most trivial gesture or movement brings about an "avalanche of sensation" (178): "if he moved a hand, stooped or said anything he dislodged the pressure of the innumerable atoms of happiness which closed and held him up again" (179). A sense of the fragility of happiness is conveyed through Stuart Elton's desire to keep the wolves at bay: "[w]ith this whole pack of famished wolves in pursuit, now worrying the little bit of biscuit he had thrown them,— those words, "I went to Kew this afternoon"—Stuart Elton raced swiftly ahead of them back to Kew, to the magnolia tree, to the lake, to the river, holding up his hand, to keep them off" (179), a metaphor underlining the necessarily personal and egotistic nature of happiness and shedding a somewhat ironic light on this self-satisfied character. However, Stuart Elton oscillates between his desire to keep himself to himself and a desire to please his long-standing friend and share his happiness with her. In the end, he exclaims: "Yes he would stop his sledge, get out, let the wolves crowd all about him, he would pat their poor rapacious muzzles" (180). This decision to share, as it were, his biscuit with the wolves is made possible by the indestructible nature of happiness: "[i]t was nothing that they could destroy" (180). Happiness is also defined as "a mystic state, a trance, an ecstasy which ... had ... some affinity with the ecstasy that turned men priests, sent women in the prime of life trudging the streets with starched cyclamen-like frills about their faces, and set lips and stony eyes; but with this difference; them it prisoned; him it set free" (180). Happiness thus turns out to be a secular form of ecstasy synonymous with freedom. It is also a form of openness to the beauty of ordinary things and sensations: "As Stuart Elton stooped and flicked off his trousers a white thread, the trivial act accompanied as it was by a slide and avalanche of sensation, seemed like a petal falling from a rose" (178). What is called happiness in the short story has close affinities with the "shower of innumerable atoms" defined by the author in her essay "Modern Fiction" and the moment of being as it appears in many of her novels, for example, in *Mrs Dalloway* between Clarissa and Sally Seton:

> Then came the most exquisite moment of her whole life passing a stone urn with flowers in it. Sally stopped; picked a flower; kissed her on the lips. The whole world might have turned upside down! The others disappeared; there she was alone with Sally. And she felt that she had been given a present, wrapped up, and told just to keep it, not to look at it—a diamond, something infinitely precious, wrapped up, which, as they walked (up and down, up and down), she uncovered, or the radiance burnt through, the revelation, the religious feeling! (*Mrs Dalloway* 38–9)

It is something one is reluctant to share and yet which can be offered to the other as a gift, something the other can share in but without appropriating it; its nature is totally contradictory since it is both fragile and indestructible, personal and yet can be shared, wonderful yet difficult to define, and therefore share.

"Together and Apart", which was first entitled "The Conversation" (Dick 309), synthesises these ideas. The narrative opens in a memorable way with "[t]he conversation began some minutes before anything was said" (189), a paradoxical sentence that in fact yields the true meaning of "conversation" for Woolf as spoken and first and foremost, silent conversation. As such, conversation becomes the paradigm of "human intercourse" (193) and its complexity. What prompts human intercourse is both the silent contemplation of beauty and spoken words. The conversation between Mr Serle and Miss Anning takes place at night at Mrs Dalloway's window, a setting already encountered in "A Woman's College from Outside" and "Moments of Being", the privileged setting for a vision, here, literally, the vision of the sky whose contemplated beauty first brings the two characters together. The conversation is also triggered by a word said at random, the word "Canterbury". By uttering it, "[Miss Anning] had touched the spring" (190) and a common love for the town unites the two characters for a while since, for Roderick Serle, "the best years of his life, all his memories, ... all had centred in Canterbury" (190) and for Ruth Anning, "her three months in Canterbury had been amazing" (192). From then on, the connection which is at the root of human intercourse can develop. Connection is first of all a form of responsiveness to the other, "responsiveness to talk" (191) for Roderick Serle, responsiveness to the other's physical presence for Miss Anning who develops some sort of body language, her senses being on the alert, "[f]ibres of her were floated capriciously this way and that, like the tentacles of a sea anemone", while "her brain received messages" (191). However, responding to the other does not entail any form of fusion; connection means rather collision with the other as is suggested through this image: "[t]heir eyes met; collided rather" (192); connection respects the other's difference even if it permits access to the other's inner and true self, "the secluded being, who sits in darkness ...; flung off his cloak; confronted the other" (192).[9] Connection is of a contradictory nature too, bringing "alternations of pain and pleasure" (193), dislike and rapturous love, "fill[ing] the veins and nerves with threads of ice and fire" (193); as Miss Anning says: "nothing is so strange as human intercourse, ... because of its changes, its extra-ordinary irrationality" (193). In the end, connection can be identi-fied as a sublime moment that brings together awe and ecstasy: "[i]t was alarming; it was terrific" (192), says Miss Anning in words rem-iniscent of Peter Walsh's on Clarissa Dalloway's approach ("What is this terror? What is this ecstasy?"[10]). Such an encounter can only be brief and followed by "that paralysing blankness of feeling ... when vacancy almost hurts ... since no emotion, no idea, no impression of any kind comes to change it, ... since the fountains of feeling seem sealed" (193–4). However this "moment of non-being", as Woolf called them in "A Sketch of the Past",[11] contains the promise of other encounters since another character, Mira Cartwright, addresses Mr Serle at that point and begins a new conversation with him.

On the whole, this short story clearly exposes what some others like "Moments of Being: 'Slater's Pins Have no Points'" had already suggested, that is, that human intercourse, in Woolf's terms, has all the characteristics of a moment of being; and conversation being, as we have shown, the paradigm of human intercourse, it can therefore be said to be a moment of being. In this short story, as in those pre-viously examined, conversation as a moment of being is clearly a moment of encounter characterised by hospitality and generosity. At that point, conversation becomes indistinguishable from love or sympathy or any other generous disposition where the self accom-modates the other without assimilating it but rather, respects its dif-ferences. Such a form of conversation certainly displays an ethical dimension.

Hate

This type of conversation is at odds with another kind of conversa-tion that can be found in other short stories where the emotion fos-tered by the encounter between the self and the other is a dark, negative one. Side by side with short stories flaunting love or sym-pathy can be found short stories where hatred or similarly negative emotions, loom large. Such is the case of "The Man Who Loved his Kind", one of the stories surrounding *Mrs Dalloway* and written after it: it stages Prickett Ellis, who comes to the party after having met his former friend, Richard Dalloway, on the same day and feels no end of contempt for the other guests whom he thinks too wealthy and spoilt. The title of the short story turns out to be an antiphrasis, relating as it does to a character who is contemptuous of the others, too proud of his own achievements and of his being an ordinary man. This conceited character is only waiting for an opportunity to flaunt his goodness, which Miss O' Keefe gives him. The encounter between "this pale, abrupt, arrogant woman" (199) and Prickett Ellis results in an unduly violent moment of horror and hatred that the courteous conversation directly leads to while trying to disguise it:

> "Have you seen the *Tempest*?"
>
> Then, (for he had not seen the *Tempest*) had he read some book?
>
> Again no, and then, putting her ice down, did he ever read poetry?
>
> And Prickett Ellis feeling something rise within him which would decapitate this young woman, make a victim of her, massacre her, made her sit down there, where they would not be interrupted, on two chairs, in the empty garden. (198)

If Prickett Ellis's murderous urge, in keeping with his physical features ("he looked hard and fierce, as if his moustache were dipped in frost. He bristled; he grated", 195) and his pricking name, stands out, the violence of his silent reaction is matched by Miss O' Keefe's: "She had no words to specify the horror his story roused in her. First his conceit; then his indecency in talking about human feelings; it was a blasphemy; no one in the whole world ought to tell a story to prove that they loved their kind" (199). Each suffers tremendously from the presence and behaviour of the other so that their "talk seemed like a frantic skeleton dance music set to something very real, and full of suffering" (198). The intolerance of these two ironically named "lovers of their kind" leads them to part "[h]ating each other, hating the whole houseful of people who had given them this painful, this disillusioning evening" (200). Irony and the hyperbolic style of caricature are the devices chosen by the author to stage this conversation which proves to be a destructive encounter.

The encounter can therefore be, as this short story shows, a dark destructive one. It can also be a moment of suffering when "things fall apart" either because two characters who were close to each other are pulled apart, as in "Lappin and Lapinova", or because a character feels rejected by the other, as in "The New Dress" or "The Introduction".

In "Lappin and Lapinova", Rosalind and Ernest, when newly wed, build themselves a world of magic and love which they inhabit with great happiness. Like Alice, they follow the rabbit down the hole and discover the pastoral dream-world of Lappin and Lapinova, an enchanted world of complicity, love and intimacy where Ernest's nose twitches and Rosalind's hands dangle like paws. However, on family occasions, Ernest escapes this magic world and comes back within his family circle from which Rosalind feels completely excluded. Suffering then begins for her. At the rigid and stifling Victorian world of Porchester Terrace, she experiences a loss of identity, a dissolution of her own self as the metaphor of the melting icicle suggests: "her icicle was being turned to water. She was being melted; dispersed; dissolved into nothingness" (265). Colour symbolism and onomastics further emphasise this: the red and gold Thorburn world does not agree with Rosalind's moonlike whiteness; the Thorburns, as their name spells out, is a burning aggressive world where ice can only thaw. From then on, Rosalind and Ernest's marriage is threatened and things go from bad to worse until their love and complicity finally die. Their conversation does not flow easily anymore from ordinary topics to their favourite one about Lappin and Lapinova. Ernest's nose stops twitching and "looked as if it had never twitched at all" (266). Their common dream-world dies away and Rosalind's self symbolically shrinks and stiffens ("she felt as if her body had shrunk; it had grown small, and black and hard", 267). She comes to resemble the stuffed hare she sees in the National History Museum, "her hands dangling empty, and her eyes glazed, like glass eyes" (267). She finally dies, symbolically shot by Ernest: "Then there was the crack of a gun.... She started as if she had been shot. It was only Ernest, turning his key in the door" (268). From then on, they start talking at cross purposes:

"Sitting in the dark?" he said.

"Oh, Ernest, Ernest!" she cried starting up in her chair.

"Well, what's up now?" he asked briskly, warming his hands at the fire.

"It's Lapinova ..." she faltered... "She's gone, Ernest. I've lost her!"

Ernest frowned. He pressed his lips tight together. "Oh, that's what's up, is it?" he said, smiling rather grimly at his wife.

"Yes," he said at length. "Poor Lapinova ..." He straightened his tie at the looking-glass over the mantelpiece.

"Caught in a trap," he said, "killed", and sat down and read the newspaper. (268)

The end of complicity, the final parting of Lappin and Lapinova is a harrowing experience for Rosalind whose self falls victim to the symbolically estranged other Ernest has become: "she waited, feeling hands tightening at the back of her neck" (268).

An equally agonising experience is evoked in "The New Dress" where Mabel Waring, a guest at Mrs Dalloway's party, is confronted with the other guests and suffers agonies while trying to behave properly and exchange a few words with the people she knows. Once steeped in the glittering world of the party, she suddenly sees her own world in a different light, as "sordid, repulsive" (170) and her own dress, made with great care and pain, as "hideous" (170). Perceiving her dress differently turns out to be a metonymic and metaphoric experience of horror. This moment of "humiliation and agony and self-loathing" (174) is presented as a moment of revelation when Mabel sees through herself and the others: "She saw the truth. *This* was true, this drawing-room, this self, the other false" (172). It is a moment which is brought about first by the mirror Mrs Barnet hands Mabel on her arrival and then by the looking-glass hung in the room where the party is held. The looking-glass, a representation of the other's pitiless eye as well as of Mabel's own self-loathing eye, becomes for Mabel a "dreadfully showing-up blue pool" (174); and little by little, as the confrontation with the other's gaze becomes more and more unbearable, Mabel, like the fly she feels herself to be, will drown into that pool. To Mabel, the other's gaze is extremely aggressive and destructive: she feels "as if spears were thrown at her yellow dress from all sides" (173). And in the devastating presence of the other, her own self experiences a particularly harrowing form of dissolution.

Mabel Waring's agony can be compared with Lily Everit's in "The Introduction". On the night of her coming out at Mrs Dalloway's party, Lily Everit is introduced to Bob Brinsley by their hostess: "Mr Brinsley—Miss Everit. Both of you love Shelley" (187). The only other spoken words in the text are those exchanged by Bob Brinsley and Lily Everit: " 'And I suppose you write?' he said, 'poems presumably?' / 'Essays,' she said" (187). Behind these nondescript words, a whole tragedy is being enacted. Lily Everit, proud of her recent intellectual achievement—a first rate essay on Swift—comes to Mrs Dalloway's party in a self-confident mood only to gradually lose it through her contact with the other guests. Unlike Clarissa Dalloway who collects herself into a diamond-shaped self when she is ready to meet the others,[12] Lily Everit's self, "sharp as a diamond" (184), dissolves when she comes face to face with the guests. The essay which she wrote and "which Professor Miller had marked that morning with three red stars" (184) becomes a metonymy of her own self which is threatened as soon as she comes into the house: "at the very first sight of people moving upstairs, down stairs, this hard lump (her essay on the character of Swift) wobbled, began melting, she could not keep hold of it, and all her being (no longer sharp as a diamond cleaving the heart of life asunder) turned to a mist of alarm" (184). These images of dissolution become images of drowning when she is introduced to Bob Brinsley, which, for her, is like "being flung into a whirlpool" (185). When Bob Brinsley starts talking to her, the butterfly that had just "come out of her chrysalis" (185), the "flower which had opened in ten minutes" (186) and that Lily is, is almost immediately crushed. Behind the perfectly banal words "And I suppose you write?", Lily perceives the insolence of her interlocutor and sees through him. She has indeed a vision of him as being much more brutal than he appears to be: "she saw him—how else could she describe it—kill a fly. He tore the wings off a fly, standing with his foot on the fender his head thrown back, talking insolently about himself, arrogantly" (187). What Clarissa Dalloway ironically interprets as a "change of expression from carelessness to conformity" (187) and a sign of coming love, is perceived by Lily as a moment of "terror" (187) in which she identifies with the fly and feels her own wings are being pulled out by the young man; her body is desecrated and her whole being crushed by him[13]:

> In spite of all she could do her essay upon the character of Swift became more and more obtrusive and the three stars burnt quite bright again, only no longer clear and brilliant, but troubled and bloodstained as if this man, this great Mr Brinsley, had just by pulling the wings off a fly as he talked (about his essay, about himself and once laughing, about a girl there) charged her light

being with cloud, and confused her for ever and ever and shrivelled her wings on her back. (188)

The various flower and insect metaphors point at the complexity and intensity of the emotion felt by Lily throughout her dialogue with the young man. Conveying the complex inner life of this hypersensitive character, a whole subterranean world of emotion and suffering is both buried under and woven with the few formal spoken words which both hide and prompt the silent conversation.

In these various short stories, the conversation between the self and the other is a moment of hatred or antipathy and suffering so that the encounter turns out to be a moment of conflict and separation. In these instances the conversation is clearly an inverted moment of being, a dark, destructive moment when the self and the other display or are perceived as displaying an intolerant disposition, a refusal of difference, that is an attitude which is anything but ethical.

The role of the party: the short story as an ethical and aesthetic space

Virginia Woolf writes in *Between the Acts* that there are "only two emotions: love; and hate" (56). On the next page, she corrects herself and adds a third one: "Peace was the third emotion. Love. Hate. Peace. Three emotions made the ply of human life" (57). In the novel, peace is synonymous with lifelessness[14] just as in "Together and Apart", it can be equated with "that paralysing blankness of feeling" (193–4) which comes after the encounter. Yet can this absence of emotion be said to be the third emotion? Couldn't the third emotion be located somewhere else in the space where the first two emotions, love and hatred, are brought together? Indeed, the self and the other often oscillate from one emotion to the other, and how volatile emotion can be, how easily love or happiness can turn into hatred or unhappiness is something that Woolf explores through various forms of conversation in such short stories as "A Summing Up".

The title of this short story is quite telling and the narrative itself summarises the possibilities offered by social encounters of bringing together, through conversation, the two main emotions. The two

main characters, Sasha Latham and Bertram Pritchard, are guests at
Mrs Dalloway's party, and are both sitting in the garden at night
while the party is going on in the house. Their geographical position
symbolically points at their being both in and out of the party, cut
off as they are from the bustle of London by the garden wall while
simultaneously standing at a distance from the other guests and thus
able to appraise the party. The ceaseless flow of words spoken by
Bertram Pritchard allows Sasha Latham to hold a silent conversation,
interwoven with his and yet private, which brings a moment of joy.
Cut off from the fun of the party without feeling excluded from it,
she can better admire the other guests and enjoy a moment of happiness and beauty, a moment of solitude and complicity with the
others, symbolised by the image of the shaft ("she looked at the
house veneratingly, enthusiastically, as a golden shaft ran through
her and tears formed on it and fell, in profound thanksgiving", 209)
and the tree ("Thinking thus, the branch of some tree in front of her
became soaked and steeped in her admiration for the people of the
house; dripped gold", 209). However, this moment lapses into a much
more prosaic one deprived of beauty and joy when the impersonal
London world intrudes upon the Dalloways' garden: "[Bertram]
peered over the garden wall. Sasha peered over too. She saw a bucket
or perhaps a boot. In a second the illusion vanished. There was
London again...Sasha could no longer spray over the world that
cloud of gold.... At that moment, ... the usual terrible sexless inarticu-
late voice rang out; a shriek, a cry" (211). With this impersonal cry in
the night, horror and fear creep into Sasha Latham's soul, the universal, time-old dark emotions that have always racked human beings
and condemned them to the torture of loneliness, the loneliness of
the "unmated" soul, "perched aloof on that tree" (210), a tree by now
"denuded of its gilt and majesty" (210). This short story thus brings
together happiness and unhappiness, feelings of being together and
apart, pointing at the capacity the self has of oscillating perpetually
between these two poles.

"A Summing Up" is the last of the short stories revolving around
Mrs Dalloway, the first one, "Mrs Dalloway in Bond Street", having
been written in 1922 before the novel, and the eight others having
been written after the novel had been completed. Each of these stories
takes place on the day of the party and except for the first one, during
the party; each deals with love or hatred, happiness or unhappiness, as

we have seen. The role of the party thus clearly seems to be to bring together different characters and expose, through conversation, through the spoken and silent words they exchange, their various emotions, what Woolf defines as "second selves", words scribbled in her diary in the margin of the following entry:

> But my present reflection is that people have any number of states of consciousness: and I should like to investigate the party consciousness, the frock consciousness etc. The fashion world at the Becks—Mrs Garland was there superintending a display—is certainly one; where people secrete an envelope which connects them and protects them from others, like myself, who am outside the envelope, foreign bodies. These states are very difficult (obviously I grope for words) but I'm always coming back to it. (*Diary* III: 13; 27 April 1925)

The role of the party is indirectly defined in "A Simple Melody", where Mr Carslake, at Mrs Dalloway's party, is seen looking at a picture, a nineteenth-century landscape, while talking to Miss Merewether about Wembley and looking out of the corner of his eyes at the other guests. Among them, he notices Mabel Waring and "her pretty yellow dress" (202), thus belying Mabel's own judgement; Stuart Elton and his paper knife, a detail turning Stuart Elton into Peter Walsh's alter ego; and that "angry looking chap with the tooth brush moustache" (202), in whom we recognise Prickett Ellis. Mr Carslake comes to include the guests he knows in the pastoral landscape represented by the picture and muses on the virtues of walking in nature which would make all these people drop their party manner and behave naturally. Walking and talking on the heath would make everyone lift their social masks, forget social conventions and smooth out their differences. Assembling these people on the heath to walk and talk functions as a metaphor of what Mrs Dalloway does in her party where she assembles many different persons who walk around the room and talk to each other. Yet a major difference between walking on the heath and being at a party is made: walking produces "a sense of similarity" (206) while "social converse...produces dissimilarity" (206). It gradually appears that the mental picture Mr Carslake is making represents a utopian world of his, a world of ease, comfort, happy thoughts and talk, a world of similarity. It is soothing to

him: "[it] had the power to compose and tranquillize his mind" (200).
This world is opposed to the party, a world of tension and conflict:

> But in this room, thoughts were jostled together like fish in a net,
> struggling, scraping each other's scales off, and becoming in the
> effort to escape,—for all thinking was an effort to make thought
> escape from the thinker's mind past all obstacles as completely as
> possible: all society is an attempt to seize and influence and coerce
> each thought as it appears and force it to yield to another. (206)

The party is a space where pleasure and pain, happiness and sadness
coexist, where "people pressed upon each other; rubbed each other's
bloom off; or, for it told both ways, stimulated and called out an
astonishing animation, made each other glow" (206); it is in a way
the space of the third emotion. Little by little we see that the pastoral
world of Mr Carslake is dead because of its uniformity and lack of
tension, whereas the party symbolises a stimulating world of tension
and exchange, that is, society itself. Like Woolf's individual short
stories, each guest retains his own individuality while belonging to
the group. As for Mr Carslake, instead of listening to the people he
meets, he only thinks of including them in "his" picture, that is of
smoothing out their identities and differences (what he calls "affectation") so as to make them fit his own uniform world (what he calls
"being natural"). This denial of difference which consists in assimilating the other rather than accommodating him is a typically non-
ethical attitude.

If Mr Carslake is a virtual artist offering an inverted image of the
author herself, the picture he looks at and reshapes functions as an
inverted image of the party (and of the author's own short stories).
From then on, the role of the party could be extended beyond the
Dalloway stories to all the short stories, and the party itself could
be said to function as a metaphor of the short stories as a whole
which stage a "gigantic conversation"[15] between many different
characters who experience various emotions. Far from erasing
difference as Mr Carslake would like to do, Woolf stages and
explores difference in her short stories. And the choice she makes
of conversation as the form of the encounter in her short stories
has at least two consequences. First, conversation being the form
of the encounter between the self and the other, it becomes the

locus of emotion, of the two main emotions as well as of the shades of emotion they can breed. Since we know that Woolf admires Greek drama for (re)presenting raw emotion, we could argue that conversation, defined as an interplay of spoken and silent words or thoughts, is Woolf's own modern transposition of Greek drama. It is the form best adapted to the mapping of the self and to the representation and presentation of emotion. And we have seen that in her short stories, conversation can hardly be distinguished from emotion. In other words, form is emotion, as Woolf explains in "An Essay on Criticism", discounting Lubbock's formalist approach, as we have seen in Chapter 1. By choosing conversation as the form of the encounter in her short stories, Woolf makes first of all an anti-formalist choice. Second, conceiving the short story as a conversation between the self and the other and the whole of her short stories as a "gigantic conversation" where difference can be staged, where love and hatred, open and intolerant attitudes, ethical and non-ethical dispositions can be explored, is a sign of the author's own ethical disposition in her writing.

"A Dialogue upon Mount Pentelicus" or conversation redefined

That the short story is for Woolf a "conversation" redefined as a form of encounter between the self and the other, as the locus of emotion and as an ethical and aesthetic space is something that Woolf syn-thesises metaphorically very early in a short story rarely mentioned by critics, "A Dialogue upon Mount Pentelicus" (1906).[16]

This somewhat cryptic narrative is about a party of Englishmen who ride down Mount Pentelicus, near Athens, on donkeys. Their Greek guides and the slopes of Mount Pentelicus whose marble blocks were transformed into the most beautiful Greek statues, are described at length. The party then stops in the shade and the Englishmen strike up a conversation which ends only when a Greek monk appears. The conversation consists mainly in a dialogue between two unnamed speakers who defend their own points of view on Greek art, the first lamenting the difference between modern and ancient Greeks as well as the loss of Ancient Greek art which was synonymous with perfection, while the second speaker, a scholar, sees no difference between modern and ancient Greeks.

This text could easily lend itself to a biographical reading. Indeed, in the notes appended to her edition of the short story, Susan Dick shows that although it is undated, it was probably written on Virginia Woolf's return from Greece which she visited in September 1906 with her sister Vanessa and her brothers Thoby and Adrian. And their climb up Mount Pentelicus together with their encounter with two (not one) monks being related in the journal she kept at the time, the biographical basis of the story cannot be questioned. Yet it does not help the reader understand the story any better.

S. P. Rosenbaum, one of the rare critics to have commented upon that piece, is more sensitive to the literary dimension of the text and suggests that the prose satire of Thomas Love Peacock, the eighteenth-century satirist mentioned in the text, serves as a model for the dialogue form Woolf uses here.[17] And it is true that the satirical mode is privileged by the writer in this text which can read as a satire of former public schoolboys indulging in a highbrow conversation, bragging about their knowledge of Greek and finally proving unable to converse with real living Greeks. The author mocks the arrogance of these pretentious Harrow boys who rather than acknowledging the limits of their knowledge, that is, that the Greek they learnt belongs to a dead past, consider the living Greeks as barbarians and adopt a spiteful attitude towards them.

These two readings could be brought together through possible reminiscences of Bloomsbury's art of conversation. Indeed, the group of Englishmen sitting around talking about various subjects reads as an image of the party Woolf went to Greece with as well as a "Bloomsbury symposium",[18] an image of the group of friends who met informally in Bloomsbury. And the satire of the Harrow boys may well be based on Woolf's own observation of her brothers and their friends from Cambridge: "the principal speakers are easily recognizable, one with his recent third in the Cambridge tripos and the other with his new MA, as Adrian and Thoby Stephen" (Rosenbaum 1994: 191).

Without excluding these two readings, I would suggest a third one. Taking into account the fact that Woolf wrote an essay entitled "A Vision of Greece" in June 1906 before going to Greece, I will argue that the story is not so much about Woolf's voyage to Greece as about Greece as a vision or a concept; and by looking at the details of the text, I will show that this satirical conversation masks a satire of conventional conversation as inadequate and a concomitant redefinition of conversation; in other words, it provides the reader with a theory of conversation.

Greek art as a conversational topic

In the text, the conversation between the two Englishmen is introduced in the following way :

> But since dialogues are even more hard to write than to speak, and it is doubtful whether written dialogues have ever been spoken or spoken dialogues have ever been written, we will only rescue such fragments as concern our story. (65)

In other words, a conversation has never been transcribed in literature or what has been transcribed is not a conversation. In this key passage, Virginia Woolf points to the impossibility of representing spoken words in a written text and therefore to the inadequacy of the literary means of representation, and particularly, of mimetic writing. After thus summarily dismissing in three lines a whole literary tradition, ranging at least from Jane Austen to the Victorian novel, she offers the reader a dialogue between two Englishmen on Mount Pentelicus. This might well appear as sheer self-contradiction if the dialogue were not introduced by these words: "the talk was the finest talk in the world" (65). If these words are obviously a sarcastic remark on the conversation the young Englishmen are indulging in, they can also be taken at face value. And here we recognise one of Woolf's favourite tricks that we shall have occasion to come back to: she takes old words and gives them new life. "[T]he finest talk in the world" is ironic if the word "talk" is understood as referring to conventional conversation and its traditional literary representation. But if "talk" is understood as referring to a new form of conversation in literature, the superlative form "the finest" then suggests that the following talk will read as an *exemplum*, a model conversation. This will become clear in the following analysis.

The topic of the Englishmen's conversation is Greek art. To my mind, it is significant that Woolf should broach the topic of Greek art, its perfection and perennial nature in a conversation. This is a main difference with the diary she kept at the time of her trip to Greece where "a trip to Mount Pentelicus near Athens is recounted, but without dialogue, and the appearance of an ancient monk carry-ing brushwood is unremarkable" (Rosenbaum 1994: 192). It is also a major change compared with "A Vision of Greece" where she specu-lates on the decadence of Greece before offering a vision of the Maiden Goddess but no dialogue.[19] By choosing, in "A Dialogue upon Mount Pentelicus", to discuss Greek art in a conversation, Woolf foregrounds conversation, a choice which inevitably reverber-ates on the nature of conversation. If Greek art and perfection have something to do with conversation, conversation must have some-thing to do with perfection and Greek art. In other words, I will argue that the topic of these characters' talk is a way for Woolf to define conversation. Since their talk is "the finest talk in the world", it is a model talk not simply because it is *about* Greek art but because it *is* Greek art. The two become interchangeable as the text shifts from Greek art as a conversational topic to a definition of conversa-tion as Greek art.

Conversation as Greek art

In the course of the talk Greek art is defined by the first speaker as "paring down the superfluous":

> the Greeks by paring down the superfluous had revealed at last the perfect statue, or the sufficient stanza, just as we obversely by cloaking them in our rags of sentiment and imagination had obscured the outline and destroyed the substance. (66)

And the conversation itself exemplifies the very process of "paring down the superfluous" that the speaker describes as typical of Greek art. It proceeds by elimination and selection both in its substance and its outline. Before the speakers come to deal with Greek art, vari-ous conversational topics are eliminated:

> It ranged over many subjects—over birds and foxes, and whether turpentine is good in wine—how the ancients made cheese—the position of women in the Greek state—that was eloquent!—the metres of Sophocles—the saddling of donkeys.... (65)

The elimination of commonplace topics in favour of a more general and weighty one ("the tough old riddle of the modern Greek and his position in the world today", 65) makes it clear that conversation is not conceived here as small talk or "conversation mondaine" which, as in Proust's case and according to Deleuze, would be the enemy of writing.[20]

As a result of the elimination of superfluous elements, the outline of the conversation becomes visible and it is presented as a fragment: "we will only rescue such fragments as concern our story", says the narrator (65). And indeed, the conversation starts *in medias res* before being interrupted by the arrival of the monk. Woolf offers "slices of conversation" as she will offer "slices of life" in her novels, which is a blunt denial of any attempt at narrativity, linearity and exhaustivity. The phrase "we will only rescue such fragments" highlights the process of elimination and selection at work in the creation of conversation. Fragmentation is thus presented as a deliberate æsthetic choice and not as a defeat of the writer.

The Englishmen's conversation is then evoked as "sinking and surging like the flight of an eagle" (65). Through this comparison, the notion of rhythm is introduced. The process of "paring down the superfluous" also results in making the rhythm of conversation perceptible and rhythm being a major component of music or poetry, conversation begins to look or sound like a piece of music or a poem.

The paring down process is also at work on the discourse of the two speakers, both on its grammar and its rhetoric. Its grammar, first. At the outset the narrative voice summarises the position of the different participants in the conversation ("some...claimed, some...expected, others...recalled") before one speaker is singled out: "Such a people he said...such a people were as sudden as the dawn, and died as the day dies here in Greece, completely" (65). Although direct discourse is used to transcribe the speaker's words, the latter are not clearly separated from the narrator's; no inverted commas appear and the narrator keeps interrupting the speaker's discourse and commenting upon it. Little by little, the narrator's voice becomes silent and the speaker's direct discourse takes over. As for the second speaker's discourse, except for the introductory verb "he said", it is direct discourse only and it is placed within inverted commas so that it comes unmediated to the reader, with no narrator, whether neutral or vaguely linked with the authorial figure, intruding upon it. It is impersonal in the sense Woolf ascribes to the term, that is, a discourse devoid of the imprint of the author's personality, a discourse as impersonal as Greek art, itself the epitome of imper-sonality according to Woolf.[21] Conversation is thus defined here as the disappearance of the author's voice and consequently appears as very close to drama.

In the substance of his speech, the first speaker, in a very pompous style, voices his unconditional admiration of the Ancient Greeks and laments the loss of Greek art, a bare and unsentimental form of per-fection. The second speaker then cannot help pointing to the contra-dictions in this eulogy of Greek art: " 'When you talk of the Greeks,' he said, 'you speak as a sentimentalist' " (66). According to him, although his interlocutor claims to admire Greek art, his verbosity and pomposity betray the Greek spirit, the Greeks' desire for bare-ness. And the scholar further suggests that what the first speaker admires in Greek art is not its "Greekness" but its beauty. He shows the other that the term "The Greeks" is synonymous neither with a people nor a specific historical period but with the unknown, "dream and desire" (66), that is, utopia, perfection, beauty, truth or the "soul of beauty" (66). Thus "The Greeks" is shown to refer to an ideal and works as a concept; any of its synonymous terms (beauty, truth, etc.) could easily be used to refer to the same thing. Therefore, the scholar comes to the conclusion that there is no point in lamenting the loss of the Ancient Greeks and Ancient Greek or in despising the Modern Greeks, since individuals have nothing to do with a concept. Consequently, the first speaker should "drop" the word Greek and talk about art or beauty, thus implementing the process of "paring down the superfluous" the Greeks advocated, a process leading to a form of impersonality, the very process Woolf implements in this conversation by depriving her speakers of names. An impersonal art would here be given an added meaning, that of an art without any grounding in space or time, an art transcending geographical and historical boundaries.

Just as, through the "paring down of the superfluous", the Greek sculptor reveals the perfect statue and the Greek poet "the sufficient stanza" (66), conversation, through the process of elimination and selection we have examined, is made perfect. This very perfection is revealed metaphorically by the arrival of the monk, himself an alle-gory of art, of what Woolf calls the "soul of beauty" (66): "he was large and finely made, and had the nose and brow of a Greek statue" (67). The monk symbolises the perfect shape of a statue or the perfect outline of a work of art. A strange and striking figure, he mainly appears as a man with a compelling gaze: "Such was the force of the eye that fixed them, for it was not only clarified by the breeze among the olive groves but it was lit by another power which survives trees and even plants them" (67). The intensity and clarity of the monk's gaze reveal the intensity and clarity that conversation has achieved in the course of the process of elimination and selection. The monk's gaze reveals the very saturation of conversation that comes with the "paring down" process. Finally, the monk addresses the Englishmen and says "good evening" in Greek. This single word brings the conversation to a close as well as to its climax; by its very bareness, it displays the intensity of perfect conversation. By then, the conversational topic, Greek art, has become the very model of the conversational form; conversation has become Greek art.

Conversation redefined

Such a reading of "A Dialogue upon Mount Pentelicus" takes us quite far from the initial biographical and satirical readings. The form of the conversation Woolf imagines is at first reminiscent of a Platonic dialogue. Indeed, the pattern of the conversation leading to the revelation of truth may appear as an illustration of the Socratic maieutical method Woolf was to describe later:

> It is Plato, of course, who reveals the life indoors, and describes how, when a party of friends met and had eaten not at all luxuriously and drunk a little wine, some handsome boy ventured a question, or quoted an opinion, and Socrates took it up, fingered it, turned it round, looked at it this way and that, swiftly stripped it of its inconsistencies and falsities and brought the whole company by degrees to gaze with him at the truth. ("On Not knowing Greek", *Essays* IV: 46)

However, the form of truth revealed by the dialogue of the Englishmen is not of a philosophical nature but of an æsthetic one. Although the talk is about beauty, the final revelation provides a vision of beauty, the vision of the monk. And although the monk is necessarily evocative of religion, the only beauty he sends back is not of a transcendental nature but belongs to the conversation leading to his appearance; he only illuminates the conversation or makes its beauty visible. Thus the religious connotations are as it were, secularised, and truth is shown to be of an æsthetic nature only. At this point the conversation comes out as doubly subversive, both of the possibility of transcendental truth and of the Platonic dialogue as a model. The model Woolf propounds instead is a form of conversation synonymous with Greek art, which is defined here as an art deprived of all superfluous detail and narration, rhythmical, impersonal and universal in its transcending of personal, geographical or historical boundaries, clear, intense and incandescent. In this short story, Woolf brings together elements that she will take up separately later in an essay and in her diary. In her essay "On Not Knowing Greek", written in 1925, she will extol in similar terms the virtues of Greek literature, the "bareness and abruptness" of drama and poetry (47), as well as those of the Greek language, its rhythm and "the compactness of the expression" (48):

> Every ounce of fat has been pared off, leaving the flesh firm. Then spare and bare as it is, no language can move more quickly, dancing, shaking, all alive, but controlled. Then there are the words themselves... so clear, so hard, so intense. (*Essays* IV: 49)

The process consisting in "paring down the superfluous" and achieving a vision of intensity and clarity is referred to later in her diary while she is writing *The Waves*, but in more neutral terms and these are linked with the creation of a new genre partaking of poetry and drama:

> The idea has come to me that what I want now to do is to saturate every atom. I mean to eliminate all waste, deadness, superfluity.... The poets succeeding by simplifying: practically everything is left out. I want to put practically everything in: yet to saturate. (*Diary* III: 210; 28 November 1928)

So the way in which, in "A Dialogue upon Mount Pentelicus", she defines and foregrounds conversation while equating it with Greek art foreshadows her "playpoem" (*Diary* III: 203; 7 November 1928) to come, *The Waves*, where the concomitant processes of elimination and saturation will be at work in a "gigantic conversation" (*Diary* III: 285; 26 January 1930). Bringing together elimination and saturation, two seemingly contradictory processes, is also a way of pointing at the necessary balance of a work of art, here particularly, of the short story. What Woolf refers to in her essay about the short story (*Essays* IV: 455) as "proportion" is clearly defined here as elimination combined with saturation.

In her early short story, although she foregrounds conversation—were it only through the title—Woolf frames it within a narrative. However the narrative only seems to function as a mirror of the conversational part, reflecting both the nature of conversation as art and the creative process itself. Indeed, at the beginning, the narrative voice evoking the ride down the mountain and then the stillness of the talkers resting in the shade is also a way of evoking the movement preceding the stasis of art, here conversation, a form of art characterised by hybridity just as Mount Pentelicus, bearing the traces of elation and suffering in her "noble scars that she suffered at the hands of certain Greek masons" (63), stands in-between beauty and ugliness, a form of art which has resisted the writer and yielded to her just as the marble blocks resisted the sculptor's chisel and yielded to it.

At the end of the short story, the narrative voice comes back and tells the story of the monk's appearance. From a structural point of view, the monk merely discloses the truth, "the soul of beauty" that was already present in the conversation, which means that there is, strictly speaking, no revelation, only recognition. In a way, this makes the role of the monk redundant.[22] Second, the figure of the monk is also a way of questioning the linear process leading up to a "revelation", a climax in a conventional story. The monk only makes what was already there apparent just as Woolf makes apparent and alive a form of beauty that has existed for ages, namely since Ancient Greek artists produced their sculptures, plays and poems: "For there is, you know, a soul of beauty that rises unchristened over the words of Milton as it rises over the Bay of Marathon yonder" (66).[23] Thus, through the figure of the monk, the author places herself within a certain tradition, within continuity as T. S. Eliot will do in his essay "Tradition and the Individual Talent".

From a metaphorical point of view, the monk reveals, with great power, through the intensity and clarity of his gaze, the very qualities the conversation has been displaying, what Woolf calls "the soul of beauty" and what Joyce also calls the "soul" in *Stephen Hero*, that is the supreme quality of beauty. So Woolf's notions of intensity and clarity are reminiscent of Joyce's concept of *claritas*, as *quidditas*, radiance or the "whatness of a thing" which is revealed through the experience of epiphanies.[24] But above all the way in which Woolf uses the figure of the monk as an allegory of art and his appearance as a metaphor of the epiphanic encounter with beauty seems to me similar to what Æschylus does with metaphors and which Woolf describes in her essay "On Not Knowing Greek":

> By the bold and running use of metaphor he [Æschylus] will amp-lify and give us, not the thing itself, but the reverberation and reflection which, taken into his mind, the thing has made; close enough to the original to illustrate it, remote enough to heighten, enlarge, and make splendid. (*Essays* IV: 45)

Similarly the monk makes the "soul of beauty" apparent or even blinding; he lays bare the whatness of conversation.

In the end, the story is about the form of conversation, and what Woolf defines as Greek art is also her own art of the short story or at least the art she yearns for. By equating conversation with Greek art and defining it as neither spoken nor written, she defines a new space for art, a space in-between spoken and written words (which makes all discussions of whether the voices' words, in *The Waves*, are sup-posed to be spoken or not irrelevant), a space in-between drama and poetry. The choice of the conversational form as the locus of art pre-supposes, even if conversation is redefined, a form of exchange between voices. Conversation is also here a space of exchange liter-ally, between the two fictional speakers but also between impersonal and personal voices—the impersonal voices of the unnamed speak-ers and the most personal voice of the author speaking through them and defending her own conception of art in a paradoxical combin-ation reminiscent of the dilemma of Gustave Flaubert who defended a new impersonal art[25] while claiming "Madame Bovary, c'est moi"). Conversation is furthermore, as we have seen in passing, a dialogue between Woolf and other artists ranging from Æschylus to T. S. Eliot or James Joyce. Conversation thus becomes synonymous not so much with intertextuality as with what Deleuze calls, in his analysis of Proust's work, "transversality",[26] that is a form of communication with other literary works. Furthermore, representing æsthetic emo-tion is a way of letting the reader enter the text, of enlarging the conversation so as to include a cooperation between the writer and the reader and turn it into an ethical space.

What the very form of conversation allows is debate. The talkers are brought together to voice their points of view and their disagreement. "Together and Apart", as in Woolf's short story of the same name, they can voice their dissent. Conversation thus appears to be an agonistic space, *agon* meaning both, as Deleuze and Guattari point out,[27] dramatic representation and verbal fight, the "rivalry of free men".[28] In other words, conversation is a democratic form, a political as well as an ethical and æsthetic space. The conventional form of the debate enables Woolf to include the political dimension within conversation,[29] a form which she has otherwise totally remodelled. In the end, under the guise of telling a satirical story, Woolf tells the story of her own art in this short story, exposing her own literary choices, creating her own lexicon at the same time as her own theory. The choice of conversation as the locus of art may at first seem paradoxical for a writer who claims to be interested in inner life. Yet, redefined as it is here as an ethical, political and aesthetic space encapsulating a specific brand of impersonality, emotion and proportion, conversation comes out as the very stuff Woolf's short stories are made of.

4

Woolf's Ethics of Reading and Writing

Conversation as the encounter between creator and reader

The definition of the short story as a space of encounter between the self and the other as characters or entities belonging to the narrative, can be extended so as to embrace the encounter between the self as creator and the other as reader. Indeed, in most short stories, a silent conversation takes place between them through the staging of the story-telling process, the story-teller and the reader. This metafictional mechanism at work in Woolf's short stories will be examined at length; how it opens onto a specific experience of alterity and a specific form of conversation involving writer and reader caught up in a collaborative process will then be analysed as well as the eminently ethical moment of encounter it creates.

Staging the story-telling process and the story-teller

If, in Woolf's short stories, story-telling is in some measure retained, it is only retained to be staged. Indeed, most of her short stories tell the story of writing and can be read as reflections on the nature of fiction as well as on the creative process itself; and there we can see fiction fade into metafiction. The most obvious representation of story-telling occurs through framing and embedding,[1] as it is the case in "An unwritten Novel", "The Shooting Party" or "The Searchlight"; these short stories set the creative process at a distance, exposing it instead of subscribing to it blindly and taking it for granted.

But what is more interesting and original is that the mechanisms of creation are laid bare in some short stories, especially in "An Unwritten Novel". In the story-within-the-story, the characters are presented as being chosen among many: Minnie Marsh will be developed while the James Moggridges will remain in the dark. And while she is imagining the life of her fellow-passenger, whom she has dubbed Minnie Marsh, while she is describing Minnie's arrival and luncheon at her sister-in-law's, the narrator suddenly comes to the fore and interrupts the description: "[But this we'll skip; ornaments, curtains, trefoil china plate, yellow oblongs of cheese, white squares of biscuit—skip—oh, but wait!...Skip, skip, till we reach the landing.]" (114). By breaking the illusion, the reader's "willing suspension of disbelief", the narrator draws attention to the fictional aspect of the story and as she does so between brackets, the distancing process is doubly underlined. She then proceeds to show the reader her own imagination at work: "(Let me peep across at her opposite; she is asleep or pretending it; so what would she think about sitting at the window at three o'clock in the afternoon? Health, money, hills, her God?)" (115). And further on she adds: "I have my choice of crimes" (115), thus displaying the creative choices she is faced with as well as the different story lines she could follow. A slightly similar, although more covert strategy, is used in "A Haunted House" where the proliferation of modal auxiliaries ("one might say", "one would be certain", "one might rise", 122) points out the shifting, unstable nature of the narrative and introduces indeterminacy. With overt self-consciousness, these narratives focus on the process of writing the text one is reading.

By drawing attention to itself through these different forms of *mise en abyme*, the text makes it clear that it is of a fictional nature, that it is the product of imagination and is first and foremost a vision. "A Haunted House" starts as a relation of facts ("Whatever hour you woke there was a door shutting", 122) but appears at the end to have been a dream, as the narrator wakes up; and at the same time, the rhythmic pulse of the house which beats first softly, then gladly, proudly, and finally wildly, appears to have been none other than the increasing beating of the narrator's heart. The embedded narratives in "An Unwritten Novel", "The Shooting Party", "The String

Quartet", and to a certain extent, "A Mark on the Wall", are also presented as visions. In the first two, the embedding of a second narrative within the first signals the beginning of the vision (114, 254). In "An Unwritten Novel", the imaginative process begins when the two characters are left alone in the compartment and ends when Minnie gets off the train. The train journey, the isolation of the characters in a closed space, is conducive to a moment of vision, the time of creation. In "The String Quartet", the beginning of the concert and the consequent unleashing of images in the listener's mind is signalled by exclamation marks and short sentences soon followed by a long flowing one:

> Flourish, spring, burgeon, burst! The pear tree on the top of the mountain. Fountains jet; drops descend. But the waters of the Rhone flow swift and deep, race under the arches, and sweep the trailing water leaves, washing shadows over the silver fish, the spotted fish rushed down by the swift waters, now swept into an eddy where— it's difficult this—conglomeration of fish all in a pool; leaping, splashing, scraping sharp fins; and such a boil of current that the yellow pebbles are churned round and round, round and round— free now, rushing downwards, or even somehow ascending in exquisite spirals into the air; curled like thin shavings from under a plane; up and up…. (139)

In most narratives, the recurrence of verbs of perception like "see", "look", "gaze", "watch", further underlines the visionary nature of the creative process under way.

The difficulty of conjuring up a vision as well as of holding on to it is represented, for instance in "A Haunted House" where, within the dream, the moments when the narrator can catch a glimpse of the characters and the object of their quest is extremely brief: "A moment later the light had faded" (122). Moreover a glass separates the narrator from the characters, literally, "[d]eath was the glass; death was between [them]" (122). Symbolically this glass acts as a barrier and a screen hiding the vision; in the same way, "the windowpanes reflected apples, reflected roses" (122) rather than the characters the narrator is trying to see and thus act as deceptive mirrors. "The screens are in the excess". What is beyond the glass is impossible to see; the glass only becomes transparent when it starts raining, a symbolic representation of the possibility of vision, which the shift from the past to the present tense further emphasises.

A vision is by nature ephemeral and soon vanishes: either the dream comes to an end, as in "A Haunted House", or a veil of some sort falls over the narrator's mind. In "The Shooting Party", the mist thickens and invades the carriage; the travellers lose their shape, "the windows were blurred, the lamp haloed with fog" (260) and the atmosphere "sepulchral"; the thickening mist and the general blurring of shapes are a symbolic rendering of the end of the vision, just as, at the beginning of the story, fog had appeared, enveloping the characters in a world of their own, isolating them so that the narrator could observe them—a symbolic representation of the beginning of the creative process. Second, the disruption of some private space can signal the end of the vision. Movement is introduced in a still place and signs the end of the quietness and peace necessary for the vision to unfold: in "The Lady in The Looking-Glass", the mirror becomes blurred as Isabella Tyson slowly walks towards the house and is gradually reflected in the hitherto still world of the looking-glass; the passenger gets off the train in "An Unwritten Novel" and the end of the journey is a moment of crisis when the imaginative process is cut short by the return to reality; someone interrupts the narrator's reverie in "A Mark on the Wall". Or conversely, movement stops, characters who had been moving suddenly come to a standstill as they do in "Kew Gardens" ("It seemed as if all gross and heavy bodies had sunk down in the heat motionless", 95); noise, the city bustle disrupts the gardens' silence and the characters consequently lose their substance ("men, women, and children...wavered and sought shade beneath the trees, dissolving like drops of water", (95). In those short stories, the intrusion of foreign elements marks the end of the vision.

The end of the vision coincides with a return to the "real" world which comes as a shock. The clash between imagination and "reality" is represented repeatedly, in different ways in several short stories. Minnie Marsh, greeted by her son at the station, is not the poor spinster the narrator had imagined her to be but merely a commonplace mother (121). Milly Masters, once in the glaring light of the station, becomes "quite an ordinary rather elderly woman, travelling to London on some quite ordinary piece of business" (260) and Isabella Tyson is not a lady with a rich social life but a dried up old maid: "She had no friends. She cared for nobody. As for her letters, they were all bills. Look, as she stood there, old and angular, veined and lined, with her high nose and her wrinkled neck, she did not even trouble to open them" (225). The "flesh and blood" character is disappointing; he loses the glamour the narrator had endowed him with in his imaginary constructs.

The antinomic nature of imagination and "reality" as well as the visionary nature of fiction are to be linked with the author's own aesthetic choices formulated in essays like "Modern Fiction", "Mr Bennett and Mrs Brown" or "Phases of Fiction" where "materialism" and realism are condemned in favour of a more modern, so-called "spiritual" form of fiction based on vision and imagination. What is interesting is that the writer's theoretical principles are woven into the fabric of her short stories and expressed there in a metaphorical or symbolic way. Under the guise of telling a story, these short stories tell the story of writing, adding a metafictional dimension to the narrative impulse.

And apart from representing the mechanisms of creation, these short narratives state what the subject-matter of fiction should be. "There is the vista and the vision", writes the narrator in "An Unwritten Novel" (120), facts and vision: what one can actually see ("Life's bare as bone" [121]) and what one imagines—the "unknown figures" (121) the narrator adores and goes back to at the very end, after the confrontation with "reality": "it's you I embrace, you I draw to me—adorable world!" (121). Vista should be superseded by vision. Thus the supremacy of imagination, which had previously been denied, is finally asserted and mimetic writing implicitly criticised. As in "Modern Fiction" or "Mr. Bennett and Mrs. Brown", writing is a far cry from what Woolf called "materialist" writing, based on verisimilitude, plot and facts.

At the same time as mimetic writing is denounced, truth is redefined first as what a writer is yearning for and what keeps eluding him: "Desiring truth, awaiting it, for ever desiring" (12). It cannot be revealed through a "story", with a plot and a clear time-line; it can only be approached in a poetic way, through sounds, colours and movements; and it comes as a revelation in "momentary sparks" (13); it is constantly covered and uncovered, veiled and bared, like the sky (13). Such a definition of truth is conveyed through "Monday or Tuesday", echoing the famous phrase in "Modern Fiction": "Examine for a moment an ordinary mind on an ordinary day. The mind receives a myriad impressions.... From all sides they come, an incessant shower of innumerable atoms; and as they fall, as they shape themselves into the life of Monday or Tuesday, the accent falls differently from of old" (*Essays* IV: 160). Truth thus appears to be plural as well as a subjective construct. On the whole, the story-telling clearly appears as an artefact, a fictional construct which, far from being a mimetic reproduction of a referential world, exposes the fallacy on which mimetic writing rests.

Truth also pertains to the "spirit" rather than the "body". "An Unwritten Novel", in which the situation is roughly the same as in "Mr. Bennett and Mrs. Brown", is probably the most explicit as well as humorous in that respect. Take for instance the character of James Moggridge, who reads the magazine *Truth*—an allusion to the true-to-life writings of the Edwardians—and is a commercial traveller selling buttons: Moggridge is no other than a caricature of the Edwardian writer's typical character as well as a humorous allusion to Woolf's own essay in which she mocks Bennett's character for being "dressed down to the last button of their coats" (*Essays* IV: 160). This humorous touch ensures that although the short stories are fictionalisations of theories developed in the essays, they are first and foremost literary pieces. Moggridge is the very antithesis of the character according to Woolf which, although ordinary, should offer infinite possibilities and thus be devised as a multi-faceted elusive self. Like the fragments of eggshell on Minnie's lap, the self is a puzzle the writer tries to piece together; like Minnie's glove, it needs mending and, as the narrator in "An Unwritten Novel" has it, it is elusive: "when you've grasped the stem the butterfly's off" (117). Woolf's character is conceived as a fictional construct besides which reality can only pale. The final coming of Isabella Tyson, in "The Lady in the Looking-glass", metaphorises this clash between the fictional and the referential world. To the observer, Isabella, whom he/she can only imagine because she is beyond the scope of his/her gaze and the mirror's gaze, "suggested the fantastic and the tremulous convolvulus rather than the upright aster, the starched zinnia, or her own burning roses alight like lamps on the straight posts of their rose trees" (222). When the observer is finally confronted with the real Isabella Tyson, "[e]very-thing dropped from her—clouds, dress, basket, diamond—all that one had called the creeper and convolvulus.... Here was the woman herself. She stood naked in that pitiless light. And there was nothing. Isabella was perfectly empty" (225). Tellingly enough, the supposedly real Isabella is empty compared to the rich construction of the mind, which has been materialised by a set of "characters" or signs on the page.

And as the narrator in "A Mark on the Wall" says:

> As we face each other in omnibuses and underground railways we are looking into the mirror.... And the novelists in future will realise more and more the importance of these reflections, for of course there is not one reflection but an almost infinite number; those are the depths they will explore, those the phantoms they will pursue, leaving the description of reality more and more out of their stories. (85–6)

In other words, fiction is genuine because it is the work of the mind and is about the mind or what we call "the self". That fiction is of an introspective nature is asserted directly in the short stories, for instance, in "An Unwritten Novel": "Life's what you see in people's eyes" (113), with an obvious pun on eye and "I", that is, the self. The short stories could indeed be read as a quest for the elusive and all-pervasive self which appears again and again under various forms, in the guise of objects mainly—whether it be letters, books, bills, diaries or rooms and houses[2]—metonymic signs of the self, multi-faceted as well as fragmented like "the little angular fragments of eggshell" (117) that Minnie drops in her lap. The writer's task is to "piece them together" as is conveyed metaphorically further on in "An Unwritten Novel" and in other narratives by images of sewing, darning, stitching, or mending,[3] images that also run though the novels, from *Mrs Dalloway* to *The Lighthouse* or *The Years*.

Such a subject matter as the self requires a form of keen perception on the part of the writer, and in the short stories, creation is represented as a sort of visual rape. In "An Unwritten Novel", observing and creating a character is presented as deciphering a secret, baring a character's soul, piercing through the envelope; it is a violent, painful, and aggressive act; in "The Lady in the Looking-Glass", the process is analogous: "one must prize her open with the first tool that came to hand" (223). If creation means raping the other, it also means raping one's own self: "she pierced through my shield; she gazed into my eyes" (113) echoes "I read her message, deciphered her secret" (114); the narrator's piercing gaze in returned by the character's.

Moreover the fact that, in "An Unwritten Novel", the first person narrator and the character come to experience a similar itching sensation points at a gradual identification between them, and we understand that under the guise of looking at Minnie, the narrator is looking at herself. The same situation is taken up again in "The Shooting Party" but this time, with an anonymous narrator. In both cases, body stigmata—an itching spot between the shoulders; a scar on the cheek of the character observed—provide an entry into the world of imagination. They connect the short stories with stories of the past, reminiscent as they are of Hawthorne's allegorical tales, especially *The Scarlet Letter*; they also open the way to the subversion of the Christian allegory—God being derided as "a brutal old bully" (115)—and its transformation into an allegory of artistic creation. Indeed, the narrator who sits watching the woman opposite her soon appears to be the very image of the writer creating a character, identifying as she does with her through the same itching sensation. This pattern lends itself to numerous variations: in "A Mark on the Wall", instead of looking at a character, the first-person narrator looks at a black dot on the wall and tries to guess what it may be. In "The Lady in the Looking-Glass", a narrator watches a mirror and invents the character the mirror does *not* reflect while in "A Haunted House", the narrator dreams about two characters, "a ghostly couple", another way of saying he creates them.

In different ways and in a more or less sophisticated manner, the imaginative process is set before us in narratives which are openly self-reflexive. The author is repeatedly staging herself in the act of creation. This metaleptic device gives a metafictional dimension to the short stories and is comparable—though perhaps more open—to the distancing process at work in several novels such as *The Waves* where Bernard, at the end of his life, takes on the role of the biographer and tries to assess the lives of his friends or in a more metaphorical way, *To the Lighthouse* and *Between the Acts* where Lily Briscoe, the painter, and Miss La Trobe, the stage producer, become images of the artist in general. If creation is presented in the short stories as self-oriented, it does not necessarily mean that it is autobiographical but rather that it privileges the self, the character's or the story-teller's self. "And the truth is, one can't write directly about the soul", Woolf wrote in her diary (*Diary* III: 60; 23 February 1926), but she certainly found an indirect way of doing so in her short stories.

Staging the origin of the creative process

If the self is the subject-matter of creation, it is also the origin of the creative process, and this is represented in the short stories as well. Indeed, some of them, in a way which is typical of the *mise en abyme*, make the invisible visible by mapping the creator's inner self, and this mainly through a symbolic use of space, colours, elements and objects.

In many narratives, the narrator is sitting either in a train compartment, a room, a concert hall or a small garden—in any case, an enclosed and intimate, womb-like space in which artistic gestation can be carried out. The setting is not so much a "mindscape" as an image of the enclosed space of the mind or subconscious mind, the privileged space of creation. It is not so much that outer space mirrors the character's inner space as Harvena Richter rightly notices in her study of Woolf's novels[4] but that, at least in her short stories, it becomes the mirror of the creative self. In "A Haunted House", for instance, the house is not so much a house haunted by a ghostly couple as the narrator's mind haunted by the ghosts of the past or dreaming up a possible past. The repetitive opening of rooms is no other than the opening up of the echoing chambers of the mind. Moreover space is fenced in either by darkness (Mrs Dalloway's garden, lit by Chinese lanterns, is enclosed by the London night), by fog (in "The Shooting Party", the train is surrounded by fog: "the fog, which came in when she opened the door, seemed to enlarge the carriage", 255), a curtain of smoke ("I looked up through the smoke of my cigarette", "A Mark on the Wall", 84), or windows and mirrors. The windows of the train are not transparent surfaces but reflecting ones, further enclosing the narrator within his own thoughts ("looking from the window and seeing...only life", 15) and underlining the introspective nature of the process under way. The mirror in "The Lady in the Looking-Glass" functions in a similar way: the narrator-observer, sitting in an empty room, looks at an Italian glass and what it reflects; but it soon becomes clear that the mirror is but her mind's eye as it only reflects—at least for the largest part of the story—what is going on in the narrator's mind. These objects symbolically seal the mind, a pre-requisite for the creative process to start.

This protected, cosy and shaded cocoon whence writing originates is a coloured world. In some short stories, it is a milky white, essentially feminine space. Indeed, words come from "ivory depths": "[f]rom ivory depths words rising shed their blackness" ("Monday or Tuesday", 137); the realm of silence is white like the veil of mist or fog which covers and uncovers the imaginary world. However the white screen of fog or mist is sometimes replaced by a curtain of flames. Indeed, creation often takes place by the fireside: in "A Mark on the Wall", the narrator is sitting by the fireside; in "Lappin and Lapinova", Rosalind lets "her fancy play with the story of the Lappin tribe" [262] when sitting over the fire). Water and fire imagery, antinomic elements with contrasted colours, thus alternate and in turn, the fog, a half-liquid element, and fire enable the flood of words to flow, a poetic way of hinting at the ambivalent origin of creation, the meeting-point of antagonistic and complementary elements, the product of feminine and masculine impulses, in short, the ultimate experience. The beginning of the creative experience is depicted in the following way in "An Unwritten Novel": "[It] floods me anew.... Oh, how it whirls and surges—floats me afresh!" (121). The flood metaphor is similar to the one used in *To the Lighthouse* to describe Mrs Ramsay's ecstasy when looking at the lighthouse beam: "[t]he ecstasy burst in her eyes and waves of pure delight raced over the floor of her mind".[5] Like Mrs Ramsay, the writer is flooded with delight; through these images, the creative process appears both as an intellectual and a sexual experience.

The short stories thus show the whole cycle of the creative process from conception through gestation to the birth of writing and, as such, can be regarded as exemplars of the modernity of Woolf's writing, eager to explore, like most subsequent writing, the circumstances of its own germination.

Staging the reader and the reading process

The representation of the creative process would not be complete if the reception of the work of art were not there to round it off. The reading of a text and in a more general way, the reception of a work of art is represented in some short stories. In an early one, "The String

Quartet" (1920), the listener to Mozart's quartet is uplifted by the music and transported into a wonderfully rich and multifaceted world. It is, as the narrator points out, a passive form of enjoyment: "I too sit passive on a gilt chair" (139). And as the listener is bombarded with sounds, the reader is bombarded with images and sounds:

> The green garden, moonlit pool, lemons, lovers, and fish are all dissolved in the opal sky, across which, as the horns are joined by trumpets and supported by clarions there rise white arches firmly planted on marble pillars.... Tramp and trumpeting. Clang and clangour. Firm establishment. Fast foundations. March of myriads. Confusion and chaos trod to earth. (141)

The alliterative and rhythmic qualities of language are to be enjoyed for their own sake in this attempt at recreating the listener's experience of music. This extreme example extols the pleasures of a passive form of reception which also appears here and there in many short stories whenever poetic rhythm is put forward—as in the refrain of "A Haunted House" that gradually gathers intensity: " 'Safe, safe, safe', the pulse of the house beat softly / 'Safe, safe, safe', the pulse of the house beat gladly / 'Safe, safe, safe', the pulse of the house beats proudly / 'Safe, safe, safe', the pulse of the house beats wildly" (122–3)—or whenever sounds take the upper hand over meaning. In those examples, Woolf seems to subscribe to the Imagists' credo according to which "a poem should not mean but be", or to echo Ford Madox Ford's words about what constitutes "the sole real province of all the arts", that is, "the beauty of music—that is to say, of music without much meaning, but of very great power to stir the emotions".[6]

However, if the writer chooses at times to directly please the reader's sensitivity, she also often, and simultaneously, solicits the reader in various ways, either through the absence of closure, which is a way of asking the reader to go on with the story or, more frequently, through denial of a plain straightforward meaning, as in "Monday or Tuesday", which is an invitation to re-reading. Such an active form of reception is represented in a short story that Woolf wrote towards the end of her life, "The Legacy" (1940). There, Gilbert Clandon is depicted reading his late wife's diary; he is inevitably attracted to the initials she used, the names she erased, and the blanks she left on the page. By trying to fill in the empty space, Gilbert becomes a detective soon leading a real inquest on the circumstances of Angela's death, and little by little, the blanks start yielding their secret. Beyond their literal meaning, one can see in the diary and its blanks representations of literary writing and of the short stories themselves, in which the unsaid is paramount; as for Gilbert's activity, it is also an exercise in reading signs, an image of the hermeneutic activity of the reader who has to read in-between the lines, thus sharing in the process of writing.

If this short story suggests that the reader may succeed in piecing together the puzzle of a story as Gilbert Clandon does, some others suggest that no final, definite reading will ever be reached. Such is the case of a little-known short story, "The Symbol", written in 1941 and first significantly titled "Inconclusions". A woman sitting on the balcony of a hotel in a mountain resort, is writing to her sister at Birmingham. In front of her, she can see an Alpine peak and climbers. While she is writing her letter, the climbers disappear in a crevasse. The lady writing can be seen as an image of the writer and the addressee as that of the reader. The climbers' death is related in a matter-of-fact way:

> As I write these words, I can see the young men quite plainly on the slopes of the mountain. They are roped together…. They are now crossing a crevasse….'
>
> The pen fell from her hand, and the drop of ink straggled in a zig zag line down the page. The young men had disappeared. (290)

Their death comes after the lady has mentioned that "the graves in the churchyard near the hotel recorded the names of several men who had fallen climbing" (288) and that "[i]n the forties of the last century two men, in the sixties four men had perished; the first party when a rope broke; the second when night fell and froze them to death" (288–9).[7] Yet the focus is not on what could be seen as a tragedy but on the mountain itself. The mountain is not depicted in detail; the whole landscape has a fantastic, "unreal" look about it to the letter-writer who sits on the balcony as in "a box at the theatre" (288); the mountain is resented as being always there, indestructible and the object of all talk. "She had written the mountain was a symbol. But of what?" (288). She tries to answer this question from the beginning to the end of the short story only to acknowledge that "there seemed no fitting conclusion" (290).

The reader simultaneously gropes for some form of meaning. A memory related by the character and prompted by a similar situation (standing on a balcony in the Isle of Wight, watching the boat on which her mother was, come into the harbour) seems to provide a clue: the lady hoped for her mother to die so that she "should be free" and "explore for [herself]. But of course, when the time came it seemed more sensible, considering our long engagement, to marry" (289). The reader can deduce from the character's memory that her desire for freedom ended up in marriage, entrapment, that is, a metaphorical death, and can make a parallel with the young climbers who, eager to explore the mountain and reach the top, met their death in the attempt. From then on, the meaning of the short story branches out into several directions: is it an attempt on Woolf's part at understanding Leslie Stephen's passion for Alpine climbing? Or is it a criticism of her father's former hobby, a condemnation of climbing as courting death and thriving on illusion or even as a death-wish? Or is it a statement on desire, on the lady's shameful desire for her mother's death and the climbers' perverse desire for death, and more generally, on the ambivalence of desire? Or could it be a metaphoric statement of the writer's own fascination with death at this late stage of her life? Or is it a story about the necessary ambivalence of symbols, the mountain being both attractive and deceptive, a symbol of freedom and death? Or is mountain climbing a metaphor of all forms of exploration and the mountain a symbol of the unreachable other, whether it be a person or any sort of aim, including the writer's own achievement? Both autobiographical and literary readings are possible without being exclusive and neither of those offered here seems to exhaust the text and be final.[8] The text purposefully requires the reader to be active and go back endlessly to his reading. Just like the creative process itself, reading is a process which can be renewed endlessly, revealing each time new possibilities in the text.

The short story as a moment of being

Throughout the short stories, staging within the story-telling process, the story-teller and the reader is a way of establishing a conversation between them. Far from seeing author and reader in antithetical and exclusive terms and suggesting, as the early Barthes will do, that the birth of the reader signals the death of the author,[9] Woolf shows she believes in their "happy alliance" (*Essays* IV: 215). Such a dynamic object as the short story requires a specific reader, the writer's partner Woolf regrets the Edwardians had not invented: "It is this division between reader and writer, this humility on your part, these professional airs and graces on ours, that corrupt and emasculate the books which should be the healthy offspring of a close and equal alliance between us" (*Essays* III: 436). In her short stories, she implements what she calls for in her essays where she writes that not only should the reader be the writer's "fellow-worker and accomplice" (*C.E.* II: 2) but there should also be a total empathy between them: "Do not dictate to your author; try to become him" (*C.E.* II: 2[10]); and their roles should be interchangeable: "Perhaps the quickest way to understand the elements of what a novelist is doing is not to read, but to write" (*C.E.* II: 2). She is in that respect very close to E. M. Forster who acknowledges that there is a "sense of co-operation" between writer and reader, a transformation of the one by the other, that turns into "an infection".[11]

Such a conception of writing and reading suggests some form of exchange and circulation between writer and reader. We have seen that in the short story, writing is represented as an endlessly renewable gift to the reader, something Woolf states more explicitly in her essays: "one of the invariable properties of beauty [beautiful writing] is that it leaves in the mind a desire to impart. Some offering we must make" (*Essays* III: 159). She finds this generous impulse in beautiful writing and especially in that of Sir Thomas Brown, one of her favourite writers, an amateur writer who is not paid for the books he writes: "He is free since it is the offering of his own bounty to give us as little or as much as he chooses" (*Essays* III: 159).

Confronted with such prose, Woolf's reader in the short stories has a double response, at once passive and active. The reader is both a passive receptacle without any preconceptions,[12] a "non-preoccupied mind" (Ford 1995: 271) or "virgin mind"(Ford 1995: 273) like Ford Madox Ford's cabman's mind modelled on Tolstoy's peasant's mind,[13] and a mind able to respond to the text, ready to give; a similar give-and-take logic of writing and reading will be explored by Derrida in *La Dissémination*[14] and by Lucette Finas who writes: "The reader's gift to the text rests on the text's gift to the reader".[15] The reader's gift consists in developing the potentialities of the text while respecting it, as we have seen, for example, with "The Symbol". Such reading is what Roland Barthes will define as "reading while looking up",[16] and what Woolf herself synthesises in a few words in "How Should One Read a Book?": "how great a part the art of not reading plays in the art of reading" (*Essays* III: 393). She will also expatiate on this generous form of reading in her essay "Reading" where, while reading Hakluyt, the narrator's "attention wanders" (*Essays* III: 148), carried along by the rhythm of the sentences and the visions of the Elizabethan age they conjure up. Yet the narrator's attention only wanders to explore further the unknown territories evoked in the narrative, broadening its scope while the text yields in return a rich, inexhaustible treasure to the reader: "And so, as you read on across the broad pages with as many slips and somnolences as you like, the illusion rises and holds you of banks slipping by on either side, and glades opening out, of white towers revealed, of gilt domes and ivory minarets. It is, indeed, an atmosphere, not only soft and fine, but rich, too, with more than one can grasp at any single reading" (*Essays* III: 149). Reading Hakluyt's book further illustrates Woolf's conception of reading and writing as a gift. "Multiplication du lu par le lisant...", Lucette Finas will write (Finas 14). Something which, according to Woolf, is only possible with one category of writers, the laymen who, like Chaucer, have her favour because "we are left to stray and stare and make out a meaning for ourselves" (*Essays* IV: 32) whereas "the priests", like Wordsworth, Coleridge, Shelley or Tennyson, "take you by the hand and lead you straight to the mystery" (*Essays* IV: 31), a move which results in morbidity and boredom rather than pleasure. The laymen guarantee a freedom of interpretation based on what Umberto Eco will call the openness of the text, what E. M. Forster calls "Expansion. ... Not completion" (Forster 1927: 116), what D. H. Lawrence refers to as its absence of fixedness when he writes: "Give me nothing fixed, set, static" (Lawrence 76).

Such active reading, for Woolf, derives from the suggestive power of words (*C.E.* II: 248) rather than their representational power or, more exactly, from their connotative rather than denotative power, an opposition that Barthes, following the linguist Hjelmlev, was to make in *S/Z* in 1970 and that Woolf made as early as 20 April 1937 in a radio broadcast entitled "Craftsmanship". A tongue-in-cheek defence of the sign language which, with one gable or one star, as in the Michelin or Baedeker's guide-books, can come to the point more clearly and concisely than words. This ironic plea clearly amounts to enhancing the power of words "not to express one simple statement but a thousand possibilities" (*C.E.* II: 246), "without the writer's will; often against his will" (*C.E.* II: 248); and reading them "allow[s] the sunken meanings to remain sunken, suggested, not stated; lapsing and flowing into each other like reeds on the bed of a river" (*C.E.* II: 248). Words are shown to exceed the writer's intentionality and disseminate meaning, thus preventing reading from turning into a hermeneutic quest.[17]

Staging the creative process thus ends up, in Woolf's short stories, in questioning the traditional boundaries between author and reader and in establishing a silent dialogue between them. The writer's offering is returned by the offering of the reader who welcomes the otherness of the text, its fullness and beauty, opening himself to the other in a moment of generosity. Reading, as well as writing, would then be better defined as a moment of openness, what Woolf calls in "A Haunted House", "love".

"A Haunted House": the short story as a "house of Love"

This extremely brief and cryptic short story only makes sense through metaphorical and metafictional expansion. Indeed, the text opposes two different states: waking and sleeping, reading and dreaming, the attempt at understanding and sudden understanding, a conscious and an unconscious process. The first leads to the failure of the quest (the narrator interrupting her reading to look for the ghosts yet failing to capture them), the second to its success (the narrator, while asleep and dreaming, gets into contact with the ghosts). What the story tells us is the story of the creative process, the narrator being both reader ("one might say, and so read on a page or two", 122) and writer ("one would be certain, stopping the pencil on the margin", 122). This process is both conscious and unconscious; it is linked to reading but more fruitful when the reading has stopped and dreaming has taken over since dreaming is conducive to a moment of revelation.

The creative process takes place in Woolf's "haunted house" whose doors are constantly opening and shutting, a welcoming house. A hospitable house is generally a house radiating love. Woolf's house of fiction, particularly in "A Haunted House", is such a house of love. "The light in the heart", "love upon their lips" is the treasure the ghosts are looking for, the buried feeling that bound them in their lifetime and which has been transmitted to their heir, the narrator. A quest for love is the hallmark of romance or of romantic stories and it would stamp Woolf's short story as a sentimental one. However, through metafictional expansion, love is here enlarged and transmuted into a concept encompassing different forms of emotion, not only the emotion that is represented (the ghosts' love) but also the emotion that is transmitted by the writer and his writing to the reader, that is, aesthetic emotion. Woolf seems to echo E. M. Forster who wrote: "All I suggest is that we call the whole bundle of emotions love" (Forster 1974: 35).[18]

In "A Haunted House", the limits between the character's and the narrator's identity are blurred. If from the beginning to the end of the text, it is clear that the ghostly couple is made of man and woman, the identity of the narrator is not so straightforward. The limits of his/her identity are now restricted now extended. Ungendered and anonymous, it is now impersonal ("one"), now single ("I"), now plural ("us", "their", a couple in the image of the ghostly one: "Sound asleep. Love upon their lips"), now referred to as "you", an ambiguous pronoun which is at times an address to the ghosts or possibly, the reader, at others, a pronoun inclusive of the narrator. The interchangeability of the ghosts and the narrator's identity suggests that aesthetic emotion depends first of all on empathy between the characters and the narrator who embodies both the writer and the reader; empathy between the created figures, their creator and the reader. Empathy is based on recognition, the recognition of familiar feelings and experiences (such as love, death, haunting memories, etc.) and of the human character of these fictitious figures. The reader thus sketched in between the lines is a reader who can only be sensitive to what he knows, what he can feel, what he can recognise, that is, the familiar, the ordinary or, more exactly, the universal—the very qualities that ensure the enduring success of Greek drama.

Aesthetic emotion further depends on the shock of language, on the sound and visual effects it creates. The contrasts between light and shadow, daylight and darkness, the beams of the sun and moonbeams give a pictorial quality to the narrative further emphasised by the recurrent references to colours ("all the leaves were green in the glass.... The apple only turned its yellow side") in ekphrastic Cézanne-like still lifes. But the house is more obviously filled with sounds (doors opening and shutting, "the wood pigeons bubbling with content and the hum of the threshing machine", 122) just as the whole narrative relies on sound-effects, on repetition (repeated motifs, repeated sounds or alliterations), on repetition and variation (" 'Safe, safe, safe', the pulse of the house beat softly/gladly/proudly/wildly") or rhythm. Visual and sound-effects, lyricism and musicality certainly bestow a poetic quality to the text, turning it into what Woolf calls "a prose poem". They contribute to make the reader see and hear just as empathy makes him feel. Through Woolf's images and words, the reader is made sensitive to the beauty of simple things, the colour of an apple, the cooing of a pigeon. Woolf meets Conrad's ambition which was "to make you hear, to make you feel..., to make you *see*".[19] She tickles the reader's senses and makes them alert to simple feelings, sounds and sights, or, more exactly, makes them alive to the power "the old words [combined] in new orders"[20] have to convey simple feelings, sounds and sights. In other words, she defamiliarises the "old, old words, worn thin, defaced by ages of careless usage" (Conrad xxv), thus rekindling their power to shock the reader and create aesthetic emotion. In the end, aesthetic emotion appears to be of an oxymoronic nature, based on recognition and "bewilderment", in Woolf's own words (*Essays* IV: 183); two antagonistic principles, the familiar and the unfamiliar, are brought together to create this extended notion of love, which is finally epitomised in the "moment of being".

Such a moment occurs at the end of the short story when the narrator wakes up. It is a moment of awakening when the reader becomes aware of a possible meaning of the story, a moment of intense pleasure both for the narrator and the reader, what Woolf calls "a moment of being": "Waking, I cry 'Oh, is this *your*—buried treasure? The light in the heart' " (123). The dash inserted by Woolf between "*your*" and "buried treasure" is a rhetorical figure of reticence or *aposiopesis*[21] which signals the beginning of the moment while deferring it: the shock of revelation is too brutal to come right away and a moment of stasis and silence is necessary before it does. The words "buried treasure" and "light in the heart" are on the one hand most familiar words as well as words "worn thin" by romance, by "Treasure Island stories" and their conventional quests for a buried treasure as well as by love stories and their conventional quests for ideal love. The shock comes from the unfamiliar association of "buried treasure" and "light in the heart", signalling the shift from a material treasure to an internal and emotional form of treasure; the shock creates both the narrator's emotion and aesthetic emotion, the very emotion the "buried treasure" and "light in the heart" come to designate in a further displacement of meaning. The "moment of being" thus epitomises the double antithetical movement of recognition and bewilderment or defamiliarisation[22] the whole narrative has led to, the encounter of the familiar and the strange which, according to Derek Attridge, is the sign that a work of art resists accommodation.[23]

Recognition and bewilderment come to a standstill and coexist in a moment of "delight" (*C.E.* II: 39), of "intensification of life" (*C.E.* II: 41), when the reader is surprised or "bewildered".[24] The coincidence of recognition and bewilderment creates a moment of being within the text and transforms the whole short story into a moment of being or aesthetic emotion or, in Woolf's terms, "love".

In "On Being Ill", Woolf theorises this and shows that surprise has a double origin. The person who is sick is evoked lying in bed "disinterested and able...to look, for example, at the sky" (*Essays* IV: 321) and discover "a strangely overcoming spectacle" which "has been going on all the time without [his] knowing it" (*Essays* IV: 321). The recumbent posture becomes the image of the reader's "disinterested contemplation"[25] and rediscovery of the ordinary world, that is, of his experience of the process of bewilderment operated by fiction that Woolf evokes in "The Russian Point of View" (Essays IV: 183). In a metaphorical way, Woolf defines what Viktor Schklovsky was to call, at about the same time, *ostranenie* or defamiliarisation. What she herself calls, in "A Sketch of the Past", "the shock-receiving capacity" (83) of the writer, which is here shown to be transferable to the reader. And Attridge will write: "the act of breaking down the familiar is also the act of welcoming the other" (Attridge 2004: 26). However illness keeps the reader's mind blurred and makes it difficult for him to understand what he is reading. But this disadvantage is turned upside down by Woolf who writes:

> Incomprehensibility has an enormous power over us in illness... In health meaning has encroached upon sound. Our intelligence

domineers over our senses. But in illness, with the police off duty,
we creep beneath some obscure poem by Mallarmé or Donne... and
the words give out their scent, and ripple like leaves, and chequer
us with light and shadow, and then, if at last we grasp the meaning, it is all the richer for having travelled slowly up with all the
bloom upon its wings. (*Essays* IV: 324)

Illness, which sharpens the reader's senses, is turned into a metaphor of the writer's attempt at drawing the reader's attention to
words as signifiers, to the musicality, sensuality or visual qualities of
language—another form of defamiliarisation—something the poetic
words "the words give out their scent, and ripple like leaves, and
chequer us with light and shadow", perform while pointing at it. On
the whole reading, for Woolf, comes out as synonymous with discovery, surprise and aesthetic involvement. Such a conception of
reading, foregrounding pleasure, paves the way for Sontag and
Barthes's erotics of reading;[26] it also turns reading into a moment of
being, the event of language and not in language, a Deleuzian
event.[27]

Taking into account Woolf's conception of reading and writing as
inextricably bound together and almost interchangeable, and as
mainly generous, open dispositions, we could finally define her art
of the short story as eminently ethical, as offering the possibility, in
Attridge's words: "to read inventively, to respond to the inventiveness of the work in an inventive way and thus affirm and prolong its
inventiveness. I would call this a responsible reading, a reading that
attempts to do justice to the alterity, singularity, and inventiveness
of the literary work; and it's here that I locate the ethical" (Attridge
2003: 33). Attridge further defines the ethical as the welcoming of
the other, which is itself understood as "an impingement from outside that challenges assumptions, habits, and values, and demands a
response"; therefore, "otherness exists only in the registering of that
which resists my usual modes of understanding" (27) and "the act of
breaking down the familiar is the act of welcoming the other" (26).
The short story as a space where recognition goes together with
bewilderment is such an ethical space.

In "A Haunted House", within the compass of two pages, Woolf
builds a house of fiction which is both very small in the actual story
it contains, and immensely large in the story of fiction onto which it

opens. As Sir Thomas Browne would say, "there is All Africa and her prodigies in [it]".[28] Built across boundaries, this house is a house of Love, the meeting-place of the narrative and the metafictional, the aesthetic and the ethical, terms whose meaning Woolf displaces and redefines. It is, in the end, the house of the short story.

5
Woolf's Short Story as a Site of Resistance

In the two previous chapters, conversation has been shown to be the form of Woolf's short stories and its aesthetic and ethical components have been examined. As a space designed to welcome the other, conversation allows for debate between the self and the other as characters or reader and writer. It is both an open space, as the analysis of "A Haunted House" pointed out, and an agonistic space, as the analysis of the tension between fragmentation and totality or the study of "A Dialogue upon Mount Pentelicus" showed. It could certainly be described in Bakhtin's terms as a dialogic space, a space thriving on diversity and interaction.[1] However, we have purposefully avoided the word "dialogic" so far. Resorting to the term "conversation", as redefined by Woolf as originating in and departing from Plato's dialogue, and with the various shades of meaning we have explored, allows indeed for a finer and more adequate appraisal of Woolf's short stories.[2] We saw that within the short story as conversation, the interplay between emotion, impersonality and proportion creates both tension and circulation, dissent and debate at a structural, thematic and metafictional level. Such a dynamic space is the specific space of the short story, an aesthetic space with an ethical turn that opens, because of its very nature, onto the political. This dimension of conversation will be explored here at length as well as the way in which the political, the ethical and the aesthetic are closely intertwined in Woolf's short stories.

Virginia Woolf has long been said to belong to the tradition of aesthetic writers whose work is supposed to be governed by purely formal considerations. In the first critical study of Woolf published in

England in 1932, Winifred Holtby, voicing what would be the position of many Woolfian critics to come, writes: "This is [Woolf's] test of disinterestedness.... [A work of art] must be an end in itself, as perfect and self-contained as a Greek vase".[3] Holtby adds that Woolf's vision of art as autonomous is that "of Arnold, of Pater, of the French symbolists, and of almost all her own contemporaries, the Georgian critics" and is antagonistic to the Edwardians who "were never interested in character itself, or in the book in itself. They were interested in something outside" (Holtby 45).

Woolf's work has therefore been considered from the start as "existing in a sphere separate from the practical and the utilitarian and governed by purely, or largely, formal considerations", to borrow Attridge's words (Attridge 2004: 11).[4] As such, it has first been accounted for by aesthetic literary criticism, that is, New Criticism and their followers. Then various forms of criticism (cultural, feminist, post-colonial studies, etc.) have exposed the preconceptions of New Criticism and pointed out that social and historical factors necessarily shape art and that the autonomy of art, in Woolf's case as in others, is bound to be deceptive. Yet such a reading of the aesthetic tradition, challenging as it is, may well be, as Derek Attridge remarks, the reading of what he calls "instrumental criticism", a form of criticism that "judges the literary work according to a pre-existing scheme of values, on a utilitarian model that reflects a primary interest somewhere other than in literature" (Attridge 2004: 13). And he adds: "there is no way [literature] can serve as an instrument without at the same time challenging the basis of instrumentality" (Attridge 2004: 13).

Those contradictory critical readings of Woolf's work seem to match Woolf's own apparent contradiction: indeed, although she was a woman of many commitments (who was involved in the Cooperative Movement, gave lectures to social workers, involved herself in preparations for an anti-fascist exhibition in London in 1935 or, to give another example, was a staunch defender of the pacifist cause, as witnessed by *Three Guineas*),[5] she could lament, as she does in her essay "The Leaning Tower", "the pedagogic, the didactic, the loud-speaker strain that dominates [the 1930s] poetry" which "feel[s] compelled to preach... the creation of a society in which everyone is equal and everyone is free" (*C.E.* II: 175). She could regret, as she does in "The Artist and Politics", that "to mix literature with politics [is] to adulterate it" (*C.E.* II: 230); "instead of bread made with flour, we [are] given bread made with plaster" (*C.E.* II: 231). These words have generally been construed as conveying her refusal of all form of commitment in literature and her fiction has subsequently been read for many years as a form of art for art's sake until, more recently, in the 1980s, feminist critics took hold of her work, most often her two long essays *A Room of One's Own* and *Three Guineas*, and exposed Woolf's commitment to the women's cause and acknowledged politicised aspects of her work.[6] Yet few critics have shown, as Moi, Bowlby[7] or Regard[8] have done, that Woolf's feminist, political and aesthetic commitments are not at odds but intimately connected.

It is this long-standing apparent contradiction in Woolf that I would like to address here by looking at her short stories. Woolf's short stories have from the start been regarded as experimental texts, the most experimental in Woolf's so-called experimental fiction. They have been called "sketches"[9] and regarded as laboratories of her fiction, and Baldwin and Skrbic back this reading by concentrating on the texts' formal experiments. Baldwin is interested in Woolf's "restless experimentation with form and technique" (Baldwin 3) and Skbric, although placing the short stories in their post-war context and pointing out that they reveal "the silent margins of the feminine" (Skbric xxi), mainly discusses in her first three chapters "the short story as form", namely "questions of genre, plot and principal narrative techniques" before devoting her last three chapters to "the issue of genre" and "the problematic question of definition in relation to Woolf's stories" (Skbric xix). To my mind, such a reading is somewhat reductive and at odds with, on the one hand, Woolf's life, and on the other with what can be read in her other works of fiction. I will argue that these self-contained texts, autonomous as they are, display forms of commitment but, just as literature in general can serve, according to Attridge, both as an instrument and a challenge to instrumentality, there is no way the short stories can be committed without at the same time challenging the basis of commitment.

While browsing through Virginia Woolf's short stories, we find here and there a few allusions to the war ("The Mark on the Wall", "Mrs Dalloway in Bond Street"), women's rights ("A Society"), religion ("An Unwritten Novel") or politics ("A Society", "An Unwritten

Novel"). However these scattered allusions to the external world are not enough to say that those texts are committed ones. Indeed, there is no open protest or denunciation; except for such texts as "A Society", the short stories on the whole are not feminist or political pleas or pamphlets. It is also obvious they do not subscribe to the rules of representational literature. However, we may wonder whether texts that do not belong to the referential category necessarily make an intransitive use of language, which is supposed to be the hallmark of modernism. My claim is that it is through aesthetics, through the autonomy of the form, that Woolf's short stories display some form of commitment.[10]

The short story as a site of resistance against silence

The short story as silent conversation

It may seem paradoxical to define the short story, as we did in Chapter 3, as, partly, a silent conversation and then attempt to analyse it as a site of resistance against silence. To define Woolf's short story as a form of conversation is to ascribe to this term a very specific meaning, as we have seen previously. Conversation is first of all to be understood as a silent form of conversation.

Indeed, conversation in the common sense of the term is rare in the short stories; dialogue between characters is rare, brief or disconnected. In most short stories, spoken words are scarce and questions or statements in direct speech remain unanswered or incomplete. In "Kew Gardens", the dialogue between two elderly women strolling past the flower-bed reads as follows:

> "Nell, Bert, Lot, Cess, Phil, Pa, he says, I says, she says, I says, I says, I says—"
> "My Bert, Sis, Bill, Grandad, the old man, sugar,
> Sugar, flour, kippers, greens
> Sugar, sugar, sugar". (93)

This parody of a dialogue from which all form of story-telling has disappeared first acts as a means of characterisation which highlights the grotesque nature of the two female characters and ironically suggests these lower middle class women may not be very different from the old man they heard "talking about spirits" (92) and whose "eccentricity, betokening a disordered brain, especially in the well-to-do", fascinated them (93). It also points out, through the use of such rhetorical devices as repetition and abruption, the meaninglessness and essential emptiness of such conversation.

In "A Summing Up", Bertram Pritchard's spoken words are summarised by the narrative voice to the same effect: "he chattered on about his tour in Devonshire, about inns and landladies, about Eddie and Freddie, about cows and night travelling, about cream and stars, about continental railways and Bradshaw, catching cod, catching cold, influenza, rheumatism and Keats" (208). In this humorous passage, words are arbitrarily and repeatedly brought together: "inns and landladies"; "cows and night travelling"; "cream and stars", etc. However, in this series of zeugmas, pairs can be formed through semantic association: cows and cream; night and stars; travelling and railways; Bradshaw, cold, influenza, and Keats, namely, Septimus's doctor in *Mrs Dalloway*, a sample of diseases and a poet notoriously suffering from tuberculosis. But if there is some sort of association of ideas, it is warped, since the words Bertram Pritchard brings together are not the expected couples we have mentioned. In a comic way, the logic of association of ideas is twisted, reverberating on the character who is therefore ridiculed. The spoken discourse of Bertram Pritchard also proceeds from phonic associations such as the repetition of the same syllables in Eddie and Freddie and alliterations in -k: cows, cream, continental, Keats (and the [k] sound may be after all the only reason for Keats being added to the list). This play on sounds comes to a climax with "catching cod, catching cold" where the repeated sounds [k] and [d] frame a semantic gap between "cod" and "cold" or paranomasia together with a repetition of "catching"—a similar number of syllables and a similar stress pattern. As in nursery rhymes, rhythm and sound prevail over meaning. Such humorous verbal play highlights the meaninglessness of Bertram Pritchard's spoken discourse and confirms Sasha Latham's intuition that meaning is to be found elsewhere: "she was thinking of him in the abstract as a person whose existence was good, creating him as he spoke in a guise that was different from what he said, and certainly the true Bertram Pritchard, even though one could not prove it" (208). Meaning is to be found in this "silence" which, as Woolf writes in *Between the Acts*, "adds its unmistakable contribution to talk" (26).

If Woolf judges Hemingway severely for "an excessive use of dialogue" (*Essays* IV: 455) in his short stories, she certainly does not give
way herself to such excess, her technique being in the end closer to
Conrad's and Ford Madox Ford's as it is described by Ford himself in his
reminiscences of his collaboration with Conrad: "[o]ne unalterable rule
that we had for the rendering of conversations—for genuine conversations that are an exchange of thought, not interrogatories or statements
of fact—was that no speech of one character should ever answer the
speech that goes before it" (Ford 1995: 279). Whatever the function
Woolf ascribes to spoken words within the economy of her narratives
(whether they adumbrate the creative process or put a stop to it, whether
they return a character to reality or make the social world and exchange
he is involved in palpable, whether they translate the difficulty to com-
municate or the inadequacy of speech to capture "reality"), it is clear
that she privileges in her short stories "genuine conversation", the
"exchange of thought" that can take a variety of forms and be a silent
exchange between characters or between one character and his/her
own self, or between a character or a narrator and the reader or the figure of the reader. As Woolf spells it out in "The Evening Party", the
silent inner world is what she favours in her short stories:

> "Speech is an old torn net, through which the fish escape as one
> casts it over them. Perhaps silence is better...."
> "It's an odd thing, silence. The mind becomes like a starless night;
> and then a meteor slides, splendid, right across the dark and is
> extinct. We never give sufficient thanks for this entertainment".
> (99)

This is in some measure what "Solid Objects" both stages and enacts.
In this short story, conversation first appears in a caricatural form,
being reduced to the meaningless words one can use in any conversation: " 'You mean to tell me ... You actually believe ...' thus the walking stick on the right-hand side next the waves seemed to be asserting
as it cut long straight stripes on the sand" (102) or "he said with the
energy that dismisses a foolish strain of thought,

> 'To return to what I was saying—'". (103)

Towards the end of the narrative, a short dialogue takes place between the two characters, John and Charles:

> "What was the truth of it, John?" asked Charles suddenly, turning and facing him. "What made you give it up like that all in a second?"
>
> " 'I've not given it up," John replied.
>
> "But you've not a ghost of a chance now," said Charles roughly.
>
> "I don't agree with you there," said John with conviction. (106)

The only time John and Charles answer each other, they talk at cross purposes, Charles referring through "it" in "What made you give it up" to John's political career while John understands "it" as referring to his quest for stones and other solid objects, his own pursuit of beauty. And the same is true of "you've not a ghost of a chance now", a statement of Charles's referring to John's now impossible election to Parliament, understood by John as bearing on his quest for stones. These few words expose the rift between the two characters, one living in a prosaic world, the other in a dream world. Although John is depicted as obsessed with lumps of glass and disconnected from reality, the very limited space devoted to John and Charles's spoken words points to the writer's preference for the richness and complexity of John's silent inner world. While Charles appears to have, like Sir George Darwin whom Woolf describes in her 1909 journal, "no feeling for beauty, no romance, or mystery in his mind" (Woolf 2003: 7) and to be very much "a solid object", a self-satisfied Victorian who "likes punctuality, good manners and tidiness" (Woolf 2003: 7), in short, a dull man,[11] John comes out as a dreamer and a man who, if slightly deranged, is sensitive to some form of beauty[12] and determined to possess "solid objects", some piece of "star-shaped china" (104) or "glass curiously marked or broken" (106), some piece of iron that "had its origin in one of the dead stars or was itself the cinder of a moon" (106). Such a solid "object mixes itself so profoundly with the stuff of thought that it loses its actual form and recomposes itself a little differently in an ideal shape which haunts the brain"(104). The shape of the object seems to materialise thought, the world of silence which in turn re-shapes it, idealises it. While making a statement about beauty and the subjective perception of beauty, this sentence also refers to the rich interaction between object and thought, to the silent conversation taking place between outer and inner world. Playing ordinary conversation against "genuine conversation", Woolf invests the words "solid objects" with two contradictory meanings and directs the reader's sympathy towards the one connected with silence and a rich inner life, at odds with a public political career that henceforth appears as superficial and unsatisfactory. This short story can thus be read as a metafictional comment on Woolf's own choice of silent conversation as a model for her short story.

Silence as a sign of inhibition

The urge for silence, the desire not to speak or not to tell, could be construed as a sign of inhibition and as such, could be traced back to the author's socio-cultural background and ascribed to her Victorian education and the taboos that went with it. For instance, "talking Greek", in "A Dialogue upon Mount Pentelicus", can be read as a euphemism of the time for "talking about homosexuality". But such an example is taken from an early short story and is quite isolated. Later, Woolf will not refrain from mentioning, in "Kew Gardens", Eleanor's memory of "the kiss of an old grey-haired woman with a wart on her nose, the mother of all my kisses all my life" (91). This "precious" kiss is ambiguous, being both a forbidden and a motherly kiss from a woman who is both a mother-figure, as the grey hair suggests, and a lover; however, she is no *femme fatale*, as the wart on the nose humorously points out. And introducing this slightly humorous note and departure from the cliché of the ideal lover may well be a means of deflating the subversive nature of the kiss.

In later stories like "A Woman's College from Outside" (written in 1920 but published in 1926), Woolf will evoke Alice's kiss to Angela without subduing it. Similarly, a comparison between the two versions of "Moments of Being" reveals her choice not to silence homosexual love. As Dick tells us, Woolf ended the first typescript of the short story with: "Julia blazed. Julia kindled. Out of the night she burnt like a dead white star. Julia opened her arms. Julia kissed her on the lips. Julia possessed it" (Dick 10), and when she published it in the American magazine, *Forum,* in 1928, she revised the ending, making it even more explicit: "She saw Julia open her arms; saw her blaze; saw her kindle. Out of the night she burnt like a dead white star. Julia kissed her. Julia possessed her" (Dick 10), a choice Leonard

Woolf ignored when he published "Moments of Being" in *A Haunted House and Other Stories*, feeling perhaps that it was not yet adapted to the British public.

Silent conversation as a way to resist repressive silence

If silence in the short story cannot be said to hide a then shameful type of sexuality, it often remains the locus of repressed feelings. Such is the case of "The Legacy" and "The Shooting Party".

In "The Legacy", Angela does not tell her husband about her love for her secretary's brother and does not even dare write about it in her diary just as, in "The Shooting Party", no mention is ever made of what happened to M. M. But Woolf is not content with simply representing a fairly commonplace type of silence; she turns silence into a powerful narrative strategy. She uses the silence inscribed in the narrative as well as the rhetorical figures of silence to denounce the repressive silence imposed by society.

In "The Legacy", through the inclusion of Angela's diary, which her husband finds and reads after her death, the power of oppression of a society where women are voiceless non-entities is denounced. Angela is indeed the type of the transparent aristocratic wife who adorns the house of her husband, an M. P. involved in active political life. She is attracted to the Marxist ideas of Miller and to Miller himself, her secretary's brother. Loving Miller is a way for her of rebelling against her husband, Gilbert Clandon, and the society and class he stands for while committing suicide is a way of acknowledging the power of society and the impossibility of changing it through rebellion: a tragic admission. Because Angela's confessions come through blanks in her diary (a name reduced to its initials, B. M., that Gilbert Clandon "could not fill in" [285]; a name repeatedly and "carefully scratched out. 'I told him I would not listen to any more abuse of...' Again the name was obliterated. Could it have been his own name?" [285]), they point out even more efficiently the power of a class-bound society where transgression of social classes is unthinkable, the power of marriage and indirectly, of religion and the Church that instil a dread of adultery. Angela's suicide, such as it is conveyed in an equally elliptical way in the diary ("'He has done what he threatened.'...He turned page after page. All were blank. But there, on the very day before her death, was this entry: 'Have I the courage to do it too?' That was the end" [286]), gives a measure of the intolerance of British society.

Accommodating the diaristic genre within the short story is a way of renewing the form of the short story; it is also a form of silent protest, of silent, indirect political commitment in favour of a more tolerant society. Silence is not only inscribed within the narrative through the blanks in Angela's diary which end up in giving her husband the clue to her love for Miller and their common suicide; it is also a narrative strategy, a way for the author of countering the silence imposed by society, its dictates and taboos by using the same tool. As Patricia Laurence writes about Woolf's novels, "Woolf's narrative coup is to subvert the sexist tradition of the silent female by infusing her silence with a new being, a new psychic and narrative life" (Laurence 41).[13]

In "The Shooting Party", silence also plays its role. The story is obviously about a shooting party Squire Rashleigh has taken part in and his triumphant return with loads of pheasants. However the story takes on a wider, metaphorical meaning through the staging of the whole Rashleigh family and of M. M. The Rashleigh family, closely connected to King Edward, consists of the squire and his two unmarried sisters, Miss Antonia and Miss Rashleigh. The grandeur of the Rashleighs, their wealth, is but a distant memory, like the Empire they helped to build; their manor-house, a metonymy of their own shabby old selves, is now draughty and decrepit. The use of metonymy extends to the pheasants which the Squire shoots and whose dying bodies metaphorise the two women's reification and approaching death. "[T]he birds were dead now, their claws gripped tight, though they gripped nothing. The leathery eyelids were creased greyly over their eyes" (256) announces the following description of the two old ladies: "Their eyes became like pebbles, taken from water; grey stones dulled and dried. And their hands gripped their hands like the claws of dead birds gripping nothing. And they shrivelled as if the bodies inside the clothes had shrunk" (259). The narrative culminates in the climatic and symbolic fall of the family shield and King Edward's photograph:

> The shield of the Rashleighs crashed from the wall. Under the mermaid, under the spears, she lay buried.
>
> The wind lashed the panes of glass; shots volleyed in the Park and a tree fell. And then King Edward in the silver frame slid, toppled and fell too. (260)

"The Shooting Party" then reads as an allegory of the end of the Edwardian period, the fall of its squirearchy, of the Empire it stood for and of the brutality that went with it ("the Rashleighs. Over there. Up the Amazons. Freebooter. Voyagers. Sacks of emeralds. Nosing round the islands. Taking captives. Maidens", 255). As such, the short story can be regarded as passing a severe judgement on this period and as a political condemnation of the Empire and the brutality both of the Imperialist and the aristocratic spirit.[14]

The narrative is framed, like "An Unwritten Novel", by two paragraphs that stage M. M., "not...exactly a guest, nor yet a maid" (254), travelling with a brace of pheasants in a railway carriage, who becomes the origin of the story, if not the narrator: "Since she was telling over the story she must have been a guest there" (254). What is immediately striking is the scar on her jaw ("she was handsome...but scarred on the jaw—the scar lengthened when she smiled", 254). The scar is the visible but silent trace of a past trauma—a trauma that will never be described. M. M. will prove to be Milly Masters, the Rashleighs' housekeeper whose son "cleaned the church" (256), and Miss Antonia and Miss Rashleigh will only make a passing allusion to her while counting their brother's female conquests:

"the girl at the tailor's," Miss Antonia murmured, "where Hugh bought his riding-breeches, the little dark shop on the right..."

"...that used to be flooded every winter. It's *his* boy," Miss Antonia chuckled, leaning towards her sister, "that cleans the church"..."Milly Masters in the still room," began old Miss Rashleigh. "She's our brother's...". (258–9)

These words and gaps in the dialogue are a brief allusion to Milly Master's affair with a Rashleigh but do not account for the scar on her jaw.

Silence surrounds this affair and the stigma it left becomes all the more blinding. Woolf chooses an indirect method to account for it. She saturates her text with images of violence, guns cracking, dogs barking and breaking carcasses of pheasants, blood streaming from the birds, the squire cursing, etc. The squire, with his "hang-dog, purple-stained face" (255), is a caricatural representation of brutality and animality while the pheasants he shoots are personified repeatedly, "swooning under their rich damp feathers" (255), or having "warm damp bodies, still languid and soft, as if in a swoon" (256), before dying, "the thighs tightly pressed to [their] sides[s]" (257). The sexual suggestiveness of the description turns the shooting party into a metaphor of sexual intercourse. And when the squire at the end lashes Miss Rashleigh on the cheek, making her stagger and die, he only reiterates the gesture that left a scar on M. M.'s cheek—the visible or symbolic sign of a silent brutal sexual relationship inflicted by one of the Rashleighs. Such a scar is also what the initial "Chk. Chk" of M. M. evokes when we read: "like somebody imitating the noise that someone else makes, she made a little click at the back of her throat: 'Chk. Chk.'" (254). Indeed, if "Chk. Chk" is a way of launching the creative process, as we saw in the preceding chapter, it is also reminiscent of *The Waste Land*, sounding as it does like "Jug. Jug"[15]: "The change of Philomel, by the barbarous king / So rudely forced; yet there the nightingale / filled all the desert with inviolable voice / And still she cried, and still the world pursues, / 'Jug Jug' to dirty ears".[16] In these lines, T. S. Eliot, drawing on Ovid's *Metamorphoses* (Book VI), evokes the rape of Philomel by her own brother-in-law and her transformation into a nightingale.

The squire lashing at his own sister may also be read in this context as metaphorising an incestuous relation. The story at that point reads as possibly deriving from Woolf's own experience of incest,[17] and therefore as autobiographical; at the same time, it stages characters that are grounded in the Edwardian period, a bygone era. The story thus collapses the personal and the collective and Woolf's fate, like Miss Rashleigh or M. M.'s fate, becomes emblematic of the fate of women in Edwardian times: whether they were sisters or housekeepers, they were often brutalised and compelled to be lovers. Silently, indirectly, long before it found its way in her autobiographical writings, the author's own scar is exposed.[18] Silently, indirectly, metaphorically, and most forcefully, the fate of Edwardian women is denounced.

Women's abuse and suffering being silent, Woolf stages the silence that weighs on Edwardian society and that conceals men's misdemeanour while re-appropriating it, through gaps in dialogues and indirect metaphorical writing, in order to counter it all the more efficiently. Several short stories staging the confrontation of women with men could be analysed along these lines. "The Introduction", beyond the confrontation of the self with the other, as we saw in Chapter 3, is a rebellion against male arrogance and a silent but vigorous plea in favour of the emancipation of women[19] and the recognition of their intellectual talents as well as a call to arms, as the last words make clear: "this civilisation, churches, parliaments and flats—this civilisation, said Lily Everit to herself, as she accepted the kind compliments of old Mrs Bromley on her appearance, depends upon me" (188). "Lappin and Lapinova", beyond the fate of Rosalind and Ernest, is, especially through the silent inferences of the last sentence, "So that was the end of *that* marriage" (268; my emphasis), a denunciation of the necessary failure of all marriages as well as of the incompatibility of male and female "characters". The confrontation between the self and the other verges on the political in "The New Dress", where Mabel's personal ordeal is also in some ways the result of the confrontation between the wealthy upper classes the Dalloways stand for and the lower poorer social layers Mabel belongs to.

These silent pleas, with a feminist and political slant, contrast with an early short story, "A Society" (1920) where Woolf stages a group of girls who form a society and set out to find out what has happened to the male children of their mothers. Their quest leads them to the Royal Navy, a Law Court, the Royal Academy and Oxbridge. The encounter with the Royal Navy is described first:

> Rose...had dressed herself as an Aethiopian Prince and gone aboard one of his Majesty's ships. Discovering the hoax, the Captain visited her...and demanded that honour should be satisfied. 'But how?' she asked. 'How?' he bellowed. 'With the cane of course!' Seeing that he was beside himself with rage and expecting that her last moment had come, she bent over and received, to her amazement, six light taps upon the behind. 'The honour of the British Navy is avenged!' he cried, and, raising herself, she saw him with the sweat pouring down his face holding out a trembling right hand. (126)

In the Law Courts, they discover that "the Judges were either made of wood or were impersonated by large animals resembling man who had been trained to move with extreme dignity, mumble and nod their heads" (127). The Royal Academy is shown to produce the worst poems imaginable, those of Burns, Browning, Tennyson or Stevenson;

and in Oxbridge, professors appear to argue endlessly about Sappho's chastity. Disappointed with their findings, the young women come to the conclusion that education, which lays the emphasis on the intellect, is responsible for this: "What could be more charming than a boy before he has begun to cultivate his intellect? ...Then they teach him to cultivate his intellect. He becomes a barrister, a civil servant, a general, an author, a professor.... Soon he cannot come into a room without making us all feel uncomfortable" (135). The remedy they advocate is to teach young girls to believe in themselves, rather than cultivate their intellect. In this short story, the Navy and its misplaced conception of honour,[20] the judges and their lack of humanity, the Royal Academy and its insensitivity to poetry, the professors and their trivial speculations are stigmatised. British institutions, the men that run them and the education that shapes these men, are derided in this biting satiric piece which reads as a forerunner of *Three Guineas* where Woolf will argue that the Establishment—Law Courts, Oxbridge, and the Church, which will be added to them—is responsible for war, educating and shaping men as it does. "A Society" also anticipates *A Room of One's Own* and its famous motto—"we think back through our mothers if we are women" (72–3)—through its feminist slant and its staging of conversations leading women to become aware of their limited role in history as mere breeders and as excluded from the life of society and its institutions. It is a direct call for women to believe in themselves—the only way to make the world change—and a vindication of women's intellectual power. Like the two later essays, "A Society" reads more like an openly committed manifesto and enables us to gauge, by contrast, Woolf's later method, her commitment to silence and indirection as both a poetic and a politically efficient strategy.

Re-appropriating silence: conversation as a poetic form of commitment

Based on elliptical narratives where nothing superfluous is stated so as to preserve proportion[21] and where typographical blanks as well as narrative ellipses silence the text, Woolf's short story is an art of silence relying on an "indirect method"[22] of suggestion and implicit statements. Silence, indeed, is not the silence imposed by censorship or social and moral coercion; it appears to be the writer's own deliberate choice. Woolf's method, in her short stories, consists in re-appropriating the silence society and respectability had imposed throughout the years—Victorian and Edwardian times mainly—and in using it to denounce these very forms of social oppression and moral coercion while redefining it in terms of rhetoric, metaphors, and generally speaking, indirection. Silence, formerly synonymous with taboos and the silencing of the inner life, is thus claimed as an asset. It therefore comes out as something new emerging from the old and is both a political and a poetic tool, a poetic form of commitment. Once again, an old word is rejuvenated and the form of the conversation redefined as silence comes out as committed form.

*   *   *

The short story as a site of resistance against authority

Silence, in its commonplace sense, is often the result of some form of oppression or at least, pressure, itself wielded by some authority. Therefore, if the short story is a site of resistance against silence, it is also a site of resistance against authority. Authority always comes from the top and is asserted through a single voice; it is monologic, whatever field it asserts itself in.

Monologism is what Woolf's short stories resist. They resist literary monoligism, the authority of binding and arbitrary literary conventions, what could be called literary norm, just as they resist other forms of monologism that some of her essays denounce and openly stigmatise, that is, the authority of Victorian patriarchy and the monologism of dictatorial political leaders.

This sends us back to the context in which Woolf was working: her early short stories belong to the Edwardian period and tend to react against the stifling and enduring Victorian way of life and values, while those written later, especially in the 1930s, are more often to be related to the traumatic post-World War I effects and above all, to the rise of fascism and Nazism. Whether these two forms of monologism—patriarchy and dictatorship—are connected and how the short story resists them is what we shall try to determine by analysing the mechanisms of resistance in the short story. We shall see how monologism is counteracted mainly through polyphony and generic hybridisation.

Resisting through polyphony

One of the early short stories will serve as a starting-point for my argument here. In "Phyllis and Rosamond", we witness the gradual disappearance of the authoritative narrative voice. Thus Woolf traces, through her own use of focalisation in this text, the way her own fiction will follow.

A first person narrator, hesitating between the singular pronoun "I" and the plural one "we", looks "at a little group" of girls, which "epitomise[s] the qualities of many" (17). Standing at a distance, observing the five girls, the narrator draws their portraits. The narrator addresses a "you" ("You must be in a position to follow these young ladies home", 18), a reader who is also an observer: "Yet you will observe also in this hour of unlovely candour something which is also sincere, but by no means ugly" (19). The narrator, who describes facts ("A few facts will help us to set them in their places", 18) and the comings and goings of the characters ("Phyllis had to go out and buy flowers and an extra dish for lunch; and Rosamond sat down to her sewing", 20), is no other than an omniscient narrator. His discourse only stops to give way to a character's direct speech: "But before she went she called Phyllis to her. 'Well my dear,' she said" (21). When it comes to the characters' thoughts, the narrator, like an omniscient god, reads them: "If one could read her thoughts, ... one would have found that she was busied in somewhat abstruse calculations" (21). The external focalisation only gives way to the internal subjective perception of the characters when Phyllis and Rosamond come to the Hibberts' house:

> Her cab stopped before some lighted windows which, open in the summer night, let some of the talk and life within spill out upon the pavement. She was impatient for the door to open which was to let her enter, and partake. When she stood, however, within the room, she became conscious of her own appearance which, as she knew by heart, was on these occasions, like that of ladies whom Romney painted. (24)

The shift from the narrator's to the young ladies' point of view occurs when the characters change places, leave the confinement of their houses where they are no better than slaves or at best, trained monkeys, and come to the Hibberts' house, a house of freedom and emancipation. The change in focalisation goes together with the geographical change and signals the girls' discovery of a freer world. At the end of the text, the last two sentences in direct free discourse enact the gradual and final disappearance of the narrator: "what did she really want, she asked herself? What was she fit for?" (28). This short story illustrates the shift from the traditional posture of the narrator to a more toned-down presence, a posture in which the narrator becomes one of the voices only. This shift from a single centre of authority to "a plurality of independent and unmerged voices and consciousnesses"[23] reads both as a shift from monologism to polyphony, as defined by Bakhtin in *Problems of Dostoevsky's Poetics*, and as a departure from the authority of Victorian patriarchal values.

In the whole of the short stories, Woolf's use of focalisation varies widely and we listen to many different voices: the narrator's, the characters' as well as the author's and the reader's. And each of these voices is plural and multi-faceted. The narrator is always present without being omniscient. He/she is either one of the characters, as in "A Society" where the narrator is one of a group of six or seven girls, or an observer, who looks at the mark on the wall or at the looking-glass and the reflected garden in "The Lady in the Looking-Glass"; rather than standing back at a distance, the narrator is part of the group or the surroundings he is describing. (S)he now assumes the identity of a historian, Rosamond Merridew, or of a diarist, Joan Martyn, in "The Journal of Mistress Joan Martyn"; now that of a biographer rewriting Miss Linsett's biography of Miss Willatt in "Memoirs of a Novelist" or of a novelist, as in "An Unwritten Novel". (S)he can impersonate a concert-goer, as in "The String Quartet", or a painter, as in "Blue and Green". Except for the early "Journal of Mistress Joan Martyn", the narrator is always anonymous, most of the time genderless, faceless and disembodied; resorting to the pronouns "one", "I" or "we", his/her identity is indeterminate and floating, as is best exemplified in "A Haunted House". Just as she redefines her characters as voices in *The Waves*, Woolf redefines in her short stories her narrator as a voice, an impersonal entity deprived of any specific gender or identity. This enables her to devise a narrator who can disappear—or nearly so—to let the other in, whether it be a character's voice, the authorial or the reader's voice. In the Dalloway stories, for example, the narrator gradually disappears to let us listen to

Clarissa Dalloway, Mabel Waring or Lily Everit's voices. Even if it is always mediated by the narrator, we have access to the character's free indirect discourse, the narrator's very facelessness and anonymity enabling him/her to give way to the character's voice.

The narrator and the characters do not prevent the author from making herself heard, either in stories with autobiographical undertones, as we have seen with "The Shooting Party", or, and especially, in caricatures and satiric stories. The author's voice can be heard through irony as it is the case, for example, in "Miss Pryme", a short story which draws the portrait of an old spinster who spends her life trying to improve the world. Improving the world first means, for Miss Pryme, caring for appearances and second, taking care of the dying and the infirm. The narrative voice analyses the first meaning as enforcing respectability and moral conventions and the second as exercising "power over the infirm, the illiterate, the drunken" (236). Miss Pryme's concern for the other appears to be but a concern for the norm and a way of fulfilling her own desire for power, or even, for oppression. Concern for the other here is no altruism or generosity but self-centredness. The portrait of Miss Pryme turns out to be a caricature of the righteous and a satire of the likes of Florence Nightingale who are intent on "improving the world", a zeal frequent in Victorian times and that Woolf witnessed in her own mother, through her philanthropic and nursing activities.[24] Through this caricature,[25] the voice of the author deconstructs what tries to pass itself off as an ethical behaviour and thus indirectly defines what she means by "ethical" (a true concern for the other) while revealing what the aim of her narrative technique and her choice of polyphony is, as we shall see in the next few pages.

However, if through irony and satire, the author's voice can criticise harshly a character, a period, or any other element and thus orientate the reading, most of the time, this voice's authority is limited by the very presence of other voices. The author's voice, in most short stories, thus comes out as only one among many. In the same way, the reader is now and then addressed, staged or solicited; he enters into a dialogue with the narrative voice, most often when the latter assumes the identity of a creator, as we have seen in our analysis of the metafictional short stories. So that instead of listening to the omniscient voice of a *Deus-ex-machina,* the reader listens to many different voices: the voices of the narrators, the author and the reader, the voices of men and women; the voices of the rich or the poor, of Clarissa Dalloway but also of Mabel Waring or John Cutbush or the widow in "The Widow and the Parrot"; the voices of the sane or the insane, like the old man's in Kew Gardens or John's in "Solid Objects"; the voices of the pleasant or the hateful ones, like Prickett Ellis and Captain Brace; the voices of those who conform to the sexual norm, like Lappin and Lapinova, or those who do not, like Fanny Wilmot and Miss Craye; the voices of "obscure figures" (17) like Joan Martyn, of "grey shadow[s]" like Miss V. (31); the voice of the voiceless like Lily Everit who stands for all women. Among the voiceless can be included the animals and the objects. Indeed, thanks to his/her disembodied nature, the narrator has access to the inanimate world and the animal world which is alive when no human presence is around: "shy creatures, lights and shadows, curtains blowing, petals falling— things that never happen, so it seems, if someone is looking" ("The Lady in the Looking-Glass" 221) or the wild beasts that are released when Nurse Lugton falls asleep—perhaps a metaphor of the subconscious mind and its wild silent life. In a way, the narrator in such cases, gives voice to the voiceless too.

Polyphony as a form of ethical commitment

On the whole, in the various short stories, we listen to voices belonging to different social classes, the voices of those society and history have either recognised or forgotten. The short stories provide a whole sample of voices in which the personal collapses into the collective and even the universal. So that the short stories can be regarded as heterogeneous pieces and as such be studied separately or they can be regarded as a "gigantic conversation"[26] in which every man and every woman is in turn allowed to speak: from the passers-by in "Kew Gardens" to Mabel Waring, Mrs Dalloway's poor relative in "The New Dress", or Mrs Gage, the penniless elderly widow in "The Widow and the Parrot". Woolf fulfils here her desire for impersonality, for doing away with "the damned egotistical self" (*Diary* II: 14; 26 January 1920); and as the depersonalised self gives way to various selves, impersonality is subsumed into personality. As in the essay "Street Haunting" where the narrator voices her love for walking through the streets because it provides the material for writing, allowing her as it does to meet many people while remaining anonymous among anonymous people ("we...become part of that vast army of anonymous trampers" (*Essays* IV: 481); in the short stories, she can be anonymous while inhabiting one character after another, adopting the voice of the other: "In each of these lives one could penetrate a little way, far enough to give oneself the illusion that one is not tethered to a single mind but can put on briefly for a few minutes the bodies and minds of others" (*Essays* IV: 490); it gives the narrator (and the reader) the illusion that one is many. Such a self-denying technique permits a movement from the personal to the impersonal and from the individual to the collective or universal, from the narrator's voice to the voice of everyman and everywoman.

This strategy favours diversity and dissimilarity, difference rather than uniformity, and erases the distinction between high and low characters. It partakes of what we could call Woolf's democratic impulse (an impulse Melba Cuddy-Keane also traces in her essays[27]) and it is comparable to what Miss La Trobe attempts in her pageant in *Between the Acts* where she gives voice to all the villagers, down to the idiot, while including, through the mirrors the actors hold back to the spectators, the gentry who are watching the performance, thus encompassing in her play the different components of society.

The word "democracy", always a keyword of British culture, was, in the 1920s and 1930s, at the centre of numerous debates and, as Melba Cuddy-Keane shows, "cultural usage was...extending the meaning of 'democratic' from a system of government to the whole framework of cultural thinking and expression within a society" (Cuddy-Keane 39). The democratic principle Woolf defends through her commitment to the Women's Co-operative Guild or to adult suffrage, can, in her writings and in reference to them, be understood as referring not to a specific political system but in a more general sense, as referring to an absence of hierarchy, of class distinctions, of racial distinctions and as a belief in the equality of all. Democracy appears as a utopian condition where authority, domination, and oppression have given way to equality and dialogue (conversation in the etymological sense of having dealings with others, "manner of conducting oneself in the world").[28] And it is as referring to a general belief in equality that we use the term "democracy" and "democratic".

A narrative technique that opens up onto plurality is certainly an anti-authoritarian one that displays a generous and tolerant disposition and a desire to encounter the other and let the other speak.

Polyphony turns the short stories into "a gigantic conversation", a site of plurality and tolerance, thus confirming that conversation is the supreme art of tolerance, as Clive Bell shows in his essay on "Civilisation" (1928).[29] Through polyphony, the short story becomes a hospitable space, that is, an ethically committed form.

This is exactly what "The Fascination of the Pool" synthesises in its evocation of a pool and its strange content. Covered as it is by the reflection of the letters of the poster advertising the sale of the nearby farm, and full as it is of thoughts and voices, the pool reads as a metaphor of the writer's mind and his writing. Like the writer's mind, the pool is inhabited by countless thoughts and voices, "not printed or spoken aloud" (226), voices of all times, ages, genders and social conditions. They are the spectral voices of the unknown, those who have been forgotten by history: a man who "came here in 1851 after the heat of the Great Exhibition" (226), a farm girl who in 1662, had been in love and then drowned herself, or a man who, on "the day Nelson fought at Trafalgar" caught a giant carp (227).

The writer's mind is represented as haunted by these anonymous voices and their emotion (love and despair, happiness and sadness), and as existing only through them. And although it encapsulates these voices—metaphorically speaking, within the compass of the pool—it cannot be said to be an all-encompassing consciousness, which would be at odds with the image of the mind hosting the others' voices. Unlike the writers of old who spoke through the monolithic voice of the omniscient narrator, Woolf's ideal writer is not "a great seer" and if she first used this phrase before cancelling it in her typescript,[30] it is not only because it has mystical or even romantic overtones but also, one may safely assume, because it is at odds with what the short story puts forward. One voice, the sad voice, threatens to muffle the others; we can recognise in that voice the voice of the author who, like Narcissus, says "Alas, alas" while looking at herself; the voice responsible for humour, irony or satire; the voice that now and again inflects the reading. However, although that voice is ever present, it never manages to stifle the others since the others continue to make themselves heard; it simply becomes one amongst the others. Indeed, the writer's mind is presented as a surface which, like the water of the pool, can be seen through. It gives access, through reflection, to what is beneath, to the thoughts and voices it harbours: "[o]ne drew closer to the pool and parted the reeds so that one could see deeper, through the reflections, through the faces, through the voices to the bottom" (227). The writer is seen as having an indefinitely layered consciousness since under each voice, another one can be heard: "yet there was always something else. There was always another face, another voice" (227). The writer therefore appears as a go-between or a "passeur", transmitting the countless voices of the others. This highly metafictional short story[31] thus reads as a perfect illustration of the polyphony and democratic spirit that runs through all the short stories.

On the whole, the short stories implement what Woolf yearns for in "The Leaning Tower". In this essay, she denounces the univocal form of literature that has prevailed, in spite of historical upheavals, since the nineteenth century, a form of literature produced by one class and one education—middle-class writers who have all received a good education at Oxbridge—that is, one voice. Woolf shows that the poets of the 1930s reacted against such uniformity: "they became communists; they became anti-fascists.... [I]t was wrong for a small class to possess an education that other people paid for; wrong to stand upon the gold that a bourgeois father had made from his bourgeois profession" (*C.E.* II: 172); but because they are the products of the society they abuse, they can only make us listen to "the pedagogic, the didactic, the loud-speaker strain that dominates their poetry" (*C.E.* II: 175). The phrasing Woolf has chosen, especially "the loud-speaker strain", very indirectly, yet inevitably, reminds her readers of the loud-speakers of the Nazi and fascist meetings of the late 1930s and of Hitler's voice that they could hear, like Woolf herself, on the radio ("we hear Hitler's voice as we sit at home of an evening" [*C.E.* II: 164]). Woolf thus subtly, if loosely, connects the monologism of dictatorship with the univocal form of literature that has dominated England for so long. And when, at the end of the essay, she pleads for a literature of "commoners", she is both pleading for a more democratic kind of literature—which "is no one's private ground", which "is common ground" (181)—and for political democracy. Variety, plurality, democracy are openly called for both in the aesthetic and political spheres. However, if her fiction were as openly committed, "we should", as she writes in "The Artist and Politics", "feel cheated and imposed upon, as if, instead of bread made with flour, we were given bread made with plaster" (*C.E.* II: 231). Woolf therefore chooses to counter monologism indirectly in her short stories, through the very form of the short story as conversation. And polyphony, a formal device, becomes a way of retrieving the voices of all, an indirect form of commitment to a democratic ideal.[32]

Resisting through generic hybridity

The democratic impulse against monologism is also exemplified in the short stories through the use of generic hybridity. It is true that Woolf indulges in formal experiments that enable her to redefine the very genre of the short story. She not only refashions the structural pattern of the short story by adopting the open beginning and ending of Chekhov's inconclusive short stories but also redefines the generic boundaries of the short story by incorporating other genres.[33] Woolf brings together elements from the three main literary forms, prose, poetry and drama, as well as elements from different art forms, music, painting, the cinema; she borrows from fictional literary genres (the epistolary in "The Symbol", the detective novel in "The Mysterious Case of Miss V.", the ghost story in "A Haunted House", etc.) and from non-fictional ones. My aim here is not to examine the various literary genres from which each short story borrows but to analyse generic hybridity as another instance of the commitment of the short story form. I shall focus here on the way Woolf's short stories resort to other genres and show that this process consists in accommodating a genre; through accommodation, the aesthetic experiment, far from resulting in merely formal generic blurring,[34] is turned into a form of ethical or/and political commitment.

Accommodating another genre can indeed be a way of giving voice to the other, of letting the other speak. It can be regarded as a way of welcoming the other (here, another genre), as a form of hospitality to the other synonymous with the valuing of impurity (here, generic impurity). And, according to Attridge, an openness to otherness—whatever the definition of the other we give—constitutes ethics itself.[35] And to illustrate such an ethical commitment in Woolf's short stories, we shall focus on "The Journal of Mistress Joan Martyn", a short story in which a fictional diary of a fifteenth-century woman is inserted. Historically speaking, diaries or journals have often been the usual and sole mode of confession or expression for women in centuries past, the only way of escaping the closed world in which they lived, as the author of the journal points out: "the whole world is barred from us...I feel the pressure of all this free and beautiful place—all England and the sea, and the lands beyond—rolling like sea waves, against our iron gates" (45). Such journals are not much valued by the old school of historians, 'la vieille histoire "chroni-queuse," as Jacques Rancière puts it,[36] and in the short story, they are not valued by the descendants of Joan Martyn. The only one interested in Joan Martyn's diary is Rosamond Merridew, the new historian who retrieves the journal and gives it pride of place within her historical narrative. In the short story, the journal appears as a way of rewriting history by giving voice to the voiceless. Similarly in "Phyllis and Rosamond", an early short story, Woolf borrows from the art of history and throws such light as "historians have begun to cast upon that dark and crowded place behind the scenes" (17) on the thwarted selves of two upper-middle class young ladies who have been raised to please their father and catch a husband with their perfect tea-table manners.

Far from being gratuitous aesthetic innovations, these generic experiments which consist in accommodating non-fictional genres, offer an opportunity to give voice to "obscure figures" (17), "not remarkable ones" (45), those who have been forgotten by history, the unknown ones, most of the time, women. Renewing the genre of the short story by inserting other genres in it is both a way of introducing ordinary characters, ordinary lives with banal and even ugly moments, and a way of introducing the other in the text. In other words, it is both a literary stance aiming at redefining the character as an anti-hero or heroine, as an ordinary anonymous character and an ethical move towards alterity. It is also a way of redefining both biography and history[37]: in the new form of biography and history, "the periphery invades the centre" (Rancière 89), the unknown ones become the heroes or displace them, as Tolstoï does in *War and Peace*.[38]

Interestingly enough, Woolf had, in her early journals, written about "obscure figures". For instance, in a 1909 entry, she writes "Carlyle's House" which focuses mainly on the "portraits of Mrs. Carlyle which seemed to look out quizzically upon the strangers" visiting the museum-house (Woolf 2003: 3) and which, to Woolf's eyes, yield the secrets of a cold, unhappy marriage, "[t]he only connection the flash of the intellect" (4). But the method she uses is the reverse of what we find in the short stories since, in her 1909 diary, Woolf inserts within the 24 February 1909 entry a text with a title, "Carlyle's House", which is a way of inserting within the diary a short story, except that it is based on people who have existed. As Frédérique Amselle writes: "In the early journals Woolf tries her hand at short story, journal and essay-writing",[39] something that will only appear incidentally in the later diaries.

Focusing on "obscure figures" is also what Woolf achieves in some of her short stories which straddle the line between prose and poetry or between writing and painting. In "An Ode Written Partly in Prose on Seeing the Name of Cutbush Above a Butcher's Shop in Pentonville", she captures the life of a John Cutbush who gives up imaginative life to make his living in the bleak reality of "cold meat" and "shrouded cadavers" in "the residue of London" (238–9). This poem, if only through its ludicrous rhyming pattern, reads as a parody of an ode and its usually romantic subject-matter. However, it also reads as a vindication of the ordinary in poetry. By turning bleak reality into a poem, traditionally regarded as a noble form, Woolf reasserts the power of imagination in a homage to Cutbush the butcher and to all the obscure ordinary workers who have relinquished their youthful romantic dreams for work and a dull life.

These workers are foreigners to the narrative voice ("These are semblances of human faces seen in passing / translated from a foreign language", 240), difficult to grasp ("how little we can grasp; / how little we can interpret and read aright / the name John Cutbush", 241): they are unusual characters for the writer and unfamiliar to Woolf herself, just as the poor "are unthinkable" for E. M. Forster.[40] Dedicating an ode to them is a way of making amends to those who enable some like the author herself, to sit in an armchair reading "the *Evening Standard* under the lamp" and lead a life of "entertainment" (241). It reads as a sort of *mea culpa* of a woman of means with socialist sympathies.

This ode also gives Woolf the opportunity to draw the portrait of a butcher just as she draws the portrait of Miss Pryme, in the preceding short story, or of a French couple obsessed with food and other characters in "Portraits", all belonging to the same period (1926–41). Whether in a poem, a short story or a gallery of portraits, Woolf captures in snapshots or visual images full of light and colour like Vanessa Bell's paintings, a couple and a marble-topped table, a vulgar stereotypical Mediterranean woman, a coarse and cruel one, etc., that is, the essence of a character. These texts, some of which are caricatures, fulfil the aim of a biography better than any traditional one while asserting the refusal of the narrative and presenting frozen moments. They bring together the qualities of the impersonal art of proportion and emotion of the short story and those of biography, poetry and painting, of different fictional and non-fictional genres and art forms[41] in examples of cross-fertilisation which point out the potentialities of generic hybridity.

Some short stories, like "The Mark on the Wall" or "An Unwritten Novel", stage a fictional situation (a narrator gazes at a mark on the wall and tries to guess what it is; a narrator looks at the passenger sitting opposite her and imagines what her life is like) while accommodating the genre of the "essai-méditation", the essay as meditation being a tradition that goes back to Montaigne. Discontinuity and openness constitute, according to Adorno, the very essence of the essay, which Montaigne calls "cette fricassée", "cette rhapsodie" (Angenot 57). And if the essay, unlike the scientific or Cartesian method, does not adopt an inductive or deductive method and a closed system, it is, Adorno goes on to explain, because it refuses the very idea of Truth or of totality. And Adorno concludes that heresy is the formal law of the essay.[42] Woolf's short stories that accommodate the essay adopt a zigzagging overall structure,[43] an associative method[44] resulting in a discontinuous development. They also become, like the essay and in Adorno's words, "the theatre of intellectual experience", "the point [being in the essay] not so much to unveil some content external to thought as to expose the intimate mechanisms through which thought selects its own objects" (Angenot 57).[45] Hence the genesis of the thinking process and consequently, of the writing or creative process is exposed in those texts. In other words, by accommodating the essay, the short story becomes metafictional. What remains to be determined is the role of metafiction. If we take as an example, "The Mark on the Wall", we see that it aims at defining fiction, the stuff modern fiction is made of. Modern fiction is about "phantoms", "the depths", that is, inner reality, the self and its numerous facets ("There is not one reflection but an almost infinite number", writes the narrator, 85), its variety, its truths: it introduces a world of freedom, "a sense of illegitimate freedom" (86). Modern fiction is neither a "description of reality" (86) nor historical fiction because external reality in the short story is equated with a set of rules, conventions, "standard things" (86) or norms, Truth, and is governed by a masculine point of view, that of professors, archbishops, policemen, Whitaker's Almanack and Table of Precedency. Indeed, the narrator says: "Yes, one could imagine a very pleasant world…. A world without professors or specialists or house-keepers with the profiles of policemen" (87) and adds, while describing Whitaker's Table of Precedency : "The Archbishop of Canterbury is followed by the Lord High Chancellor; the Lord High Chancellor is followed by the Archbishop of York" (88). Refusing to describe external reality therefore appears to be both a refusal of binding, authoritative literary norms (the norms of mimetic fiction) and a refusal of social conventions, of their authority, of the masculine authority of the Law, the University, the Church,[46] and other patriarchal institutions[47]: it amounts to a refusal of "the masculine point of view which governs our lives" (86).[48] A literary decision is thus doubled by a political one.

Whereas in her essay *Three Guineas*, published in 1938, Woolf openly and directly criticises British institutions, in her short stories, through the appropriation of the form of the essay and the introduction of metafictional reflections, she points to a strong connection between literature and the external world just as Adorno does when he chooses to define the essay as "heretical" and refusing Truth and all form of totality. The same conventions and lack of freedom governing the world and the world of fiction, literature cannot be dissociated from the social and historical world. Woolf also implicitly suggests that by transforming literature, the world will be, if not transformed, at least questioned; by transforming literary conventions, social conventions will be challenged. Metafiction here is far from being the hallmark of a self-reflexive, narcissistic, intransitive literature; although in a very submerged way, it points out the political power of literature.[49] We could say that form is politicised.

The eulogy of impurity

Generic hybridity in Woolf's short stories thus appears to be a way of accommodating other literary genres and of refusing the binding authority of a single literary genre. These literary choices, which have ethical as well as political resonance, amount to a eulogy of the impurity of the short story form. As such, they can be compared to the eulogy of the impurity of language that Woolf makes in a late essay, "Craftsmanship", which was first broadcast on the BBC in 1937. There she explains that "Words, English words, are full of echoes, of memories, of associations" (*C.E.* II: 248). Dissemination, the "power of suggestion" (248) of words therefore appears not simply as a formal choice in favour of open meaning in an open text. It is also connected with history, both with literary history—as in the example Woolf takes of "the splendid word 'incarnadine'...who can use it without remembering also 'multitudinous seas'?" (248)—and with the country's history: "They have been out and about, on people's lips, in their houses, in the streets, in the fields, for so many centuries" (248), the history of the people, of everyman and everywoman. Words are the living palimpsests and memory of English history. Woolf points here not only to a phenomenon that critics, in the wake of T. S. Eliot will study under the banner of intertextuality, but also to the grounding of words and fiction in history, a historical context that precludes the autonomy of fiction.

In the same essay, Woolf adds: "they [words] are so stored with meanings, with memories, ... they have contracted so many famous marriages" (248) and she expatiates on this metaphor, further personifying words by referring to the necessity they feel to change: "it is their nature to change" (251), what she also calls their "falling in love, and mating together": "Royal words mate with commoners. English words marry French words, German words, Indian words, Negro words, if they have a fancy" (250). The evolution of language is here linked with historical circumstances: the invasion of England, the wars she fought, and the reality of Empire. History has altered language and necessarily weighs on the writing of fiction. What Woolf also insists on in this passage is the mating of royal words with commoners, of uneducated words with educated ones as well as of Indian or Negro words with English ones. Language is depicted as a democratic space where social hierarchies are blurred ("They are highly democratic, too; they believe that one word is as good as another", 250) and where different cultures enter into a dialogue with each other. These statements are first of all an indirect way of taking into account the origin of words, the social class that coined them, the nation they were born in, that is, their socio-cultural background, dismissing once more a conception of language and the fiction that uses it as autonomous. They also extol the virtues of impurity and point out the dialogic forces at work in language, implicitly stating the political nature of language, its submerged but nonetheless real capacity to defend a pluralistic and democratic ideal. In a very light, humorous and metaphorical manner, Woolf unmasks the unconscious of language which precludes its autonomy, something that Bakhtin examines at length, especially in "Discourse of the Novel", written at about the same time, in 1934–5.[50] If language enables the writer to make aesthetic choices, it also, as "a social and historical construct" (Lecercle 1999: 223), constrains the writer in a double movement that Lecercle identifies as its "enabling constraints" (Lecercle 1999: 116).[51]

Like words, the short story is anchored in history and literary history and is the result of literary genres "falling in love, and mating together", thus creating a pluralistic and democratic space, an impure form. However, impurity is not only valued in the form of the short story, it is also valued as such. In "A Society", the "impure woman" (129), who shocks some of her contemporaries when she becomes pregnant without being married, is presented as the woman of the future: she gives birth to the first girl who, rather than being taught to perform the tasks traditionally allotted to women or to believe in the male principle, "the intellect", will be taught to believe in herself. Impurity becomes the springboard to a new era and a new woman. Apart from sexual impurity, racial impurity is praised in "Gipsy, the Mongrel", the story of "a wretched little mongrel, a regular gipsies' dog" (274) that proves to be "a dog of remarkable character" (274) whereas her companion, a dog with "a pedigree as long as your arm" (275) has none at all. Found when a puppy after the Gypsies had been around, she left her masters one day, years afterwards, when she heard again the Gypsies' whistle. Although it is a mere "dog story", it is interesting to notice that Woolf wrote it in 1940 when Chambrun asked her for a "dog story" (Dick 318) and set her narrative in 1937. Choosing to write about a mongrel rather than any other dog and to show that that dog is "remarkable" when the purebred is not may not be anodyne; further than pointing at Woolf's love for animals, it also highlights her choice of racial impurity, as it is made clear in the very title—a political stance at a time the Nazis were promoting "racial purity".

This short story is reminiscent of *Flush* that traces the progress of Flush, a pure-bred spaniel which, after having been locked in a Victorian invalid's room, Elizabeth Barrett Browning's, is turned loose in Italy and starts roaming the streets of Florence, heartily mixing with all the mongrels of the town, thereby discovering life and freedom. The "pure-bred Cocker of the red variety marked by all the characteristic excellences of his kind" (*Flush*, 10) becomes "daily more and more democratic.... All dogs were his brothers.... Flush embraced the spotted spaniel down the alley, and the brindled dog and the yellow dog—it did not matter which" (77; 79) until he loses his flea-ridden coat, "the insignia of a cocker spaniel" (89), his pedigree, and becomes indistinguishable from all the other mongrels. In this humorous, yet efficient, criticism of pedigree and pure race, Woolf indirectly states, as E. M. Forster will do in his 1939 essay "Racial Exercise", that "we are all mongrels, dark-haired and light-haired, who must learn not to bite one another",[52] a statement her short story "Gipsy, the Mongrel" echoes, were it only through its title.

Flush also offers an interesting parallel to the short stories in so far as it not only extols the virtues of racial impurity but also of aesthetic impurity. Indeed, it exemplifies the new type of biography that Woolf wants to write. Rather than relying on facts and dates and producing "an amorphous mass... in which we go seeking disconsolately for voice or laughter, ... for any trace that this fossil was once a living man" ("The New Biography", *Essays* IV: 475); rather than "preserv[ing the subject] under glass", as "a wax work" (74) as the imaginary Miss Linsett does in her biography of Miss Willat, in "Memoirs of a Novelist",[53] Woolf indulges in "scene-making" in order "to express not only the outer life of work and activity but the inner life of emotion and thought" (*Essays* IV: 474). Rather than worshipping heroes, she deals with "obscure figures", both Flush the dog and his mistress, Elizabeth Barrett Browning, a poet dwarfed by her husband's fame. *Flush* departs from the biographical tradition, in Woolf's own words "a bastard, an impure art" (Lee 1996: 10) and ironically enough, the very words Woolf used to criticise Victorian biography are redefined throughout the book as tokens of perfection and renewal, and once divested of their derogatory meaning, are claimed as the very hallmarks of her own new form of biography, "a bastard, an impure art".[54] *Flush* thus comes out as a successful example of this new impure art Woolf had in mind.

Similarly, in the short stories, racial and sexual impurity are extolled and impurity is exemplified in the generic hybridity of the form itself. The short story thus appears to be "a bastard, an impure art". Impurity is claimed as an asset; a negative moral judgement is turned upside down and retrieved to encapsulate the aesthetic, ethical and political nature of the short story.

Are there limits to Woolf's ethical impulse?

However if we believe what some critics of the short story have written, there might be limits to Woolf's valuing of impurity since in some short stories, the encounter with the other turns into a rejection of the other. I am not referring to the short stories where the encounter with the other is presented thematically as a violent encounter and a moment of hatred, as in "The Introduction" or "The Man who Loved his Kind": those stories are either caricatures or in any case, clearly condemn the character who is guilty of hatred and cruelty or violence. I am referring to the stories where the other might be condemned as other by the narrative voice and implicitly by the author. Such is the case of "The Duchess and the Jeweller", or at least of the reading of this short story that has been offered by various critics up to David Bradshaw in his latest edition of the text in 2001.[55] For Bradshaw, this story is anti-Semitic and "comes as quite a shock" (Bradshaw 2001: xxix) describing as it does "the stereotype Jew" (xxix), and he is definitely ill-at-ease to account for what he feels to be "Woolf's single most controversial piece of work, largely inexcusable, perhaps, definitely untypical, but well-crafted in spite of its offensive subject-matter" (xxxi). Julia Briggs goes the same way when she writes about the short story's "explicit anti-Semitism" (Briggs 181). Such analyses introduce a contradiction and a blatant incoherence in Woolf's short stories while creating great uneasiness in the reader. All the more so as Woolf has not been found guilty of such prejudice in the representation of Jews that she offers in other works of fiction, especially in *The Years* which Bradshaw himself analyses as "a philo-Semitic novel" (xxix),[56] and in *Three Guineas* which, according to Briggs, "adopts a very different attitude to Jews, comparing their persecution as outsiders to the oppression of women" (Briggs 182).[57]

A close reading of the short story might help us out of this critical difficulty. This short story was meant to be part of a book of caricatures and the two characters it stages, the duchess and the jeweller, are caricatured through animal similes: the duchess is compared with a peacock and the jeweller with an elephant, a hog, a horse and a camel. The jeweller is conceived as the typical self-made man who went from rags to riches, having "beg[u]n life in a filthy alley... selling stolen dogs to fashionable women in Whitechapel" (248) and having become "the richest jeweller in England" (249) with a shop in Piccadilly and wearing clothes cut "by the best scissors in Savile Row" (248). He is also the stereotypical Jew—although the word is never couched on the page—bearing the offensive name of Oliver Bacon, having "long pointed nails" (248) and a "nose, which was long and flexible, like an elephant's trunk" (249)—all the attributes anti-Semitism has saddled Jews with. Such features may be construed as deeply offensive if they are taken at face value. However in the story, the jeweller is confronted with a duchess who is not only extremely ugly ("she was very large, very fat, tightly girt in pink taffeta, and past her prime", 251) but also clearly derided by the narrator, if only through the use of repetition, plosives and hyperbole, as the epitome of what is most hateful in the aristocracy: "Then she loomed up, filling the door, filling the room with the aroma, the prestige, the arrogance, the pomp, the pride of all the Dukes and Duchesses swollen in one wave" (251). The duchess is also presented as a swindler who does not hesitate to sell false pearls to the jeweller in order to wipe off her gambling debts and recover her honour. The jeweller appears as the willing victim of the woman's strategy since he accepts being fooled by the pearls which he knows to be false, in order to be invited by the duchess to spend a weekend with her daughter with whom he is in love. The jeweller comes out as a tender-hearted noble man who can relinquish money for the sake of love and happiness whereas the duchess appears as the shrewd, dishonest money-lover. Just as the cliché of the necessarily noble aristocrat is taken to task, the cliché of the Jew as jeweller, money-lover, saddled with all the traditionally offensive features (long nose, pointed nails, etc.), is undermined as Woolf shows there is a human being, noble and tender-hearted behind the mask society has devised for Jews. But probably because the short story was written around 1932, in troubled times, and published in 1938, Woolf could not run the risk of having her main character misunderstood. She therefore repeatedly presents the jeweller as taking off his mantle when he is on his own: "But he dismantled himself often and became again a little boy in a dark alley" (248); "And again he dismantled himself and became once more the little boy playing marbles in the alley" (250). The mantle is like a mask Oliver wears when he is with the others. Climbing the social ladder, having a rich shop, loving money is the mask the others make him wear. In private, he can take off the mask and become his own original self. Through this metaphor, Woolf exposes Jewishness as a social construction, a construction that is so powerful that the Jews can only inhabit it; in other words, they can only conform to the clichés society has devised for them and escape them when far from the others' gaze. The mantle and the dismantling also read as a metaphor of what Woolf herself does here and which, to my mind, is not different from what she does in other short stories: that is, just as she accommodates silence in "The Legacy", just as she accommodates various genres in her short stories, she accommodates here a cliché, the cliché of the Jew and she inhabits it in order to deflate it and subvert it from inside (exemplifying as she does so what Adorno explains about Kafka and Beckett and modernist writers in general who have a much more efficient way of commenting upon the world than representational literature and are much more committed than openly committed literature: "the avant-garde abstraction…is a reflex response to the abstraction of the law which objectively dominates society…. By dismantling appearance, they explode from within the art which committed proclamation subjugates from without, and hence only in appearance"[58]). The result is a story in keeping with her literary democratic impulse and, needless to add, her marrying a Jew. Rather than being an anti-Semitic story, it reads as a committed story but relying as it does on irony and indirection, it runs the risk of being misunderstood.[59]

As such, "The Duchess and the Jeweller" is reminiscent of an entry in Woolf's 1909 diary, one of the sketches David Bradshaw edited in 2003 under the title "Jews" (Bradshaw 2003: 14–15). In this entry for 3 November, Woolf draws the portrait of Mrs Loeb, an acquaintance, taking up the clichés usually appended to Jewish women who are stereotypically said to be coarse, fat, flattering, and ostentatious; the sentence "[h]er food, of course, swam in oil and was nasty" (14) confirms, if need be, through the "syntactic slight" (44), "of course", that Bradshaw notices, the use of clichés. Mrs Loeb is described as "a fat Jewess", as a synecdochic representation of the set she belongs to and with the title, "Jews", generalisation and anti-semitism become even more palpable, genericity "distribut[ing] characteristics to a group regardless of individuals", a distinctive feature of hate speech.[60]

However, this offensive portrayal also stands out as an attempt at capturing the different facets of Mrs Loeb. Woolf underlines Mrs Loeb's desire to be appreciated by her guests as well as her fear of being criticised by them. She describes how the lady manages to adapt her discourse to her different guests, hence the difficulty for the diarist to pinpoint the truth about her and the necessity of resorting both to factual and imaginary elements ("I imagine her to be...", 14) in order to capture her essential being. As a result, Mrs Loeb comes out as a character who has redeeming features ("she wishes to be popular, and is, perhaps, kind, in her vulgar way, ostentatiously kind to poor relations", 14–15) even if she is certainly "unpleasant". Unlike Sylvia Loeb's own portrait of her grandmother as "a lady of leisure, large, fat and gregarious" (Bradshaw 2003: 41), Woolf's portrait is not monolithic and as such, is in keeping with the portraits of various other persons she draws in the 1909 diary— Miss Reeves, for instance, is said to be full of energy "even though [her] capacities were not of the finest"(5)—, the attempt at capturing the different facets of the character combining with the sharp tone of the caricaturist.

If the diary entry for 3 November 1909 stopped there, one could only agree with Bradshaw that "Jews" "will bear the doubtful distinction of being Woolf's first significant anti-Semitic smear" (40). The double-sided portrait, even if it is an improvement compared with Sylvia Loeb's evocation of her grandmother, would not be enough to dispel the accusation of anti-Semitism on which Bradshaw expatiates for many pages.

What is interesting, though, is that "Jews" appears in the holograph notebook together with "Divorce Courts": " 'Jews' and 'Divorce Courts' appear under the same title in the notebook ('Jews and Divorce Courts') with a clear break in the text between 'and very unpleasant' (the last words of 'Jews' in this edition) and 'Curiosity took me' (the opening of 'Divorce Courts')" (Bradshaw 2003: xxvii). Woolf therefore leads us to read the two texts—a single entry for 3 November 1909—together. And indeed, "Divorce Courts" seems to take up where "Jews" end: "I imagine her to be ... ostentatiously kind to poor relations. The one end she aims at for them, is the society of men and marriage. It seemed very elementary, very little disguised, and very unpleasant" ("Jews", 14–15). After Mrs Loeb the match-maker comes the humdrum torture of the unhappy married life of Mr and Mrs Whittingstall, of ill-suited man and wife. Although an early feminist streak runs through these lines (the power of the male word is underlined and indirectly, denounced when the narrator evokes the man who "vindicated the position of the ideal husband" [16] and "the whole male world was against her" [17]), what is striking is the unpleasantness of all the characters involved: the selfish, cruel, hypocritical clergyman, the hysterical and waspish wife, the coarse lesbian, Miss Lewis, who both protected and seduced her. The diarist guesses—rightly, as it turned out—that even if Mr Whittingstall is "a man without pity or imagination" (17), his wife, after a while, will go back to him "and be received with due Christian charity" (17). The narrator describes them with the eye of the caricaturist, the eye that dissected Mrs Loeb, and displays the same sharpness and irony. So much so that, even if Mr Whittingstall is a clergyman, "Divorce Courts" appears as a sequel to "Jews". Indirectly, and iron-ically, the two texts put together show that match-making, ill-suited and failed marriages are not a Jewish or an Anglican speciality but a universal problem. Thus the offensiveness of the title "Jews" takes on a different meaning; instead of referring to Jews in the usual stereo-typical sense, of categorising Jews and separating them from the rest of human beings, of branding certain man and women with an offensive, anti-Semitic name, the name "Jews" opens up so as to include all men and women. Subtly, Woolf deflates the offensiveness of the word "Jews" or rather displaces it. First, by showing the title is partly inadequate (it should be "Jewesses", since the person described is a woman). Second, when the two texts are read together, "Jews" comes to encompass unpleasant men and women (Mrs Loeb, the clergyman, his wife, and her lover—all with faults of their own: flat-tery, hypocrisy, hysteria, etc.) and the unpleasant relationship in which they get entangled (match-making, marriage, vindication of their rights). And the word Jews in the end, even includes the person attending the divorce in court, the narrator: "It was human nature rendering an account to human nature" (16). Woolf thus dissolves the boundaries between religion and mocks men's faults, whatever their faith. Instead of using the words "unpleasant men and women", she uses the word "Jews", displacing its meaning, "re-investing" the word with another meaning that finally derides the usual one. She finally shows that the clichés usually appended to Jews can be appended to many other human beings.

In the end, although "Jews and Divorce Courts" belongs to Woolf's early journal and offers portraits of people Woolf met, the method she uses is comparable to the one she resorts to in her short stories where imaginary characters appear: she inhabits clichés and dismantles them, thus rejuvenating "old words".

Bradshaw chose to separate the two texts; he writes: "Since the two sketches are entirely unconnected and Woolf's title is misleading, I have decided to separate them into two distinct sketches for this edition—even though by doing so 'Jews' is brought into even sharper focus" (xxviii). By doing so, he can only conclude that the sketch is offensive and anti-Semitic. One can only regret this editorial choice which renders Woolf's meaning illegible or at least, prevents the reader from making up his mind about the diarist's position.

What Woolf's short stories—especially short stories like "The Duchess and the Jeweller" and diary entries like "Jews and Divorce Courts"—finally call for is a responsible form of reading since the presence or absence of limits to Woolf's valuing of impurity is for the reader to decide. Woolf requires a respectful and inventive reader,[61] in other words, an ethically committed one.

The reading of Woolf's short stories shows that they cannot be reduced to the generic features they display since Woolf's formal choices exceed aesthetics and branch out into politics and ethics. Like Flaubert, she makes the choice of the ordinary and the anonymous, retrieving in a democratic impulse the voice of the voiceless. Through its refashioning of norms that realise new possibilities, through its openness to the other and to other genres, her short story writing displays an ethical commitment and results in "a form without formalism", to use Attridge's own words (Attridge 2004: 119).[62]

Conclusion

Virginia Woolf's short stories have been read, in the light of her own essays, as an impersonal art of proportion and emotion, an art based on tension which plays fragmentation against totality, which conceives form as emotion and intensity and where the impersonal meets the collective. The form of Woolf's short story, we have argued, is the form of the conversation, a dialogic fictional space, a space of debate, plurality, tolerance and openness, a space of generic hybridity and impurity, a democratic and ethical space.

The short story as conversation therefore comes out as a committed form and foregrounds connection. Reactivating the etymological sense of commitment ("bringing together"), Woolf's commitment is neither action nor direct protest but connection, connecting as it does aesthetics with politics and ethics. The paradigm of modernism that equates modernist literature with an intransitive use of language, a pure and autonomous form of art, is thus questioned unless we remember with Rancière that in the word autonomy, "the Greek *nomos* has a plurality of meanings [referring] non only [to] the law but [to] the *sharing* on which it is based, and the *melody*, the song of the community on which it is grounded."[63] Autonomy would then read as an oxymoron referring both to its own law and to a law founded on sharing and the community. In other words, autonomy would meet commitment.

Because conversation is the form of the short story, the short stories as a whole can be read as a "gigantic conversation" in which the various characters share, as in a party, the metaphor used in the Dalloway stories which are therefore emblematic of all the short stories but also part of the whole, and which, for that reason, should not be isolated from them.

Through their generic hybridity as well as the narrative strategies they implement and the aesthetic principles they display, the short stories also connect to Woolf's other works while connecting them. "Only connect...", E. M. Forster's epigraph to *Howards End*, could well be their motto and, in a way, the circulation between texts that the manuscripts display[64] is emblematic of their general make-up. In the end, far from being peripheral to Woolf's work, the short stories appear to be definitely part of the network of Woolf's writings. They cannot be described as simply experimental, as a mere testing ground for her novels or a minor genre; they are neither marginal nor central. They are part and parcel of Woolf's rhizomatic work. Through the very concepts of connection and circulation they put forward, through those of democratic space and conversation they redefine and re-appropriate, they point to the necessity of coming to Woolf's work without establishing any hierarchy between her novels, her biographies, her essays, her letters, her diaries, or her short stories. And if we have argued that the term "short story" should be retained, it is because the short stories as such take part in the general process of re-appropriation that Woolf is implementing, which, to an important degree, consists in re-appropriating or "rejuvenating" old words.

Finally, because they are based on connection and re-appropriation, Woolf's short stories are "rich, ... with more than one can grasp at any single reading" (*Essays* III: 149) and offer an "obstinate resistance" to reading (*Essays* III: 158), an endless deferral of meaning, which constitutes both their difficulty and their inexhaustible gift to the reader.

Notes

Introduction

1. Virginia Woolf, *The Letters of Virginia Woolf* (1888–1941) 6 vols, ed. Nigel Nicolson and Joanne Trautman (London: Hogarth Press, 1975–80) V, 16 October 1930.
2. Woolf, *Letters*.
3. Leonard Woolf, ed., *A Haunted House and Other Stories* (1944; London: Harmondsworth: Penguin, 1973), "Foreword by Leonard Woolf", 7.
4. Virginia Woolf, *The Diary of Virginia Woolf*, 5 vols, ed. Anne Olivier Bell (London: Hogarth Press, 1977–84; Harmondsworth: Penguin, 1981) V: 188; 22 November 1938.
5. On this subject, see Susan Dick, ed., *Virginia Woolf: The Complete Shorter Fiction* (1985; London: Triad Grafton Books, 1991) 314–15.
6. Elena Gualtieri, *Virginia Woolf's Essays* (London: Macmillan, 2000) 69.
7. Nena Skrbic, *Wild Outbursts of Freedom: Reading Virginia Woolf's Short Fiction* (Westport, CT; London: Praeger, 2004) xiii.
8. "But Nessa and I quarrelled ... over the get up of Kew Gardens, both type and woodcuts; & she firmly refused to illustrate any more stories of mine under those conditions.... An ordinary printer would do better in her opinion" (*Diary* I: 279; 9 June 1919).
9. "I much doubt if M & T [Monday or Tuesday] will sell 500, or cover expenses" (*Diary* II: 111; 17 April 1921).
10. Both *Kew Gardens* and *Monday or Tuesday* were published by the Hogarth Press, the first in May 1919, with two woodcuts by Vanessa Bell, the second in 1921, with woodcuts by Dora Carrington.
11. Among the short stories collected in *A Haunted House*, those in italics had been published by Virginia Woolf herself in *Monday or Tuesday* together with "A Society" and "Blue and Green", six had been published in magazines between 1922 and 1941 ("The New Dress", "The Shooting Party", "Lappin and Lapinova", "Solid Objects", "The Lady in the Looking-Glass" and "The Duchess and the Jeweller") and six had never been published. Woolf, *Haunted House*.
12. Stella McNichol, ed., *Mrs Dalloway's Party: A Short Story Sequence by Virginia Woolf* (London: Hogarth Press, 1973).
13. Except for "The Journal of Mistress Joan Martyn", which was published in *Twentieth Century Literature* in 1979 and "A Dialogue upon Mount Pentelicus", that was published in *The Times Literary Supplement* in 1987. See Dick for further detail.
14. Previously published in *Redbook* (July 1982).
15. David Bradshaw, ed., *Virginia Woolf: Carlyle's House and Other Sketches* (London: Hesperus Press, 2003). It includes "Carlyle's House", "Miss Reeves",

"Cambridge", "Hampstead", "A Modern Salon", "Jews", "Divorce Courts". Whether these texts are short stories or not will be discussed further on.

16. Leonard Woolf, for instance, wrote that by publishing a collection of short stories and omitting from it "A Society" and "Blue and Green", he tried to respect Virginia's intention: "in 1940, she decided that she would get together a new volume of such stories and include in it most of the stories which had appeared originally in *Monday or Tuesday*, as well as some published subsequently in magazines and some unpublished" (*AHH* 7). And he adds, "The two omitted by me are 'A Society' and 'Blue and Green'; I know that she had decided not to include the first and I am practically certain that she would not have included the second" (*AHH* 8).

17. McNichol's editorial procedures were severely criticised by J. F. Hulcoop on *Virginia Woolf Miscellany* 3 (Spring 1975). For a discussion of McNichol's edition and possible mistakes, see Daugherty who argues that Dick's later edition "establishes a more reliable text of Woolf's short story sequence, although not, of course, in the form of a separate book", Beth R. Daugherty, "'A Corridor Leading from *Mrs Dalloway* to a New Book': Transforming Stories, Bending Genres", *Trespassing Boundaries: Virginia Woolf's Short Fiction*, ed. Kathryn N. Benzel and Ruth Hoberman (New York and Basingstoke: Palgrave Macmillan, 2004) 101–24, 123, n. 11.

18. For instance, Nena Skrbic mentions, in the fourth chapter of her book "Woolf's Unpublished Juvenilia", stories which "concentrate on pure atmosphere": "The Manchester Zoo" (1906), "The Penny Steamer" (1906), "Sunday up the River" (*c.* 1906) and "Down the River to Greenwich" (1908). Skrbic, *Wild Outbursts*, 90.

19. Dick justifies her choice by quoting Woolf's letter to Ethel Smyth: "I wrote The Mark on the Wall—all in a flash" but omits the following sentence: "The Unwritten Novel was the great discovery, however" (Woolf, *Letter*), which would point to a different landmark in Woolf's short story writing from the one Dick herself chooses.

20. For instance, Joseph Conrad's short stories grew into novels: "Dollars" grew into *Lord Jim;* and some of James Joyce's short stories, like "The Dead", constituted the germs of *A Portrait of the Artist as a Young Man.*

21. For example, Woolf wrote "The Lady in the Looking-Glass" while trying to begin *The Waves.*

22. For example, Woolf wrote "Moments of Being" while finishing *To the Lighthouse.*

23. B. R. Daugherty has adumbrated such a study in a very interesting essay devoted to this unusual phenomenon where, after reminding us that "*Night and Day* generated the stories in *Monday or Tuesday*" (112) and that as she was finishing *Mrs Dalloway*, *To the Lighthouse* or *Between the Acts* Woolf was working on several short stories, she shows that, in Woolf's case, "novels grow out of short stories and short stories grow out of novels" (Daugherty 113).

24. "After being ill and suffering every form and variety of nightmare and extravagant intensity of perception—for I used to make up poems, stories, profound and to me inspired phrases all day long as I lay in bed, and

thus sketched, I think, all that I now, by the light of reason, try to put into prose (I thought of the Lighthouse then, and Kew and others, not in substance, but in idea)—after all this, when I came to, I was so tremblingly afraid of my own insanity that I wrote Night and Day mainly to prove to my own satisfaction that I could keep entirely off that dangerous ground" (Woolf, *Letter*).

25. Virginia Woolf, *Virginia Woolf. A Passionate Apprentice: The Early Journals 1897–1909*, ed. Mitchell A. Leaska (London: The Hogarth Press, 1990).

26. Jean Guiguet, *Virginia Woolf et son œuvre. L' Art et la quête du réel* (Paris: Didier, 1962) 326–38. Let us add that the word "sketch" is also the one chosen by Elena Gualtieri to define Woolf's essays.

27. Guiguet's own words are "esquisses", "pochades impressionnistes" and "contes" (Guiguet 326–38).

28. Leila Brosnan, *Reading Virginia Woolf's Essays and Journalism* (Edinburgh: Edinburgh University Press, 1997) 140.

29. Dean R. Baldwin, *Virginia Woolf: A Study of the Short Fiction* (Boston, MA: Twayne Publishers, 1989).

30. We should also mention Dominic Head's chapter on Woolf's short stories in *The Modernist Short Story* (Cambridge: Cambridge University Press, 1992).

31. Christine Reynier, ed., *Journal of the Short Story in English*, Special Virginia Woolf Issue, 50 (Spring 2008).

32. Andrew Maunder has partly corrected this in his *Companion to the Short Story* which includes articles on Woolf's short stories. *The British Companion to the Short Story*, ed. Andrew Maunder (New York: Facts on File, 2007).

33. "A draft of this story (probably written in July 1920) is located in *JR*I, where it is chapter X. The undated typescript, with holograph revisions, which has *Jacob's Room* written at the top and then cancelled, is also headed X, and the pages numbered 47–52, thus suggesting that VW was still planning to use it in *Jacob's Room*. The 'chapter' was not included in the novel, however, but was published in November 1926 as 'A Woman's College from Outside' in *Atalanta's Garland: Being the Book of the Edinburgh University Women's Union*" (Dick 304).

34. "On 6 October [1922] she made an outline of a book to be called 'At Home: or The Party' in which 'Mrs Dalloway in Bond Street' figured as the first chapter (*JR*III)" (Dick 305).

35. See Clare Hanson, ed., *Re-reading the Short Story* (New York: St Martin's Press, 1989) 3.

36. See on that subject Frédérique Amselle, *Virginia Woolf et les écritures du moi: le journal et l'autobiographie* (Montpellier: Presses Universitaires de la Méditerranée, 2008).

37. See (Dick 306).

38. A title Woolf first chose, incidentally, for "The Symbol".

39. On this subject, see (Dick 316–17). See also Laura Marcus, " 'In the Circle of the Lens': Woolf's 'Telescope' Story, Scene-Making and Memory" (Marcus in Reynier 2008; 153–69).

40. Baldwin argues that "[s]ince Virginia Woolf experimented continually
    with the short story form, sometimes writing stories that seem more like
    essays, at other times stories that approach the lyric poem, critics may
    legitimately argue over which of her prose pieces are in fact stories.
    Rather than engage in this argument, I have decided to accept as short
    stories all of the works included in Susan Dick's edition, *The Complete
    Shorter Fiction*" (Baldwin xi).
41. Virginia Woolf, *The Essays of Virginia Woolf* (1925–8), vol. 4, ed. Andrew
    McNeillie (London: Hogarth Press, 1994) 157–65.

1 Virginia Woolf's definition of the short story

1. A first version of the first pages of this chapter, here considerably aug-
   mented and modified, has been published in "Virginia Woolf's Ethics of
   the Short Story", *Etudes Anglaises* 60/1 (January–March 2007): 55–65.
2. Virginia Woolf, "On Re-Reading Novels", revised version, *Collected
   Essays II* (1966; London: Hogarth Press, 1972) 127. The original version
   can be found in McNeillie's edition (*Essays* III: 336–46).
3. See especially chapter 1: "'I Am One Person—Myself': Virginia Woolf's
   Practitioner Criticism" (Skrbic 2004). See also Nena Skrbic's "'Excursions
   into the Literature of a Foreign Country': Crossing Cultural Boundaries
   in the Short Fiction" (Skrbic in Benzel and Hoberman 25–38) in which
   she compares Woolf's "Happiness" (1925), "The Lady in the Looking-
   Glass" (1929) and "Uncle Vanya" (1937) with Chekhov's "Happiness" and
   Valery Brussof's "In the Mirror" (both published in English in 1918), tra-
   cing the Russian influence in Woolf's narrative method. Skrbic notes
   that Woolf reveals the impact that the Russians had on her aesthetic and
   intellectual concerns in "Modern Novels" (1919), an essay where "Woolf's
   theorizing about the Russians is at its most powerful" (Skrbic in Benzel
   and Hoberman 31).
4. Virginia Woolf, "An Essay in Criticism", *The Essays of Virginia Woolf*
   (1925–28), vol. 4, ed. Andrew McNeillie (London: Hogarth Press, 1994)
   449–56.
5. Virginia Woolf, "The Russian Point of View" (*Essays* IV: 181–90).
6. Virginia Woolf, "On Re-Reading Novels" (*C.E.* II: 122–30).
7. The references here are to the original version of "On Re-reading Novels".
   See note 1.
8. "And butterflies flew out of the wardrobe", my translation.
9. "Félicité was grateful to her as if it had been a godsend and from then on,
   loved her with a bestial devotion and a religious veneration", my translation.
10. Clive Bell, *Art* (1914; Oxford: Oxford University Press, 1987).
11. E. W. Tomlin, *Wyndham Lewis* (London: Longman, 1955) 33.
12. Roger Fry, *Vision and Design* (1920; Oxford: Oxford University Press, 1981)
    126.
13. Also quoted in Woolf, "The Russian View" (*Essays* II: 341–4) and "Modern
    Fiction" (*Essays* IV: 157–65).

14. Impersonality and Emotion are central notions to Modernism as has been shown in our volumes: Christine Reynier and Jean-Michel Ganteau, eds, *Impersonality and Emotion in Twentieth-Century British Literature* (Montpellier: Presses Universitaires de la Méditerranée, collection *Present Perfect* 1, 2005) see especially the introduction, 1–15; Jean-Michel Ganteau and Christine Reynier, eds, *Impersonality and Emotion in Twentieth-Century British Arts* (Montpellier: Presses Universitaires de la Méditerranée, collection *Present Perfect 2*, 2006).

15. Edgar Allan Poe, "Twice-Told Tales", *Selected Writings* (Harmondsworth: Penguin Books, 1979) 446.

16. See (*Essays* IV: 455).

17. Alberto Moravia, "The Short Story and the Novel", *Short Story Theories*, ed. Charles E. May (Athens: Ohio University Press, 1976) 147–51.

18. Julio Cortazar writes, "Le symbole, la métaphore du conte parfait est la sphère.... ce pourrait être un cube, en tout cas une forme parfaite" ("the symbol, the metaphor of the perfect short fiction is the sphere.... it could be a cube, in any case, a perfect form", my translation). Julio Cortazar, *Entretiens avec Omar Prego* (Paris: Gallimard, 1984) 81, quoted in Liliane Louvel et Claudine Verley, *Introduction à l'étude de la nouvelle. Littérature contemporaine de langue anglaise* (Toulouse: Presses du Mirail, 1993) 14.

19. And, discussing Coleridge, Woolf adds: "Perhaps a mind that is purely masculine cannot create, any more than a mind that is purely feminine", Virginia Woolf, *A Room of One's Own* (1929; London: Granada, 1977) 94.

20. T. S. Eliot, "Tradition and the Individual Talent" in *Selected Essays* (1932; London: Faber & Faber, 1999) 17.

21. Woolf's notion of impersonality owes probably more to the eighteenth-century tradition of "sympathy", the ability to assume others' identities and to the Romantic vision of Shakespeare, especially Coleridge's "myriad-minded Shakespeare" who "becomes all things, yet for ever remaining himself", S. T. Coleridge, *Biographia Literaria* (1817; London: J. M. Dent & sons, 1975) chapter 15, II, 175, 180.

22. "The ordinary reader resents the bareness of their [the Greeks'] literature. There is nothing in the way of anecdote to browse upon, nothing handy and personal to help oneself up by; nothing is left but the literature itself, cut off from us by time and language, unvulgarized by association, pure from contamination, but steep and isolated" (*C.E.* II: 274–5).

23. Brenda Silver, ed., "Anon" and "The Reader", reprinted in the special Woolf issue of *Twentieth Century Literature*, 25 (Fall/Winter 1979): 382.

24. Gillian Beer, *Virginia Woolf: The Common Ground* (Edinburgh: Edinburgh University Press, 1996) 3. Beer uses this phrase in reference to Woolf's Anon that she compares with Walter Benjamin's "storyteller".

25. Elena Militsina and Mikhail Saltikov, "The Village Priest" (by Militsina), *The Village Priest and Other Stories*, trans. Beatrix L. Tollemache (London: T. Fischer Unwin, 1918), 34.

26. On this subject, see Frédéric Regard, "Penser, sentir, écrire. Quelques réflexions sur la notion de *feeling* dans l'histoire de l'esthétique britannique", *Etudes britanniques contemporaines* 9 (June 1996) 69. Yet it should

be noted that Woolf departs from the Romantics in her definition of the self: "It is apparently easier to write a poem about oneself than about any other subject. But what does one mean by 'oneself'? Not the self that Wordsworth, Keats, and Shelley have described—not the self that loves a woman, or that hates a tyrant, or that broods over the mystery of the world. No, the self that you are engaged in describing is shut out from all that. It is a self that sits alone in the room at night with the blinds drawn. In other words the poet is much less interested in what we have in common than in what he has apart" ("A Letter to a Young Poet", *C.E.* II: 189).

27. G. E. Moore, *Principia Ethica* (1903; Cambridge: Cambridge University Press, 2000) 238.
28. We follow here Henri Meschonnic who, in *Critique du rythme* (Paris: Verdier, 1982) considers that all these echoes go into the making of rhythm.
29. "Life and the Novelist" (*Essays* IV: 401).
30. "The idea has come to me that what I want now to do is to saturate every atom. I mean to eliminate all waste, deadness, superfluity: to give the moment whole; whatever it includes" (*Diary* III: 210; 28 November 1928).
31. On this subject, see Christine Reynier: "The Impure Art of Biography: Virginia Woolf's *Flush*", *Mapping the Self: Space, Identity, Discourse in British Auto/Biography*, ed. Frédéric Regard (St Etienne: Publications de l'Université de St Etienne, 2003) 187–202. Woolf's position in relation to impurity is comparable to E. M. Forster's in his essay "Racial Exercise" in *Two Cheers for Democracy* (1938; London: Harvest Book, 1979) 17–20.
32. John Wain, "Remarks on the Short Story", *Les Cahiers de la Nouvelle* 2 (1984): 49–66, quoted in Louvel, *Introduction à l'étude de la nouvelle*, 12.
33. Eileen Baldeshwiler, "The Grave as Lyrical Short Story", *Studies in Short Fiction* I, 216–21.
34. John Gerlach, *Towards the End, Closure and Structure in the American Short Story* (Alabama: The University of Alabama Press, 1985) 7.
35. My translation. Pierre Tibi writes: "la nouvelle semble être le lieu et l'enjeu d'une rivalité entre le poétique et le narratif" in "La nouvelle: essai de définition d'un genre", *Cahiers de L'Université de Perpignan* 4 (Spring 1988): 7–62.
36. Andrew Gibson, *Postmodernity, Ethics and the Novel: From Leavis to Levinas* (London: Routledge, 1999) 25.
37. Derek Attridge, *The Singularity of Literature* (London: Routledge, 2004) 32.
38. For Attridge, who is closer to Derrida and Lyotard, "the other" has a different or rather, a larger meaning: "The other"...is...not, strictly speaking, a *person* as conventionally understood in ethics or psychology; it is once again a relation—or a relating—between me, as the same, and that which, in its uniqueness, is heterogeneous to me and interrupts my sameness" (Attridge 2004: 33).
39. The absence of Manichaeism is also what Woolf praises in Henry James's ghost stories, especially in *The Turn of the Screw* where "the inner world gains from the robustness of the outer,...beauty and obscenity twined

together worm their way to the depths" ("Henry James's Ghost Stories", *Essays* III: 325).
40. Spinoza, *Ethique*, trans. Charles Appuhn (Paris: Flammarion, 1965) 242; "nothing is undoubtedly good or bad ...", my translation.
41. Gilles Deleuze, *Spinoza. Philosophie pratique* (1970; Paris: Minuit, 1981) 36. "Ethics...takes the place of Morals ...; morals is God's judgement, a system of judgement. But ethics takes this system of judgement upside down", my translation.
42. Geoffrey Harpham, *Getting It Right: Language, Literature and Ethics* (Chicago, IL: University of Chicago Press, 1992) 48.
43. Letter to Janet Case, Tuesday 1 September 1925.
44. "Bewilderment" being the term Woolf uses, it will be retained rather than "defamiliarisation". Indeed, as Attridge rightly remarks, for the Russian Formalists, defamiliarisation refers to "the use of literary devices [that] render unfamiliar that which through habit has become scarcely noticeable" and "what shines through by virtue of these devices is 'reality'"; He comments: "The other is not the real, but rather a truth, a value, a feeling, a way of doing things" (Attridge 2004: 39), which applies perfectly to Woolf's vision.
45. "*Admiratio* is when the soul is bewildered by the imagination of something because this particular imagined thing is not connected with any other", my translation.
46. It is also what Attridge calls "surprise": "[Surprise] denotes, here, the experience of a reordering of habitual modes of thought and emotion, an experience which arises from an encounter with an entity, an idea, a form, a feeling that cannot be accounted for, cannot even be registered, by those habitual modes" (Attridge 2004: 84).
47. Lorenzo Vinciguerra, *Spinoza* (Paris: Hachette, 2001) 142. "Not only does bewilderment signal a break in the flow of thought but it can also be the moment which crystallizes a new way of thinking", my translation.
48. See John Keats's Letter to George and Thomas Keats (21, 27 [?] December 1817) in *Selected Letters by John Keats*, ed. Jon Mee (Oxford: Oxford University Press, 2002).
49. Roland Barthes, *S/Z* (Paris: Seuil, 1970) 10. Barthes makes a distinction between "le texte lisible" ("the readerly text") and "le texte scriptible" ("the writerly text").
50. Derek Attridge, "Ethics, Otherness, and Literary Form", *The European Messenger*, XII/1 (Spring 2003): 33–8, 33.

2   Woolf's short stories as a paradoxical and dynamic space

1. Eliot, "Tradition and Individual Talent".
2. Virginia Woolf, *Between the Acts* (1941; London: Penguin, 2000) 56.

3. E. M. Forster, *Aspects of the Novel* (1927; London: Edward Arnold, 1974) 60.

4. For Woolf's short stories, all references will be to Dick's 1991 edition, if not otherwise stated.

5. A distinction made recurrently in Woolf's fiction and particularly, in *Between the Acts*, where the narrative voice says of Mrs Swithin: "It took her five seconds in actual time, in mind time ever so much longer" (*Between the Acts* 8). "Actual time" and "mind time" could also be compared with Henri Bergson's concepts of duration as distinct from scientific time, as developed in *Time and Free Will: An Essay on the Immediate Data of Consciousness* (1910).

6. Virginia Woolf, "A Sketch of the Past", *Moments of Being*, ed. Jeanne Schulkind (1976; London: Triad/Granada, 1981) 142.

7. See Walter Benjamin, *Charles Baudelaire. Un poète lyrique à l'apogée du capitalisme* (Paris: Payot, 1990) chapter 1.

8. T. S. Eliot, "Burnt Norton", *Four Quartets, The Complete Poems and Plays of T. S. Eliot* (London: Faber and Faber, 1969) 171.

9. In this short story, memory also stands as a metaphor of story-telling as we shall see later on.

10. Yet excluded from Stella McNichol's *Mrs Dalloway's Party*.

11. Gilles Deleuze and Félix Guattari, *A Thousand Plateaus: Capitalism and Schizophrenia,* trans. and foreword by Brian Massumi (1980; Minnesota: University of Minnesota Press, 1987) 24.

12. *The New Republic*, 10 March 1917.

13. Patricia Ondek Laurence, *The Reading of Silence: Virginia Woolf in the English Tradition* (Stanford, CA: Stanford University Press, 1991) 94.

14. Jonathan Culler, *Framing the Sign: Criticism and Its Institutions* (Oxford: Blackwell, 1988) ix.

15. Philippe Lacoue-Labarthe and Jean-Luc Nancy, *L'Absolu littéraire. Théorie de la littérature du romantisme allemand* (Paris: Seuil, 1978).

16. My translation. Lacoue-Labarthe and Nancy write: "il désigne autant, si l'on peut dire, les bords de la fracture comme une forme autonome que comme l'informité ou la difformité de la déchirure" (62).

17. My translation. "Pareil à une petite oeuvre d'art, un fragment doit être totalement détaché du monde environnant, et clos sur lui-même comme un hérisson" (quoted in Lacoue-Labarthe and Nancy 63).

18. My translation. Lacoue-Labarthe and Nancy write: "Ecrire en fragment, c'est écrire en fragments" (64).

19. My translation. Lacoue-Labarthe and Nancy write: "Le fragment ... comprend un essentiel inachèvement" (62).

20. Walter Benjamin, *The Origin of the German Tragic Drama*, trans. Peter Osborne (London: NLB, 1977) 28.

21. My translation. Roland Barthes writes: "lire en levant la tête"; in "Ecrire la lecture" (33–6), *Le Bruissement de la langue. Essais Critiques* (Paris: Seuil, 1984) 33.

22. Quoted in David S. Ferris, ed., *The Cambridge Companion to Walter Benjamin* (Cambridge: Cambridge University Press, 2004) 5.

23. Benjamin quoted in Ferris 14.
24. Virginia Woolf, "On Re-reading Novels" (*Essays* III: 340).
25. Ferris writes about Benjamin: "As a result of refusing... traditional under-
    standing, the significance of the parts is no longer dependent on the
    whole. But, as Benjamin insists, this does not mean that the parts have
    no relation to the overall picture or underlying idea. Rather, it means
    that the relation between them is no longer imposed from the top down,
    instead, it has to be thought from the bottom up, from what Benjamin
    terms 'immersion in the most minute details of the material content'
    (Origin 29)" (Ferris 6).

3 Conversation, emotion and ethics or the short story as conversation

1. This list has been partly quoted in Chapter 1 but our perspective being
   wider in this chapter and Attridge's definition being central to our point,
   we quote here a fuller version of the text.
2. Clive Bell, *Civilization: An Essay* (1928; West Drayton: Penguin, 1947) 96.
3. Nathalie Sarraute's own term, in *L'Ere du soupçon. Essais sur le roman*
   (Paris: Gallimard, 1956) 114, is "la sous-conversation" .
4. Virginia Woolf, *The Voyage Out* (1915; London: Granada, 1978) 220.
5. James Joyce, *A Portrait of the Artist as a Young Man* (1916; London: Granada,
   1977) 222.
6. Ford Madox Ford, *The Good Soldier* (1915; London: Norton, 1995) 15.
7. Katherine Mansfield, *Bliss and Other Stories* (Harmondsworth: Penguin,
   1962) 106.
8. Although it is not explicitly stated in the short story, we gather that the
   scene is taking place at Mrs Dalloway's since Elton Stuart is mentioned
   again by Mr Carslake as being one of the guests in "A Simple Melody"
   (204), a story set at Mrs Dalloway's party.
9. As Anne Besnault-Levita writes in her analysis of "The Introduction" and
   "Together and Apart" based on pragmatics and narratology, conversation
   "implies an agonistic yet creative exchange with the other". "Speech
   Acts, Represented Thoughts and Human Intercourse in 'The Introduction'
   and 'Together and Apart'" (Besnault in Reynier 2008; 67–83).
10. Virginia Woolf, *Mrs Dalloway* (1925; London: Penguin, 2000) 213.
11. In "A Sketch of the Past", Woolf writes: "These separate moments of being
    were however embedded in many more moments of non-being.... in a
    kind of nondescript cotton wool" (Woolf 1981: 81).
12. "That was her self—pointed; dartlike; definite. That was her self when
    some effort, some call on her to be her self, drew the parts together, she
    alone knew how different, how incompatible and composed so for the
    world only into one centre, one diamond, one woman who sat in her
    drawing-room and made a meeting-point, a radiancy no doubt in some
    dull lives, a refuge for the lonely to come to perhaps" (*Mrs Dalloway* 40).

13. The feminist undertones of this short story will be studied in chapter V.
14. Peace is evoked in *Between the Acts* when a character in the pageant dies and is clearly equated with lifelessness and the absence of all feeling.
15. A phrase Virginia Woolf uses in her diary about *The Waves*, while writing it: "it might be a gigantic conversation" (*Diary* III: 285; 26 January 1930).
16. A first version of this analysis, modified here, has been published in "Conversation Redefined: Notes on 'A Dialogue upon Mount Pentelicus'", *Etudes britanniques contemporaines*, "Conversation in Virginia Woolf's Works", numéro hors série (Autumn 2004): 167–80.
17. S. P. Rosenbaum, "Virginia Woolf: 'A Dialogue upon Mount Pentelicus'", *TLS* (September 11–17; 1987) 979; *Charleston Newsletter* 19 (September 1987) 23–32.
18. S. P. Rosenbaum, *Edwardian Bloomsbury: The Early History of the Bloomsbury Group*, Vol. 2 (London: Macmillan, 1994).
19. S. P. Rosenbaum writes that "A Vision of Greece" "begins with a map and goes on to speculate how disillusioning the place will be to the classically educated, with the monuments all ruined and the Greeks unable to understand their own classical language. At night, however, an image of 'the great statue of the Maiden Goddess' appears, as if to inspire the words of her lovers, Plato, Sophocles, Pericles. The vision lasts until the morning, when a farmer, after impiously cursing her, leaves a carrot on her altar because his priest had told him there is but one God. The shift here from disillusionment to the visionary and back to ordinary reality is a familiar pattern in Woolf's later writing" (Rosenbaum 1994: 182).
20. See Gilles Deleuze, *Proust et les signes* (Paris: Presses Universitaires de France, 1964).
21. "Greek literature is the impersonal literature", Woolf writes in "On Not knowing Greek", and goes on explaining that we know very little about Greek writers' lives (*Essays* IV: 39); see on that subject in Chapter 1.
22. It would also explain why Woolf will be able to dispense with narration in *The Waves* and resort only to conversation, the latter including the metaphors, allegories and other figures which are external to it here.
23. See also the image of the "ring of gold" and the "golden chain" running "through ages and races" (68) and the following sentence: "Such a flame as that in the monk's eye...had been lit once at the original hearth" (68).
24. "*Claritas* is *quidditas*.... This is the moment which I call epiphany. First we recognize that the moment is one integral thing, then we recognise that it is an organised composite structure, a *thing* in fact: finally, when the relation of the parts is exquisite, when the parts are adjusted to the special point, we recognise that it is *that* thing which it is. Its soul, its whatness, leaps to us from the vestment of its appearance". *Stephen Hero*, 213, quoted by Maurice Beebe, "Joyce and Aquinas: The Theory of Æsthetics (1957)" in *James Joyce*, 166.
25. Gustave Flaubert, "L'auteur dans son œuvre, doit être comme Dieu dans l'univers, présent partout, et visible nulle part", *Correspondance*, 4 vol. (Paris: Gallimard, 1973–98). Lettre à Louise Colet, 9 December 1852.

26. Deleuze writes: "La nouvelle convention linguistique, la structure formelle de l'œuvre, est donc la transversalité, qui traverse toute la phrase, qui va d'une phrase à une autre dans tout le livre, et qui même unit le livre de Proust à ceux qu'il aimait, Nerval, Chateaubriand, Balzac...Car si une œuvre d'art communique avec un public, bien plus le suscite, si elle communique avec les autres œuvres du même artiste, et les suscite, si elle communique avec d'autres œuvres d'autres artistes, et en suscite à venir, c'est toujours dans cette dimension de transversalité, où l'unité et la totalité s'établissent pour elles-mêmes, sans unifier ni totaliser objets ou sujets" (Deleuze 1964: 201–2).
27. See Gilles Deleuze and Félix Guattari, *Qu'est-ce que la philosophie?* (Paris: Minuit, 1991).
28. Jean-Jacques Lecercle and Ronald Shusterman, *L'Emprise des signes* (Paris: Seuil, 2002) 238.
29. We shall come back at length to the political dimension of Woolf's short stories in chapter V.

4   Woolf's ethics of reading and writing

1. See Chapter 2 on that subject.
2. As in "The Lady in the Looking-Glass", "Sympathy", "The Legacy" or "The Symbol" to quote only a few examples.
3. See for instance, "The Shooting Party" or "Lappin and Lapinova".
4. Harvena Richter writes: "People, objects, landscapes...become a series of mirrors reflecting the many aspects of the character himself", *Virginia Woolf: The Inward Voyage* (Princeton, NJ: Princeton University Press, 1970) 99.
5. Virginia Woolf, *To the Lighthouse* (1927; London: Hogarth Press, 1982) 103–4.
6. "Les Jeunes and Des Imagistes", first published in *Outlook* 33 (9 May 1914) 653. Ford admired this quality in Imagiste poetry which had found a new form for the narrative of emotion whereas the novel was still groping for one, according to him (Ford 2002: 154).
7. Although Woolf seems to be mistaken about the dates, the broken rope may be an allusion to the tragedy faced by Edward Whymper, a famous climber and contemporary of Lesley Stephen who related the circumstances of the event in *Scrambles amongst the Alps in the Years 1860–1869* (1871; Washington, DC: National Geographic Adventure Classics, 2002).
8. Julia Briggs first mentions this short story and reads it as exploring "the obscure connections between desire...death, and language" in " 'Cut Deep and Scored Thick with Meaning': Frame and Focus in Woolf's Later Short Stories" (Benzel and Hoberman 190; 175–91). See also on "The Symbol", Liliane Louvel, "Telling 'by' pictures: Woolf's Shorter Fiction" (Louvel in Reynier 2008; 185–200).
9. Roland Barthes writes: "la naissance du lecteur doit se payer de la mort de l'Auteur" (Barthes 1984: 69).

10. A considerably revised version of this lecture given in 1926 at Hayes Court, a girls' school, is published in (*Essays* IV: 388–400); the wording, if not the substance, is different.
11. E. M. Forster writes: "What is so wonderful about great literature is that it transforms the man who reads it towards the condition of the man who wrote, and brings to birth in us also the creative impulse" (Forster 1979: 84).
12. In "How Should One Read a Book", Woolf defines her ideal reader thus: "Most commonly we come to books with blurred and divided minds, asking of fiction that it shall be true, of poetry that it shall be false, of biography that it shall be flattering, of history that it shall enforce our own prejudices. If we could banish all such preconceptions when we read, that would be an admirable beginning" (*C.E.* II: 2).
13. Ford writes: "Now the one sensible thing in the long drivel of nonsense with which Tolstoi misled this dull world was the remark that art should be addressed to the peasant" (270) and adds that "in Occidental Europe the non-preoccupied mind—which is the same thing as the peasant intelligence—is to be found scattered throughout every grade of society" (271) but is certainly not an English gentleman, the latter being too much concerned with conventions. The cabman is the very opposite and embodies the ideal reader's "non-preoccupied mind". "On Impressionism", Second article, *Poetry and Drama* 2.6 (December 1914) 323–34. Reproduced in (Ford 1995: 264–74).
14. See especially "La Pharmacie de Platon" about reading and writing being one and about what he calls "adding" or "supplement": "ajouter n'est pas ici autre chose que donner à lire…. Le supplément de lecture ou d'écriture doit être rigoureusement prescrit mais par la nécessité d'un *jeu*, signe auquel il faut accorder le système de tous ses pouvoirs" (Derrida 1972: 80).
15. My translation. Finas writes: "Le don du lecteur au texte suppose le don du texte au lecteur" (Finas 14).
16. Barthes writes about "lire en levant la tête" (Barthes 1984: 33).
17. "Dissemination" would then synthesise more adequately than "polysemy" what Woolf describes in this essay. Derrida defines dissemination in the following way: "S'il n'y a donc pas d'unité thématique ou de sens total à se réapproprier au-delà des instances textuelles,…le texte n'est plus l'expression ou la représentation…de quelque *vérité* qui viendrait se diffracter ou se rassembler dans une littérature polysémique. C'est à ce concept herméneutique de *polysémie* qu'il faudrait substituer celui de *dissémination*" (Derrida 1972: 319).
18. Jeanette Winterson, a great reader and admirer of Woolf, adopts the same stance. See my "Jeanette Winterson's Cogito—'Amo Ergo Sum'—or Impersonality and Emotion Redefined" (Reynier and Ganteau 2005: 299–308).
19. Joseph Conrad, Preface to *The Nigger of the 'Narcissus'* (1897; London: Everyman's Library, 1974) xxvi.
20. Virginia Woolf, "Crafstmanship" (*C.E.* II: 249).
21. Omitted in Leonard Woolf's edition (*AHH:* 11).

22. See chapter I, n. 43.
23. See especially (Attridge 2004: 44–9). The double antithetical movement of recognition and defamiliarisation could also be compared with Benjamin's "arrested dialectics", a concept he uses in *The Origin of German Tragic Drama*.
24. E. M. Forster compares Woolf and Sterne's capacity for bewilderment (Forster 1974: 12), a term Woolf herself uses about reading Chekhov in "The Russian Point of View" (*Essays* IV: 183); see chapter 1 on that subject.
25. A Kantian concept Fry, Bell or Woolf resorted to so as to evoke the contemplation of a work of art or, in Woolf's case, the reading of a book. On that subject, see (Froula 2005: 1–32).
26. Barthes, in 1973, makes a distinction between le "[t]exte de plaisir: celui qui contente" and the "[t]exte de jouissance: celui qui met en état de perte ... met en crise son rapport au langage" (Barthes 1973: 25–6). As for Sontag, she argues in favour of an art that would make us "recover our senses" and, paraphrasing Conrad, she writes: "We must learn to *see* more, to *hear* more, to *feel* more.... In place of a hermeneutics, we need an erotics of art" (Sontag 312).
27. According to Deleuze, the event cannot be captured by language; it can only exist in language. Deleuze and Guattari write: "l'événement n'est pas du tout l'état de choses, il s'actualise dans un état de choses ... mais ... ne cesse de se soustraire ou de s'ajouter à son actualisation" (Deleuze and Guattari 1991: 147–8). See also Gilles Deleuze, *La Logique du sens* (Paris: Minuit, 1969). On that subject and while referring to "Kew gardens", Lecercle writes that Woolf's moments of being are "the best illustrations I know of the Deleuzian event" (Lecercle 2002: 151).
28. Sir Thomas Browne, *Religio Medici* (1642) quoted in Virginia Woolf, "The Elizabethan Lumber Room" (*Essays* IV: 58–9).

5 Woolf's short story as a site of resistance

1. See Mikhail Bahtin, *The Dialogic Imagination: Four Essays*, ed. Michael Holquist, trans. Caryl Emerson and Michael Holquist (Austin, TX: University of Texas Press, 1981).
2. Melba Cuddy-Keane, in her analysis of Woolf's essays, shows that "Woolf proposed her own version of the dialogic by casting a review of Joseph Conrad as a debate between two readers ['Mr Conrad: A Conversation' (1923)]" (136) but "abandoned her scheme for using explicit dialogue" and "embedded the dialogue within the essayist's voice" (137). Woolf then "achieves the rhetorical effect of conversation by employing a single voice that undergoes constant shifts in focalization" (141). In this way, the readers "are urged simultaneously to form opinions and never to allow opinion to harden into 'truth'" (141). Through a different use of voice and a different technique, a different genre, the essay, foregrounds debate or conversation as the short story does.
3. Winifred Holtby, *Virginia Woolf: A Critical Memoir*, with a new introduction by Marion Shaw (1932; London: Continuum, 2007) 44.

4. This is Attridge's definition of the aesthetic tradition.
5. On this subject, see Michael Whitworth, *Authors in Context: Virginia Woolf*, Authors in Context Series (Oxford: Oxford University Press, 2005).
6. For a synthetic account of Woolf's critical reception, see Jane Goldman, *The Cambridge Introduction to Virginia Woolf* (Cambridge: Cambridge University Press, 2006). Goldman writes that in the 1960s, Jean Guiguet's first full-length study of Woolf's œuvre "set a trend against materialist and historicist readings of Woolf by his insistence on the primacy of the subjective and the psychological" (129). In the 1970s and 1980s, "[t]here were ... many points of critical friction between those interpreting Woolf as an aesthete and those who followed her feminism" (130). In the 1990s, "Woolf in social, historical and political context has been addressed by a number of critics" (135).
7. See Toril Moi, *Sexual/Textual Politics: Feminist Literary Theory* (London: Methuen, 1985); Rachel Bowlby, *Feminist Destinations and Further Essays on Virginia Woolf* (Edinburgh: Edinburgh University Press, 1997). As Elena Gualtieri writes, "Like Moi, Bowlby sets out to dismantle the kind of impassable oppositions that have regulated the reading of Woolf's work as either a modernist or a feminist, an essayist or a novelist, a refined aesthete or a committed socialist revolutionary" (Gualtieri 15).
8. In *La Force du féminin* (Paris: La Fabrique, 2002), Frédéric Regard studies three of Woolf's essays and points out that Woolf's political, aesthetic and ethical commitments go hand in hand.
9. Jean Guiguet in the chapter he devotes to Woolf's short stories uses the words "esquisses", "pochades impressionnistes" and "contes" (Guiguet 326–38). David Bradshaw also uses the word "sketch" (Bradshaw 2003: xviii). On this subject, see my introduction.
10. In a recent article, Charles Sumner, basing his argument on three short stories, shows that the exploration of "damaged beauty" in these texts is politically committed, but he discounts all ethical dimension. Charles Sumner, "Beauty and Damaged Life in Virginia Woolf's Short Fiction" (Sumner in Reynier 2008; 33–47).
11. The journal entry is that of "29 February 1909, Cambridge" (Woolf 2003: 6–9). As David Bradshaw writes in a footnote to this entry, "[a solid object] was one of Woolf's preferred terms for the obstructiveness, burdensomeness and tweed-clad predictability of the Victorian patriarchal world" (20, n. 4). And Woolf suggests the dullness of the man as well as his lack of taste through her description of his room: "In the drawing room, the parents' room, there are prints from Holbein drawings, bad portraits of children, indiscriminate rugs, chairs, Venetian glass, Japanese embroideries: the effect is of subdued colour, and incoherence; there is no regular scheme. In short the room is dull" (Woolf 2003: 6).
12. See on that subject the insightful analysis of Charles Sumner (Sumner in Reynier 2008; 33–47).
13. In her study of silence in Woolf's novels, Laurence further engages "the multiple levels and the meaning of silence that one experiences in a

Woolf novel" and shows that "the meanings of silence shift, as do the methods used to represent it" (3).
14. It is interesting to remember here that "The Shooting Party" was published in 1938 when *Three Guineas* was as well.
15. "Jug. Jug" is also taken up in *The Waves:* "Jug, jug, jug I sing like the nightingale whose melody is crowded in the too narrow passage of her throat" (126).
16. T. S. Eliot, "A Game of Chess", *The Waste Land* (1922; London: Faber and Faber, 1969) 64.
17. See "A Sketch of the Past", 79.
18. "The Shooting Party" was written in 1932 and published in 1938; "A Sketch of the Past", where Woolf relates what her half-brother submitted her to, was written in 1939 and published in *Moments of Being* in 1976.
19. Women, as Lily's name, "Ever-it", suggests, have always been labelled as objects and should rebel against this.
20. This is obviously based on the Dreadnought hoax, a joke Woolf and her friends played on the Navy and which led Woolf's cousin and some officers to react somewhat aggressively, feeling as they did that the honour of the Navy had to be saved. For a fuller account, see Quentin Bell, *Virginia Woolf,* vol. 1 (St Albans: Triad/Paladin, 1976) 157–60. Woolf will take the Navy to task once again in "Scenes from the Life of a British Naval Officer", a caricature of Captain Brace, presented as cut off from the others and totally dehumanised and at one with his navigating instruments, dials compasses and a telescope; the only trace of potential humanity in this character, "the photograph of a lady's head" (232), cannot rise to its promise, placed as it is in the centre of the instruments.
21. On this subject, see *Essays* IV: 455 and my first chapter.
22. A phrase Katherine Mansfield used about her own short stories in her *Letters and Journals.*
23. Mikhail Bakhtin, *Problems of Dostoevsky's Poetics* (Manchester: Manchester University Press, 1984) 6.
24. See on that subject, Martine Stemerick, "Virginia Woolf and Julia Stephen: the Distaff Side of History", *Virginia Woolf: Centennial Essays*, eds, Elaine K. Ginsberg and Laura Moss Gottlieb (Troy, NY: Whitson, 1983) 51–80.
25. In this caricature Woolf retrieves the tone she used in the portraits she drew of some of her acquaintances in *Carlyle's House*, for example, Miss Reeves who is both praised for being full of stamina, a great talker, and very human, and subtly criticised for her likeness to a snake, her lack of discrimination and mystery, and finally condemned: "one figures her always in flight; so much determined to embrace everything that she fails" (Woolf 2003: 5).
26. This was Woolf's project for *The Waves;* see *Diary* III: 285; 26 January 1930.
27. See Melba Cuddy-Keane, *Virginia Woolf, the Intellectual, and the Public Sphere* (Cambridge: Cambridge University Press, 2003).
28. It is close to the vision defended by Walt Whitman, the self-styled poet of democracy whom Woolf admired; see on that point (Cuddy-Keane 41–5).

29. Clive Bell analyses the notion of civilisation and takes the Greeks as his model; he refers to Plato's *Symposium* and shows that "[c]onversation is a delight known to the civilized alone" (Bell 1947: 113).
30. See Dick's notes in (Dick 311).
31. Cuddy-Keane reads this short story as a "fictional essay" and as a refiguration of the myth of Narcissus where "the mirror image is read not as a projection of self but as an alterity" (126), "a textual collective unconscious" (131).
32. In a very perceptive analysis of *Between the Acts*, Christine Froula comes to a similar conclusion: "Against the enforced univocality of totalitarianism, parodied and deconstructed by the megaphone, the music gathers up in its aural mirror a dialogic community, to which real differences, as Hannah Arendt says, are so much less dangerous than indifference; a community of spectators who enact a public 'form of being together' where 'no one rules and no one obeys', where people seek to 'persuade each other'. It is almost as if the pageant gives voice to the 'we' Churchill vowed would 'fight in the fields' against the Nazis' scapegoating perversion of community, at the same time as it bodies forth the outsiders' wish to 'give to England first what she desires of peace and freedom for the whole world'". "The Play in the Sky of the Mind: Dialogue, 'The Tchekov Method', and *Between the Acts*", *Etudes britanniques contemporaines*, "Conversation in Virginia Woolf's Works", ed. C. Reynier (Autumn 2004): 181–96.
33. See on that subject Benzel and Hoberman, especially the articles collected in the second chapter, "Crossing Generic Boundaries".
34. On that subject, see Skbric xv.
35. The other can be defined as another human being, as Hegel does, or as God, as Levinas does, or the colonised as in post-colonial studies, or as "the new"—here, as another genre—as Derek Attridge suggests in *The Singularity of Literature* (Attridge 2004: 32).
36. Jacques Rancière, *Politique de la littérature* (Paris: Galilée, 2007) 88.
37. For an analysis of the new type of history Woolf advocates in this short story, see Leena Kore-Schroeder: "Who's afraid of Rosamond Merridew? Reading Medieval History in 'The Journal of Mistress Joan Martyn'" (Kore-Schroeder in Reynier 2008: 103–19).
38. Rancière writes that in Tolstoï's work, "la périphérie a envahi le centre" (89) and explains that he bases his narrative on narratives, letters and documents of the anonymous people who took part in the war and were the actors of battles. He argues that Tolstoï's fiction anticipated the new form of history that would be based on the silent ones' testimonies, unlike the old form of history, based on "chronicles", that is, on the official archives of princes and military officers.
39. My translation. Amselle writes: "Dans le *Journal d'adolescence*, Virginia Woolf s'essaie à la nouvelle, au journalisme et à l'essai. Elle ne développe pas autant ce caractère expérimental dans les autres journaux, hormis quelques essais, en 1926, par exemple", Postface au *Journal Intégral*, 1915–41 (Paris: Stock, la Cosmopolite, 2008) 1531.

40. E. M. Forster, *Howards End* (Harmondsworth: Penguin, 1989) 58.
41. For a specific analysis of writing and painting in Woolf's short stories, see Liliane Louvel: "Telling 'by' pictures"; of writing and cinema, see Laura Marcus on "The Searchlight": "In the Circle of the Lens"; and of writing and music, see Emilie Crapoulet, "Beyond the Boundaries of Language: Music in Virginia Woolf's 'The String Quartet'" (Reynier 2008; 185–200; 153–69; 201–15).
42. T. W. Adorno, "L'essai comme forme", *Notes sur la littérature* (1958; Paris: Flammarion, 1984) 5–29.
43. "une méditation errante déréglée", according to Marc Angenot, *La Parole pamphlétaire. Typologie des discours modernes* (Paris: Payot, 1982) 57.
44. Marc Angenot writes: "le passage d'une proposition à une autre se fait non par l'essentiel mais par l'accessoire: l'image intuitive y a plus de force que le syllogisme" (Angenot 57).
45. Marc Angenot writes: "il s'agit en tout cas moins de dévoiler un 'contenu', extérieur à la pensée que de montrer les mécanismes intimes par lesquels la pensée se donne des objets" (Angenot 57).
46. See also the Church and the aggressive God represented in "An Unwritten Novel" ("Minnie Marsh prays to God.... this seeing of Gods! More like President Kruger than Prince Albert", 115) and pronounced dead one page afterwards ("who thinks of God?...there's nothing but grey in the sky", 116).
47. This is what Woolf will denounce much more bluntly in *A Room of One's Own* when she writes, for example: "I do not believe that even the Table of Precedency which you will find in Whitaker's Almanac represents a final order of values, or that there is any sound reason to suppose that a Commander of the Bath will ultimately walk in to dinner behind a Master of Lunacy. All this pitting of sex against sex, of quality against quality; all this claiming of superiority and imputing of inferiority, belong to the private-school stage of human existence where there are 'sides', and it is necessary for one side to beat another side.... As people mature they cease to believe in sides" (*A Room* 100–1).
48. The power and violence of patriarchy is also denounced through the caricature of the Squire in "The Shooting Party" but is not necessarily represented by male characters as it is the case in "Lappin and Lapinova" where Mrs Thorburn, who embodies the violence of patriarchal society, is called the Squire.
49. As Adorno phrases it: "On peut douter que les oeuvres d'art interviennent effectivement dans la politique; lorsque cela se produit, c'est le plus souvent de façon périphérique...leur véritable effet social est hautement indirect". Theodor Adorno, *Théorie esthétique*, trans. E. Kaufnolz et Marc Jimenez (1970; Paris: Klincksieck, 1995) 334.
50. Bakhtin broaches the same topics as Woolf through the concepts of heteroglossia, polyglossia, ideologem, and more widely, dialogism, especially in "Discourse in the Novel", where he shows that "the word does not exist in a neutral and impersonal language" and that "[l]anguage is

not a neutral medium ...; it is a populated—overpopulated—with the intentions of others" (Bakhtin 1981: 294).

51. Lecercle echoes here Jameson's famous statement: "there is nothing that is not social and historical... everything is 'in the last analysis' political" (Jameson 20) and comments Judith Butler's conception of the subject as both actor and acted, a position comparable to the writer's (and reader's) in Woolf's essays.

52. Forster, "Racial Exercise", 20.

53. In "Memoirs of a Novelist" (1909), the narrator adopts the posture of a reviewer of a fictitious biography and in his criticism of this traditional biography, comes to write an essay about the new biography, long before Woolf herself wrote the essay of the same name.

54. For a more detailed analysis of *Flush* as an art of cross-fertilisation and impurity, see my "Impure Art of Biography".

55. Virginia Woolf, *The Mark on the Wall and Other Short Fiction*, ed. David Bradshaw (Oxford: Oxford University Press, 2001).

56. David Bradshaw, "Hyams Place: The Years, the Jews and the British Union of Fascists" in *Women Writers of the 1930s: Gender, Politics and History*, ed. Maroula Joannou (Edinburgh: Edinburgh University Press, 1999) 179–91.

57. However, Briggs reads *The Years* as anti-Semitic and argues that in this novel, "the Jew is more explicitly associated with contamination" (Briggs 182).

58. Theodor Adorno, "Commitment", *Aesthetics and Politics*, ed. Fredric Jameson (London: Verso, 1980) 191.

59. In her preface to the French edition, Geneviève Brisac, writes about Bradshaw's reading of this short story and of "Jews", included in *Carlyle's House and Other Stories*: "une magnifique érudition se met au service de la misogynie et des préjugés", *La Maison de Carlyle et autres esquisses*, trans. Agnès Desarthes (Paris: Mercure de France, 2003) 13.

On "The Duchess and the Jeweller", see also Leena Kore Schröder, "Tales of Abjection and Miscegenation: Virginia Woolf's and Leonard Woolf's 'Jewish' Stories", *Twentieth Century Literature* 49.3 (Autumn 2003): 298–327; and Kate Krueger Henderson, "Fashioning Anti-Semitism: Virginia Woolf's 'The Duchess and the Jeweller' and the Readers of *Harper's Bazaar*" (Henderson in Reynier 2008; 49–65). Quoting Chambrun who first accepted the synopsis of the short story, but later rejected it "on the grounds that it was 'a psychological study of a Jew' and thus, because of widespread racial prejudice in America, unacceptable to his (unnamed) client", Henderson convincingly argues that Chambrun's comments indicate that, rather than the author, "the *audience* is anti-semitic" (50) and shows that the short story deals in fact with the consumers' practices that are the readers' of *Harper's Bazaar*.

60. Jean-Jacques Lecercle, *Interpretation as Pragmatics* (Macmillan: Basingstoke, 1999) 176.

61. The type of reader Derek Attridge evokes in his *The Singularity of Literature* and in "Ethics, Otherness and Literary Form", 33–8.

62. As Adorno phrases it: "[i]t is not the office of art to spotlight alternatives, but to resist by its form" (Adorno 1980: 180).
63. Rancière writes: "le *nomos* grec a une pluralité de significations; non seulement la loi mais le *partage* qui la fonde, et la *mélodie*, le chant de la communauté, où elle s'incarne" (104).
64. See my introduction.

Bibliography

Adorno, Theodor W., "L'essai comme forme", *Notes sur la littérature* (1958), Paris: Flammarion, 1984, 5–29.

——, *Théorie esthétique*, trans. E. Kaufnolz et Marc Jimenez (1970), Paris: Klincksieck, 1995.

——, "Commitment", *Aesthetics and Politics*, ed. Fredric Jameson, London: Verso, 1980, 177–95. Amselle, Frédérique, *Virginia Woolf et les écritures du moi: Le journal et l'autobiographie*, Montpellier: Presses Universitaires de la Méditerranée, 2008.

Amselle, Frédérique, Virginia Woolf et les écritures du moi. Le journal et l'autobiographie. Montpellier: Presses Universitaires de la Méditerranée, 2008.

——, Postface, *Journal Intégral* (1915–41), Paris: Stock, la Cosmopolite, 2008, 1529–37.

Angenot, Marc, *La Parole pamphlétaire. Typologie des discours modernes*, Paris: Payot, 1982.

Attridge, Derek, "Ethics, Otherness, and Literary Form", *The European English Messenger* XII (1) (Spring 2003): 33–8.

——, *The Singularity of Literature*, London: Routledge, 2004.

Bakhtin, Mikhail, *The Dialogic Imagination: Four Essays*, ed. Michael Holquist, trans. Caryl Emerson and Michael Holquist, Austin, TX: University of Texas Press, 1981.

——, *Problems of Dostoevsky's Poetics*, Manchester: Manchester University Press, 1984.

Baldeshwiler, Eileen, "The Grave as Lyrical Short Story", *Studies in Short Fiction* I (Winter 1982), 216–21.

Baldwin, Dean R., *Virginia Woolf: A Study of the Short Fiction*, Boston, MA: Twayne Publishers, 1989.

Barthes, Roland, *S/Z*, Paris: Seuil, 1970.

——, *Le Plaisir du texte*, Paris: Seuil, 1973.

——, *Roland Barthes par Roland Barthes*, Paris: Seuil, 1975.

——, "La Mort de l'auteur" (1968) (63–9); "Ecrire la lecture" (33–6), *Le Bruissement de la langue. Essais critiques IV*, Paris: Seuil, 1984.

Beebe, Maurice, "Joyce and Aquinas: The Theory of Æsthetics (1957)", *James Joyce: Dubliners and a Portrait of the Artist as a Young Man*, ed. Morris Beja, London: Macmillan, 1973, 163–8.

Beer, Gillian, *Virginia Woolf: The Common Ground*, Edinburgh: Edinburgh University Press, 1996.

Beja, Morris, ed., *James Joyce: Dubliners and a Portrait of the Artist as a Young Man*, London: Macmillan, 1973.

Bell, Clive, *Art* (1914), Oxford: Oxford University Press, 1987.

——, *Civilization: An Essay* (1928), West Drayton: Penguin Books, 1947.

Bell, Quentin, *Virginia Woolf*, vol. 1, St Albans: Triad/Paladin, 1976.

Benjamin, Walter, *Sens unique*, trans. Jean Lacoste (1928), Paris: Maurice Nadeau, 1998.

——, *The Origin of the German Tragic Drama*, trans. Peter Osborne, London: NLB, 1977.

Benzel, Kathryn N. and Ruth Hoberman, eds, *Trespassing Boundaries: Virginia Woolf's Short Fiction*, New York & Basingstoke: Palgrave Macmillan, 2004.

Bernard, Catherine, "Virginia Woolf essayiste ou l'écriture sans pédigrée", *Virginia Woolf: Le Pur et l' impur*, eds C. Bernard and C. Reynier, Rennes: Presses Universitaires de Rennes, 2002, 247–58.

Bernard, Catherine and Christine Reynier, eds, *Virginia Woolf. Le Pur et l' impur*, colloque de Cerisy-la-Salle 2001, Rennes: Presses Universitaires de Rennes, 2002.

Besnault-Levita, Anne, "Speech Acts, Represented Thoughts and Human Intercourse in 'The Introduction' and 'Together and Apart' ", *Journal of the Short Story in English*, ed. Christine Reynier, 50 (Spring 2008): 67–83.

Bowlby, Rachel, *Feminist Destinations and Further Essays on Virginia Woolf*, Edinburgh: Edinburgh University Press, 1997.

Bradshaw, David, "Hyams Place: The Years, the Jews and the British Union of Fascists", *Women Writers of the 1930s: Gender, Politics and History*, ed. Maroula Joannou, Edinburgh: Edinburgh University Press, 1999, 179–91.

——, ed., *The Mark on the Wall and Other Short Fiction*, Oxford: Oxford University Press, 2001.

——, ed., *Carlyle's House and Other Sketches*, London: Hesperus Press, 2003.

Briggs, Julia, " 'Cut Deep and Scored Thick with Meaning': Frame and Focus in Woolf's Later Short Stories", *Trespassing Boundaries: Virginia Woolf's Short Fiction*, eds, Kathryn N. Benzel and Ruth Hoberman, New York & Basingstoke: Palgrave Macmillan, 2004, 175–91.

Brisac, Geneviève, Préface, *La Maison de Carlyle et autres esquisses*, trans. Agnès Desarthes, Paris: Mercure de France, 2003.

Brosnan, Leila, *Reading Virginia Woolf's Essays and Journalism*, Edinburgh: Edinburgh University Press, 1997.

Bullen, J. Barry, ed., "Introduction to Roger Fry", *Vision and Design* (1920), Oxford: Oxford University Press, 1981, xi–xxv.

Coleridge, S. T., *Biographia Literaria* (1817), London: J. M. Dent & sons, 1975.

Conrad, Joseph, Preface to *The Nigger of the "Narcissus"* (1897), London: Penguin, 1987, xlvii–li.

Couturier, Maurice, *La Figure de l'auteur*, Paris: Seuil, 1998.

Crapoulet, Emilie, "Beyond the Boundaries of Language: Music in Virginia Woolf's 'The String Quartet' ", *Journal of the Short Story in English*, ed. Christine Reynier, 50 (Spring 2008): 201–15.

Cuddy-Keane, Melba, *Virginia Woolf, the Intellectual and the Public Sphere*, Cambridge: Cambridge University Press, 2003.

Culler, Jonathan, *Framing the Sign: Criticism and Its Institutions*, Oxford: Blackwell, 1988.

Daugherty, R. Beth, " 'A Corridor Leading from *Mrs Dalloway* to a New Book': Transforming Stories, Bending Genres", *Trespassing Boundaries: Virginia*

Woolf's Short Fiction, ed. Kathryn N. Benzel and Ruth Hoberman, New York & Basingstoke: Palgrave Macmillan, 2004, 101–24.

Deleuze, Gilles, *Proust et les signes*, Paris: Presses Universitaires de France, 1964.

Deleuze, Gilles, *La Logique du sens*, Paris: Minuit, 1969.

——, *Spinoza. Philosophie pratique*, 1970; Paris: Minuit, 1981.

Deleuze, Gilles and Félix Guattari, *A Thousand Plateaus: Capitalism and Schizophrenia*, trans. and foreword by Brian Massumi (1980), Minnesota: Minnesota University Press, 1987.

——, *Qu'est-ce que la philosophie?* Paris: Minuit, 1991.

Derrida, Jacques, *La Dissémination*, Paris: Seuil, 1972.

——, *La Carte Postale*, Paris: Aubier-Flammarion, 1980.

——, *Psyché, Inventions de l'autre*, Paris: Galilée, 1987.

——, *Signéponge*, Paris: Seuil, 1988.

——, *Politiques de l'amitié*, Paris: Galilée, 1994.

Dick, Susan, ed., "Introduction; Notes and Appendices", *Virginia Woolf: The Complete Shorter Fiction*, (1985), London: Triad Grafton Books, 1991–5, 294–367.

Eco, Umberto, *L'Œuvre ouverte* (1962), Paris: Seuil, 1965.

Eliot, T. S., "Burnt Norton", *Four Quartets*, 171–6; "A Game of Chess", *The Waste Land* (1922), 64–6, *The Complete Poems and Plays of T. S. Eliot*, London: Faber and Faber, 1969.

——, "Tradition and the Individual Talent" (1919), *Selected Essays*, London: Faber and Faber, 1999.

Ferris, S. David, ed., *The Cambridge Companion to Walter Benjamin*, Cambridge: Cambridge University Press, 2004.

Gerlach, John, *Towards the End, Closure and Structure in the American Short Story*, Alabama: The University of Alabama Press, 1985.

Finas, Lucette, *La Toise et le Vertige*, Paris: Des Femmes, 1986.

Flaubert, Gustave, *Correspondance*, 4 vols, Paris: Gallimard, 1973–98.

Ford Madox Ford, *The Good Soldier*, ed. Martin Stannard (1915), London: Norton, 1995.

——, *Critical Essays*, ed. Max Saunders and Richard Stang, Manchester: Carcanet, 2002.

Forster, Edward Morgan, *Aspects of the Novel* (1927), London: Edward Arnold, 1974.

——, "Racial Exercise" (17–20); "Anonymity: An Enquiry" (77–87); "Art for Art's Sake" (88–94), *Two Cheers for Democracy* (1938), New York & London: HBC, 1979.

——, *Howards End* (1910), Harmondsworth: Penguin, 1989.

Froula, Christine, "The Play in the Sky of the Mind: Dialogue, 'The Tchekov Method', and *Between the Acts*"; "Conversation in Virginia Woolf's Works", *Etudes britanniques contemporaines*, ed. C. Reynier, numéro hors série (Autumn 2004): 181–96.

——, *Virginia Woolf and the Bloomsbury Avant-Garde: War-Civilization-Modernity*, New York: Columbia University Press, 2005.

Fry, Roger, *Vision and Design* (1920), Oxford: Oxford University Press, 1981.

Ganteau, Jean-Michel and Christine Reynier, eds, *Impersonality and Emotion in Twentieth-Century British Arts*, Montpellier: Presses Universitaires de la Méditerranée, collection *Present Perfect* 2, 2006.

Gibson, Andrew, *Postmodernity, Ethics and the Novel: From Leavis to Levinas*, London: Routledge, 1999.

Giles, Steve, *Theorizing Modernism: Essays in Critical Theory,* London: Routledge, 1993.

Goldman, Jane, *The Cambridge Introduction to Virginia Woolf,* Cambridge: Cambridge University Press, 2006.

Goldman, Mark, *The Reader's Art: Virginia Woolf as Literary Critic,* The Hague: Mouton, 1976.

Gualtieri, Elena, *Virginia Woolf's Essays,* London: Macmillan, 2000.

Guiguet, Jean, *Virginia Woolf et son œuvre. L' Art et la quête du réel,* Paris: Didier, 1962.

Hanson, Clare, ed., *Re-reading the Short Story,* New York: St Martin's Press, 1989.

Harpham, Geoffrey, *Getting It Right: Language, Literature and Ethics,* Chicago, IL: University of Chicago Press, 1992.

Head, Dominic, *The Modernist Short Story: A Study in Theory and Practice,* Cambridge: Cambridge University Press, 1992.

Henderson, Kate Krueger, "Fashioning Anti-Semitism: Virginia Woolf's 'The Duchess and the Jeweller' and the Readers of *Harper's Bazaar*", *Journal of the Short Story in English,* ed. Christine Reynier, 50 (Spring 2008): 49–65.

Holtby, Winifred, *Virginia Woolf: A Critical Memoir,* with a new introduction by Marion Shaw (1932), London: Continuum, 2007.

Jameson, Fredric, *The Political Unconscious: Narrative as a Socially symbolic Act,* New York: Cornell University Press, 1981.

Joyce, James, *A Portrait of the Artist as a Young Man* (1916), London: Granada, 1977.

Kaufmann, Michael, "A Modernism of One's Own: Woolf's TLS Reviews and Eliotic Modernism", *Virginia Woolf and the Essay,* ed. B. C. Rosenberg and J. Dubino, New York: St Martin's Press, 1997, 137–55.

Keats, John, *Selected Letters by John Keats,* ed. Jon Mee, Oxford: Oxford University Press, 2002.

Kore-Schroeder, Leena, "Tales of Abjection and Miscegenation: Virginia Woolf's and Leonard Woolf's 'Jewish' Stories", *Twentieth Century Literature* 49 (3) (Autumn 2003): 298–327.

——, "Who's Afraid of Rosamond Merridew? Reading Medieval History in 'The Journal of Mistress Joan Martyn'", *Journal of the Short Story in English,* ed. Christine Reynier, 50 (Spring 2008): 103–19.

Lacoue-Labarthe, Philippe and Jean-Luc Nancy, *L'Absolu littéraire: Théorie de la littérature du romantisme allemand,* Paris: Seuil, 1978.

Laurence, Patricia Ondek, *The Reading of Silence: Virginia Woolf in the English Tradition,* Stanford, CA: Stanford University Press, 1991.

Lawrence, D. H., "Poetry of the Present", *Selected Critical Writings,* Oxford: Oxford University Press, 1998, 75–9.

Lecercle, Jean-Jacques, *Interpretation as Pragmatics,* London: Macmillan, 1999.

——, *Deleuze and Language,* Basingstoke: Palgrave Macmillan, 2002.

Lecercle, Jean-Jacques and Ronald Shusterman, *L'Emprise des signes,* Paris: Seuil, 2002.

Lee, Hermione, *Virginia Woolf,* London: Chatto & Windus, 1996.

Louvel, Liliane, "Telling 'by' Pictures: Woolf's Shorter Fiction", *Journal of the Short Story in English*, ed. Christine Reynier, 50 (Spring 2008): 185–200.

Louvel, Liliane and Claudine Verley, *Introduction à l'étude de la nouvelle. Littérature contemporaine de langue anglaise*, Toulouse: Presses Universitaires du Mirail, 1993.

Low, Lisa, "Refusing to Hit Back: Virginia Woolf and the Impersonality Question", *Virginia Woolf and the Essay*, ed. B. C. Rosenberg and J. Dubino, New York: St Martin's Press, 1997, 257–73.

Mansfield, Katherine, *Bliss and Other Stories*, Harmondsworth: Penguin, 1962.

——, *Letters and Journals*, ed. C. K. Stead, Harmondsworth: Penguin, 1977.

Marcus, Laura, "'In the Circle of the Lens': Woolf's 'Telescope' Story, Scene-making and Memory", *Journal of the Short Story in English*, ed. Christine Reynier, 50 (Spring 2008): 153–70.

Maunder, Andrew, ed., *The British Companion to the Short Story*, New York: Facts on File, 2007.

Meschonnic, Henri, *Critique du rythme*, Paris: Verdier, 1982.

Moi, Toril, *Sexual/Textual Politics: Feminist Literary Theory*, London: Methuen, 1985.

Moore, G. E., *Principia Ethica* (1903), Cambridge: Cambridge University Press, 2000.

Poe, Edgar Allan, "Twice-Told Tales", *Selected Writings*, Harmondsworth: Penguin, 1979, 437–47.

Rancière, Jacques, *Politique de la littérature*, Paris: Galilée, 2007.

Regard, Frédéric, "Penser, sentir, écrire. Quelques réflexions sur la notion de *feeling* dans l'histoire de l'esthétique britanique", *Etudes britanniques contemporaines* 9 (June 1996): 65–77.

——, *La Force du féminin. Sur trois essais de Woolf*, Paris: La Fabrique, 2002.

——, ed., *Mapping the Self: Space, Identity, Discourse in British Auto/Biography*, Saint-Etienne: Publications de l'Université de Saint-Etienne, 2003.

Reynier, Christine, "The Impure Art of Biography: Virginia Woolf's *Flush*", *Mapping the Self: Space, Identity, Discourse in British Auto/Biography*, ed. Frédéric Regard, Saint-Etienne: Publications de l'Université de Saint-Etienne, 2003, 187–202.

——, ed., "Conversation in Virginia Woolf's Works", *Etudes britanniques contemporaines*, numéro hors série (Autumn 2004), 167–80.

——, ed., "Introduction", *Insights into the Legacy of Bloomsbury, Les Cahiers Victoriens et Edouardiens* 62 (October 2005): 13–24.

——, "Jeanette Winterson's Cogito—'Amo Ergo Sum'—or Impersonality and Emotion Redefined", *Impersonality and Emotion in Twentieth-Century British Literature*, eds, Christine Reynier and Jean-Michel Ganteau, Montpellier: Presses Universitaires de la Méditerranée, collection *Present Perfect 1*, 2005, 299–308.

——, ed., *Journal of the Short Story in English*, special Virginia Woolf issue, 50 (Spring 2008).

Reynier, Christine and Jean-Michel Ganteau, eds, *Impersonality and Emotion in Twentieth-Century British Literature*, Montpellier: Presses Universitaires de la Méditerranée, collection *Present Perfect 1*, 2005.

Richter, Harvena, *Virginia Woolf: The Inward Voyage*, Princeton, NJ: Princeton University Press, 1970.

Rosenbaum, S. P., "Virginia Woolf: 'A Dialogue upon Mount Pentelicus'", *TLS* (September 11–17, 1987): 979; *Charleston Newsletter* 19 (September 1987): 23–32.

——, *Edwardian Bloomsbury: The Early History of the Bloomsbury Group*, vol. 2, London: Macmillan, 1994.

Rosenberg, Beth Carol and Jeanne Dubino, eds, *Virginia Woolf and the Essay*, New York: St Martin's Press, 1997.

Sarraute, Nathalie, *L'Ere du soupçon: Essais sur le roman*, Paris: Gallimard, 1956.

Sheppard, Richard, "The Problematics of European Modernism", *Theorizing Modernism: Essays in Critical Theory*, ed. Steve Giles, London: Routledge, 1993, 1–51.

Silver, Brenda, ed., "'Anon' and 'The Reader': Virginia Woolf's Last Essays", *Twentieth Century Literature*, 25 (3/4) (Fall/Winter 1979): 356–424.

Skrbic, Nena, "'Excursions into the Literature of a Foreign Country': Crossing Cultural Boundaries in the Short Fiction", *Trespassing Boundaries: Virginia Woolf's Short Fiction*, eds, Kathryn N. Benzel and Ruth Hoberman, New York & Basingstoke: Palgrave Macmillan, 2004, 25–38.

——, *Wild Outbursts of Freedom: Reading Virginia Woolf's Short Fiction*, Westport, CT; London: Praeger, 2004.

Sontag, Susan, *Against Interpretation and Other Essays* (1966), New York: Picador, 2001.

Spinoza, *Ethique*, trans. Charles Appuhn, Paris: Flammarion, 1965.

Stemerick, Martine, "Virginia Woolf and Julia Stephen: The Distaff Side of History", *Virginia Woolf: Centennial Essays*, eds, Elaine K. Ginsberg and Laura Moss Gottlieb, Troy, NY: Whitson, 1983, 51–80.

Sumner, Charles, "Beauty and Damaged Life in Virginia Woolf's Short Fiction", *Journal of the Short Story in English*, ed. Christine Reynier, 50 (Spring 2008): 33–47.

Tibi, Pierre, "La nouvelle: essai de définition d'un genre", *Cahiers de L'Université de Perpignan* 4 (Spring 1988): 7–62.

Tomlin, E. W., *Wyndham Lewis*, London: Longman, 1955.

Vinciguerra, Lorenzo, *Spinoza*, Paris: Hachette, 2001.

Whitworth, Michael, *Authors in Context: Virginia Woolf*, Authors in Context Series, Oxford: Oxford University Press, 2005.

Whymper, Edward, *Scrambles amongst the Alps in the Years 1860–1869* (1871), Washington, DC: National Geographic Adventure Classics, 2002.

Woolf's works

Novels

Woolf, Virginia, *The Voyage Out* (1915), London: Granada, 1978.

——, *Mrs Dalloway* (1925), London: Penguin, 2000.

——, *To the Lighthouse* (1927), London: Hogarth Press, 1982.

——, *A Room of One's Own* (1929), London: Granada, 1977.

——, *Flush* (1933), Oxford: Oxford University Press, 1998.

——, *Between the Acts* (1941), London: Penguin, 2000.

Short stories

Woolf, Virginia, *A Haunted House and Other Stories*, ed. Leonard Woolf (1944), London: Harmondsworth: Penguin, 1973.
——, *Mrs Dalloway's Party: A Short Story Sequence by Virginia Woolf*, ed. Stella McNichol, London: Hogarth Press, 1973.
——, *Virginia Woolf: The Complete Shorter Fiction*, ed. Susan Dick (1985), London: Triad Grafton Books, 1991.
——, *The Mark on the Wall and Other Short Fiction*, ed. David Bradshaw, Oxford: Oxford University Press, 2001.
——, *Carlyle's House and Other Sketches*, ed. David Bradshaw, London: Hesperus Press, 2003.
——, *La Maison de Carlyle et autres esquisses*, trans. Agnès Desarthes, Paris: Mercure de France, 2003.

Essays

Woolf, Virginia, "How Should One Read a Book" (1–11); "Hours in a Library" (34–40); "Phases of Fiction" (56–102); "On Re-Reading Novels" (122–30); "The Leaning Tower" (162–81); "A Letter to a Young Poet" (182–95); "The Artist and Politics" (230–2); "Walter Sickert" (233–44); "Craftsmanship" (245–51); "Personalities" (273–7); "The Moment: Summer's Night" (293–7), *Collected Essays II* (1966), London: Hogarth Press, 1972.
——, *The Essays of Virginia Woolf* (1904–28), 4 vols, ed. Andrew McNeillie, London: Hogarth Press, 1986–94; New York: HBJ, 1989–94.
——, "The Russian View" (341–4), *The Essays of Virginia Woolf* (1912–18), vol. 2., ed. Andrew McNeillie, New York: HBJ, 1990.
——, "Modern Novels" (30–7); "The Russian Background" (83–6); "Reading" (141–61); "Henry James's Ghost Stories" (319–26); "On Re-Reading Novels" (336–46); "Mr Bennett and Mrs Brown" (384–89); "Character in Fiction" (420–38), *The Essays of Virginia Woolf* (1919–24), vol. 3., ed. Andrew McNeillie, New York: HBJ, 1988.
——, "The Common Reader" (19); "The Pastons and Chaucer" (20–38); "On Not Knowing Greek" (38–53); "The Elizabethan Lumber Room" (58–9); "Notes on an Elizabethan Play" (62–70); "Modern Fiction" (157–65); "The Russian Point of View" (181–90); "The Patron and the Crocus" (212–15); "The Modern Essay" (216–27); "On Being Ill" (317–29); "How Should One Read a Book?" (388–400); "Life and the Novelist" (400–6); "An Essay in Criticism" (449–56); "Is Fiction an Art?" (457–65); "The New Biography" (473–80); "Street Haunting" (480–91); "The Art of Fiction" (599–603), *The Essays of Virginia Woolf* (1925–8), vol. 4., ed. Andrew McNeillie, London: Hogarth Press, 1994.
——, "A Sketch of the Past", *Moments of Being: Unpublished Autobiographical Writings*, ed. Jeanne Schulkind (1976), London: Triad Granada, 1981.

Diaries and Journals

Woolf, Virginia, *The Diary of Virginia Woolf* (1915–41), 5 vols, ed. Anne Olivier Bell, London: Hogarth Press, 1977–84; Harmondsworth: Penguin, 1979–85.

——, *The Diary of Virginia Woolf* (1915–19), vol. I., ed. Anne Olivier Bell, Harmondsworth: Penguin, 1979.

——, *The Diary of Virginia Woolf* (1920–4), vol. II., ed. Anne Olivier Bell and Andrew Mc Neillie, Harmondsworth: Penguin, 1981.

——, *The Diary of Virginia Woolf* (1925–30), vol. III., ed. Anne Olivier Bell and Andrew Mc Neillie, Harmondsworth: Penguin, 1982.

——, *The Diary of Virginia Woolf* (1931–5), vol. IV., ed. Anne Olivier Bell and Andrew Mc Neillie, Harmondsworth: Penguin, 1982.

——, *The Diary of Virginia Woolf* (1936–41), vol. V., ed. Anne Olivier Bell and Andrew Mc Neillie, Harmondsworth: Penguin, 1985.

——, *Virginia Woolf. A Passionate Apprentice: The Early Journals* (1897–1909), ed. Mitchell A. Leaska, London: The Hogarth Press, 1990.

——, *Journal Intégral* (1915–41), Paris: Stock, la Cosmopolite, 2008.

Letters

Woolf, Virginia, *The Letters of Virginia Woolf* (1888–1941), 6 vols, ed. Nigel Nicolson and Joanne Trautman, London: Hogarth Press, 1975–80.

Index

Adorno, T.W., 136, 137, 143, 165, 166, 167
"The Art of Fiction", 174
"The Artist and Politics", 112, 132
Attridge, D., 29, 30, 31, 33, 34, 35, 60, 61, 108, 109, 112, 113, 133, 146, 154, 155, 157, 161, 162, 164, 166
autonomy, 8, 40, 47, 52, 56, 112, 113, 114, 138, 139, 147

Bakhtin, M., 111, 127, 139, 163, 165, 166
Baldwin, D., 11, 13, 15, 16, 113, 151, 152
Benzel, K., 12, 13, 150, 152, 159, 164
Between the Acts, 8, 14, 40, 50, 75, 97, 115, 130, 150, 155, 156, 158, 164
bewilderment, 32, 33, 35, 107, 108, 109, 155, 161
"Blue and Green", 9, 127, 149, 150
Bradshaw, D, 5, 7, 8, 9, 115, 141, 143, 144, 146, 149, 162, 166

Chekhov, A., 9, 16, 19, 20, 22, 24, 28–9, 30, 31, 32, 50, 54, 133, 152, 161
commitment, 17, 112, 113–14, 119, 120, 124–5, 129–33, 143, 146, 147, 162, 166
Complete Shorter Fiction, 4, 5, 7, 11, 12, 15, 149, 152
Conrad, J., 107, 116, 150, 160, 161
conversation, 17, 46, 60, 63, 69, 82, 84, 85, 88, 90, 114, 116, 119, 124, 131, 147, 157, 158, 161, 164
craftsmanship, 34, 104, 138

Deleuze, G., 30, 35, 44, 83, 88, 89, 155, 156, 158, 161, 159, 164
Derrida, J., 103, 154, 160
"A Dialogue upon Mount Pentelicus", 5, 37, 79–89, 111, 118, 149, 158
Diary, 2, 3, 7, 15, 23, 47, 77, 86, 98, 119, 135, 143, 144, 146
"Divorce Courts", 144, 145, 146, 150
"The Duchess and the Jeweller", 2, 5, 53, 141, 143, 146

Eliot, T.S., 3, 24, 35, 36, 42, 87, 88, 122, 138, 153, 155, 156, 163
emotion, 22, 25, 60, 153
"An Essay in Criticism", 19, 20, 23, 152, 158
"The Evening Party", 5, 45, 116
ethics, 60, 90, 155

Flush, 14, 27, 139, 140, 166
Ford, M. F., 62, 100, 103, 116, 157, 159, 160
Forster, E.M., 3, 26, 37, 39, 44, 103, 106, 135, 140, 147, 154, 156, 160, 161, 165, 166
fragment, 15, 17, 37, 38, 44, 47, 50, 55–6, 58, 60, 83

"Gipsy, the Mongrel", 5, 37, 139, 140
Greek art, 79, 81–5, 86, 88

"Happiness", 5, 43, 67, 152
A Haunted House, 4, 6, 9, 53, 91, 92, 93, 97, 98, 100, 105–10, 111, 127, 133, 149
"A Haunted House and Other Stories", 4, 8, 10, 119, 149
Hoberman, R., 12, 13, 150, 152, 159, 164
hospitality, 70, 133

"How Should One Read a Book",
25, 26, 57, 104, 160
hybridity, 27, 28, 87, 133–7,
140, 147

impersonality, 24, 26, 35, 36, 84,
89, 111, 129, 153
impurity, 133, 137–41
"In the Orchard", 7, 52
incompletion, 15, 56
intensity, 21, 23–7, 38–40
"Is Fiction an Art?", 18

"Jews", 141, 142, 143, 144–6
"The Journal of Mistress Joan
Martyn", 5, 44, 62, 127, 133

"Kew Gardens", 2–3, 8, 41, 46, 48,
63, 114

"The Lady in the Looking-Glass",
51, 93, 95, 96, 97, 98, 127, 149
"Lappin and Lapinova", 2, 5, 54,
71–2, 73, 123
"The Leaning Tower", 112, 132
"The Legacy", 39, 100, 119, 143, 172
"Life and the Novelis", 154
love, 22

"The Man Who Loved his Kind", 5,
6, 39, 70
"The Mark on the Wall", 4, 7, 48,
92, 93, 96, 97, 99, 136
"Memoirs of a Novelist", 127,
140, 166
"Miss Pryme", 128, 135
"Modern Fiction", 16, 29, 31, 32,
37, 94, 136, 174
"Modern Novels", 152
moment of being, 25, 67, 68, 70,
102, 107, 108, 109
"Monday or Tuesday", 4, 8, 51, 94,
100, 149, 150
"Mr Bennett and Mrs Brown", 10,
11, 16, 94, 174
"Mrs Dalloway in Bond Street", 7,
13, 41, 52, 53, 76, 113

Mrs Dalloway, 6, 38, 64, 68, 70,
76, 115
"The Mysterious Case of Miss V.",
5, 133

"The New Biography", 174
"The New Dress", 6, 39, 43, 52, 73,
123, 129
"An Ode Written Partly in Prose on
Seeing the Name of Cutbush
Above a Butcher's Shop in
Pentonville", 5, 12, 135
"On Being Ill", 32, 108, 174
"On Not Knowing Greek", 86,
88, 158
"On Re-Reading Novels", 18, 19,
23, 27, 28

party, 37, 42–3, 51, 73, 75–9, 101
"The Pastons and Chaucer", 174
"The Patron and the Crocus", 174
"Personalities", 24, 174
"Phases of Fiction", 32, 33, 94
"Phyllis and Rosamond", 5, 38,
126, 134
polyphony, 125, 126, 128, 129–33
"Portraits", 5, 15, 135
proportion, 20, 22, 23, 25, 27, 36,
87, 136

reading, 7, 16, 17, 21, 33, 35, 57–9,
80, 85, 99, 104–5, 109, 112, 141
recognition, 53, 106, 108, 109, 176
"The Russian Background", 50, 59
"The Russian Point of View", 19,
22, 24, 28, 108, 161
"The Russian View", 25, 152

saturation, 26, 85, 86–7
"Scenes from the Life of a British
Naval Officer", 5, 163
"The Searchlight", 5, 15, 42, 51,
54, 90
"The Shooting Party", 5, 14, 51,
55, 93, 97, 119, 120, 121, 128,
163, 165

silence, 40, 62, 114, 116, 118–20,
    124–5
"A Simple Melody", 5, 43,
    77, 157
"A Sketch of the Past", 58, 70, 108,
    156, 157, 163
Skrbic, N., 11, 19, 113
"A Society", 3, 113, 114, 123, 124,
    127, 139, 149, 150
"Solid Objects", 5, 37, 38, 59,
    116, 129
"The String Quartet", 3–4, 9,
    92, 127
"A Summing Up", 5, 6, 52, 75,
    76, 115
"The Symbol", 5, 14, 53, 101,
    104, 133
"Sympathy", 5, 43

tension, 17, 36, 50, 57, 78, 111
"Three Guineas", 112, 113, 124, 141
"Three Pictures", 7, 40
To the Lighthouse, 8, 96, 97, 99, 172
"Together and Apart", 5, 6, 39, 54,
    69, 75, 89, 157

"An Unwritten Novel", 3, 4, 10,
    47, 50, 54, 55, 90, 91, 92, 93,
    94, 95, 96, 97, 99, 113, 121,
    127, 136, 150, 165

The Voyage Out, 62

"Walter Sickert", 27
"The Watering Place", 5, 14, 45
"The Widow and the Parrot: a True
    Story", 5, 15, 54, 129